It Ain't The Coffee That's

Bitter

A NOVEL

Other novels by Kristofer Clarke

One Day You Will

Don't Ask My Neighbor

Second Thoughts

'Til It Happens To You

Less Than Perfect Circumstance

Published by Second Twin Publishing

This book is dedicated to women and men who bravely share their stories, and to those who heal in silence.

Never feel alone.

It Ain't The Coffee That's

Bitter

Kristofer Clarke

Second Twin Publishing

Acknowledgment

Thanks to God for a creative mind, to be able to tell stories
that entertain and enlighten.
To friends and family, thank you for your understanding,
your encouragement, your support, and your selfless love.
To the readers, thank you for giving me the opportunity to
share my craft.

Love and Happiness,

Kristofer Clarke

Visit me at www.kristoferclarke.webs.com

It Ain't The Coffee That's

Bitter

One

Kennedie...

Lightning doesn't strike the same place twice. Those were words often spoken from my grandmother's own mouth whenever she saw worry on my face. As much as I tried to conceal whatever troubled me, a quiet stare in my direction and she had me figured out. She knew me well. She was the same grandmother who, when I went to live with her, told me I wasn't the first grandchild to call her house home, and all those who had given her trouble were buried in the backyard. I was only ten years old. I didn't have any proof— I knew better than to question my grandmother—but I figured, if she was crazy enough to admit her crime, I wasn't going to match her crazy and go digging for bones. After her warning, because that's exactly what it was, I dreaded the day I would awake to find one of my aunts, dressed in all black, standing in the rain, sobbing at an unmarked grave.

I decided I would wait for the biggest rainstorm or tornado to unearth the remains. While I waited, I abided by my grandmother's rules. I was in the house before the streetlights came on. I acknowledged my elders as sir or ma'am, and I sat with my knees together and with both feet on the ground, just as instructed. I wore pigtails and dresses, which bothered me more than I dared to say. Thank God we lived in the south, miles away from the bitingly cold winters that often paralyzed the north. Yes, occasional cold fronts teased us, but they paled in comparison. I knew better than to rebel during my teenage years, especially if I wanted to live to enjoy them. Every time the thought crossed my mind—and that wasn't often—the image of my grandmother with shovel in hand, digging the hole she would bury me in, came flashing in my mind.

My grandmother, Geraldine Rose Lamar, was born and raised in Thomasville, Georgia, a town about four hours south of Atlanta. Thomasville was a place where everybody knew everybody. It was a Mayberry kind of town. I remember my grandmother and I taking the two-and-a-half hour drive to the Georgia National Fair, held every October in Perry, Georgia. It was 1990; the same year her house became my home, permanently. A few months earlier, just before the start of summer and right before my eleventh birthday, my mother had an epiphany: she just couldn't do it anymore. *She* was Natalie Lamar. *It* was sharing her space, time, and love with a child she never wanted in the first place. I could recall every single time she spoke those exact words. My mother knew words hurt—she's heard some hurtful words in her lifetime—still she often spoke them without regrets, and usually with an intent expression on her face. You had to be an unselfish person to bring another human being into this world. As I got older, I realized my mother was as selfish as they came. It didn't take long to realize, while my grandmother had a heart of gold, my mother had a heart that had been dipped in cement.

Geraldine was a slender woman, but there was nothing fragile about her. Her mother, my great-grandmother, died exactly two years after Geraldine was born. Her father followed five years later. She was raised tough, but she had no choice in the matter. Years after she was orphaned, my grandmother had to fight the blame and criticism she received from her older siblings. She was the complication that killed her mother and the extra mouth to feed that caused their hardworking father to work even harder, suffering that fatal heart attack. She was the Cinderella in a family of ugly blood sisters who robbed her of an education because she was busy playing maid, catering to their needs while she and everyone else abandoned her own. When she thought she wouldn't survive, he swooped in and saved her. He was Russell Lamar, my grandfather.

I wanted to have a marriage that lasted as long as my grandparents', then I remembered people in hell wanted water. We can't have everything we want. It was actually death that did them part. Their marriage was a sign of their time. All the signs I've seen in my time forecast an entirely different outcome. Still, I didn't exactly feel like all the odds were stacked against me. I did get to pull out my grandmother's wedding dress—my something old—that hung in the back of my walk-in closet. I'd promised to wear it only when I met the man who treated me the way my poppa treated my grandmother. He didn't have to be the man of my dreams, because the men I dreamed about definitely were not marriage material. To say Poppa worshipped the ground my grandmother walked on wouldn't give justice to the love he had for her. She was the air he breathed, and her smiles began and ended his day.

"I want to see my oldest granddaughter in this before my eyes close." My grandmother made her wish clear. Actually, at the time I was her only granddaughter, which probably explained why she took me in without apprehension that spring evening when my mother packed me up and sent me on my way. She didn't even care to drive me to Thomasville. I was looking out the window of a cold Greyhound bus with tears running down my face. She never even waved goodbye.

Geraldine held the lace bodice antique wedding dress against her body and swayed. She smiled as if she remembered her own stroll down the aisle as a young, blushing bride in the magnificent piece forty-three years earlier. She said she was exactly my size when she wore it. My grandmother was still my size. I was going to honor her request, but marriage wasn't on my list of priorities, unless I was going to walk down the aisle by myself. I needed a faithful man, and the boys I had been meeting—'cause that's exactly what they were—hid from faithful, had a Peter Pan complex, and avoided commitment like it was the world's worst plague. Funny, they could never figure out what they kept doing wrong. Frankly, it was as clear as day. They were little boys trying to play a grown man's game, except they hadn't quite learned the important rules, the simple rules.

I had dreams of how good married life would be, and even lived it briefly. Unfortunately, good times never last too long, and I had Windsor Oliver to thank for making sure I knew firsthand. I didn't think he had the heart to hurt me, but I was the unlucky woman who found out he didn't have the heart to love me either. He was damn good at pretending. I just wished he had the balls to tell me. He went from the man who I would wake to see staring into my face, to the man who created an immeasurable distance between us, even though he was just on the other side of the bed. He had abandoned his spontaneous nature for the predictable shell he had become.

The only thing people are obligated to do is tell the damn truth. Everything else becomes so simple. I forgot how difficult simple shit could be sometimes. Some men just don't get it. Some men made it difficult. I was fine going to work, coming home, settling on the couch with a glass of Shiraz, nestling between my pillows with a good book, with my dog lying at my feet. That was my routine, and that was exactly how I liked it. I didn't need to add him, but I allowed him to convince me otherwise. How the hell did I let that happen? Oh, that's right. It was the well-executed proposal, beginning with the serenade from an orchestra, playing one of my favorite songs, "I Wanna Grow Old With You", and ending with the diamond engagement ring at the bottom of the champagne glass. It was the bouquet of flowers, and kisses on my neck that had my body tingling. So, I decided to give love and this marriage thing a try, since I gave everything else before that night a chance. The night was just as I described it to him six months earlier, though I was telling him with no expectation for him to actually pull it off.

Well, he did pull it off. How could I lose? With reservations, my grandmother loved him, and my sister adored him like the brother she never had. She thought the sun rose and set on him. Talk about pulling the wool over our eyes. It took some time, but eventually we learned Windsor's first name was Full Of, and his last name was Shit.

$\mathcal{T}$wo

Kennedie...

I was in love with my husband right up until the day I turned into my driveway and saw her leaned against her white Mercedes, in waiting, as if she had perfectly timed my arrival. Since last year's Christmas party, I hadn't seen or spoken two words to her, and since she's never set foot in our house or in our yard, her presence puzzled me. I geared my car into park, and then unbuckled T.J.'s seatbelt. I opened the door and exited. She posed with her hands at her small waist, and held her long coat open. Just like the silver gown she wore to the Christmas party, the black dress, hemmed just below her calves, showcased healthy curves. I was still dressed in scrubs. I had rushed from work and didn't get a chance to change into something more appropriate to meet my uninvited guest. She maintained a businesslike poker face, as if it pained her to smile. I approached her with a genuine grin on my face, dismissing her serious demeanor. She was my husband's boss's wife, so I assumed her pop-up visit had everything to do with unfinished work business. A few things ran across my mind before I finally spoke. I was certain she knew my husband wasn't home. *I hope nothing bad happened to him,* I thought, but I did not allow the troubling intrusion to show on my face. T.J. busied himself, running around the yard with both arms stretched to his sides, simulating a flying aircraft. He paid no attention to Selecia Lassiter, the silky, black haired stranger his mother approached.

"Selecia," I said in a cheerful greet.

I extended my arms to embrace her, but she stared at me from head to toe with coldness in her eyes. As far I knew, I hadn't done anything to warrant her scolding. I did not understand her undeserved rejection, which came quickly and without a second thought. The grin on my face disappeared as I stepped back to assess the sinister look that fell upon her. I placed my handbag on my shoulder, folded my arms across my chest, and gazed at her with unbothered eyes.

"My husband isn't home," I added.

"Kennedie, Honey, I don't need you to apprise me of Windsor's whereabouts," she snarled. "I always know exactly where he is."

"Well, you must have my husband in your back pocket for you to always know where he is." I enjoyed a muted chuckle, obviously entertained by my own retort. "Which leads me to the question, why the hell are you here? I don't know of another reason why I would come home to find you standing here in my driveway." I turned to dismiss her presence.

I was in no mood to waste precious time entertaining this snob for whom my affinity was, at best, pretense. There was something about her I didn't like. From the stories Windsor told, her attitude had more to do with the fact that the position she held in the company was by default, and it was off-putting. She'd turned up her nose at her coworkers, threatened by the fact that the only thing she had over them was the bed she shared with the boss, although the jury was still out on that. For Windsor's sake, I humbled myself. Now she was on my turf, and after she brushed off my cordial approach and added her snide comeback about my husband, I was more than ready to abandon that friendly decorum. Yes, I was this close to giving her directions to the side of my ass I needed her to place her Restylane-filled lips.

I ignored Selecia's giggle. What I said wasn't for her

amusement, but there she was, laughing in my face. I called for my son, who had begun making his way toward the front door.

"I can't stand a dumb bitch," Selecia declared. Her statement stopped me in my tracks.

I dropped my bag from my shoulder and into my hand.

"What the hell did you say?" I turned to face her and waited for the audacious heifer to respond.

"You heard me," she snapped. "My mother warned me about the entertainment of fools."

Selecia's words echoed in my ears.

"When it comes to weak women like yourself, men either walk all over you or they walk away from you," she asserted. She walked closer to me as she spoke. She carefully placed her heels on the concrete. Just like the words that fell from her mouth, her walk was with purpose, an appearance that she had control. "You lie quietly like welcome mats at your doorstep. You see the comings and goings, but you are ignorant to anything happening inside."

With that, I decided to entertain that simple bitch.

"And it's just your luck that they walk away to you, an insecure, pathetic jade who's completely satisfied with the iota of attention any man gives you. You're dressed in this smidgeon of confidence you selected from your closet, but you'll still have to face the fact that you can't be me, not even on your best day. So, when you speak of weak, look in the damn mirror and you'll see weak gazing back at you."

T.J. stood between two towering figures. He looked up as we spoke. He was the only thing that saved her from the ass beating she was begging for, because I prided myself in not introducing my son to violence of any kind.

"He's not just any man," Selecia explained. "He's Windsor Sebastian Oliver. I've waited all of my life for a man like him, and he wants me 'cause I'm not you."

"I'm baffled," I said. I laughed at the absurdity of her statement.

I moved T.J. to the side and stepped closer to lessen the space between Selecia and me. She matched me in height, and I stared into her eyes.

"So, you're weak and pathetic. Seriously, the best reason you can come up with is that my husband wants you because you're not me? I see he didn't need to say much to have you spreading your legs from east to west like the slut you are."

"It's the only reason I need."

"Then you must be satisfied with the fact that all you're getting is a fraction of him and his time. His mornings or his nights will never be yours, and the beginning and end of any amount of time he spends with you is dictated by an alarm that is a constant reminder that, bitch, you are just temporary. He'll use you for the instant satisfaction you were there to give him, and as quickly as he came, he'll be gone."

She laughed.

"If telling yourself that makes this pill easier for you to swallow, have at it. And the only thing temporary is your marriage and this little family you're trying so desperately to keep." She nodded her head at T.J. and smiled.

"You're actually standing here, thinking you have a chance?"

"I don't need chance." Selecia was so sure of herself, as if she and Windsor had sat around and etched out this plan.

I guess Windsor didn't have the balls to break this news to me, so he sent Selecia. His confession came from his whore's mouth. I kept my peace and gave Selecia her one shining moment. She held nothing back. She began with the moment they first met, the day she sat in her husband's office and Windsor walked in. She smiled as she traveled back down memory lane. She couldn't take her eyes off him, and the moment they first touched, she'd felt a surge inside her like none before. She revealed her pretense in not understanding a report Windsor had shared and, at her husband's request, Windsor had taken time to explain the report's contents. She closed her eyes and inhaled as she remembered being stifled by a breath of the intoxicating pheromone that had her wanting him instantly. She bravely relished in her recount of the whirlwind romance, the perfect love affair they embarked on almost immediately. They dismissed the fact that both he and she had spouses to whom they were supposed to be devoted. I didn't ask any questions, but, without apprehension, Selecia provided many answers. She made certain not to omit their romantic getaways, those taken under the guise of business trips. Windsor had taken his time exploring her walls, making her juices flow from the pleasurable pain he'd inflicted on her love nest. Those nights she felt he'd given the best he had, including the pillow talks that usually followed. She bragged because she thought of all the reasons Windsor deserved to be with her, and to her, it all made sense.

"And your husband," I finally interrupted, "does he know?"

She was bold enough to expose her relationship with my husband to me, I wondered if she'd had a similar conversation with hers, or if it was happening right under his nose and he was clueless.

"What goes on between me and my husband is not your business. But since you asked, what my husband and I have is an arrangement."

Again, she continued her speech with pride. She

wanted me to believe her husband had been privy to her clandestine affair, and I was the only person with my head buried in the sand. I knew better. Little by little, as night closed in, I realized this conniving snake had grown tired of hiding in the grass.

"Fine, but you're forgetting one thing," I corrected.

"And what's that?"

"This arrangement with your husband does not include mine."

"Not only does it include your husband," she shot back, "it includes any man I decide is worth the time of day."

Selecia showed up classless and shameless, and dropped a bomb in my lap. I had no time to prepare for its explosion. T.J. sat on the steps. He looked gloomy and lethargic, a far cry from the energetic little boy he had been about an hour earlier. Selecia's uninvited intrusion had interrupted my evening plans with my son.

Had my crazy-ass mother raised me, my confrontation with Selecia would've ended like an episode of First 48. She needed to be counting her blessings as she reversed from the driveway with nothing to show she had just confessed to sleeping with another woman's husband. I was raised right. I knew better than to show my ass in public, though I had every right. I had to set an example for my child, and I wouldn't dare embarrass my grandmother.

Selecia had admitted to having her talons secured in my husband and was still able to leave unscathed.

After I dismissed Selecia, I walked away as if my ego had not been bruised by her revelation. Inside a home that immediately felt broken, my husband's infidelity and betrayal grabbed at me. I busied myself, fulfilling my duties of a devoted mother. I stifled the humiliation that built inside me, but I was slowly getting to the point of raising the white flag to surrender. I laughed out of anger because what had occurred was surreal. I'd picked up my phone several times to call Windsor, and when I finally called, I received his familiar directive, *"This is Windsor. You know what to do."* He was right. I did know what to do, but I hadn't figured out how to get away with murder.

*T*hree

Michaela...

They were right, when a woman's fed up, there's absolutely nothing you can do about it. Five-and-a-half years of marriage, but after two years, my happily ever after began to fade. Away from the light, I fought hard to keep myself from crumpling. I walked tall when in the company of men, but at home I lived in a situation that painted a happy face on misery. I was just keeping up appearances. Conveniently, I forgot the last two years, even though I lived every single one of them, of course, with regrets. He was still uninteresting, humorless, and he still made love as if he were just learning his way around a dark cave. I hung on hoping he would get better in bed. Damn! I'd gotten so used to being disappointed, I forgot what being satisfied felt like. He had lost it. Actually, he never had it to begin with.

Not long after meeting Zachary McKnight, I had to become perfect at the one thing I hated the most: lying. Every time we had one of our intimate moments—that's what he called it—I had to lie. To me, they were the moments I immediately teleported to a world where the man who made love to me was the man I actually loved, and when my eyes rolled to the back of my head, it was the result of his thrusts that also sent my body pulsing from immeasurable pleasure, and not because I wanted the torture to be over. That's exactly what him being on top of me was, torture.

So often, in the middle of his lackluster performance—cause that's what it was at best—when he was hitting it from behind—which I enjoyed, just not with him— I wanted to look at him and ask, "Are you done yet?" But there were Emmys and Oscars that had my name on them for my portrayal. My act would trigger his inquests. "Does it feel good?" Zachary would ask, putting the brakes on my fantasy and jarring me back to a reality that, unfortunately, included him. He was predictable. And his next question would be, "Damn, Daddy put in work, didn't he?" as he collapsed next to me, as I lie still, feeling dissatisfied. First, I wanted to remind him he was not my damn daddy. Second, what I felt was anything but good. His reflection in the mirror had tricked him into believing he had been. He was disappointing to no end, but to appease his tired-ass ego, I said, "You did your thing." There, I said the lie he'd gotten used to hearing and always believed, when all he'd done was messed up a good perm, smeared his nasty sweat all over me, and made me yearn for the men in my fantasies even more. Truthfully, Zachary wouldn't have known the difference if I'd fucked up while I faked it. He was too busy making sure he got to his climax, not giving a damn if I drizzled or rained. He lay on the bed next to me, heaving as if he'd just rolled a fucking bolder up a damn mountain, when he had barely skipped a pebble along the surface of a pond. Thankfully, my days of embellishing were over, and now I just wished his occupancy in my house was over, too.

"Michaela, did you pick up my gray suit from the cleaners?" Zachary yelled from the second level of our NE DC row house.

I tilted my face toward the ceiling in the kitchen and I wished he could see the scorn on it. Only Zachary could make my face twist when I hear my own name.

"Why the hell can't he just choke on it?" I said in a whisper.

I could hear him pacing the upstairs, and he talked with the toothpaste still in his mouth. Damn, I hate when he does that. It was the same routine every morning: he wakes up, spends a lifetime in the shower, and then begins to work my freaking nerves. How the hell was I supposed to know which gray suit he was talking about? It's not like it was the only one he had. It was a gray suit. Close your eyes and pick one. It wasn't going to make him look any more in shape than the four striped ones that hung in the back of the closet, or the other gray ones—charcoal or otherwise—that he wore only in the middle of the week.

"I picked it up on Saturday. It's in the closet, to the right," Alison answered. She looked at me and shook her head.

Alison Tyson, my friend and semi-confidant, was a referred nanny hired three days after it was confirmed that Zachary and I would be parents. A few months later, I was rushed to the hospital to save our child after the heartbeat we had heard just three weeks earlier disappeared. Our rush and the doctors' desperate attempt to avoid the inevitable were to no avail. Following a Dilation and Curettage procedure and weeks of recovery, we'd decided to keep Alison after Zachary and I agreed we would try to conceive again. We both wanted children, so while we were disappointed by the loss of our first child, we were already looking forward to growing our family of two and experiencing love as parents. A year after completely healing from my operation, Nyla Melanie was born. I thought there was no greater love than marrying Zachary McKnight, but it was nothing compared to the heart-melt I experienced when I first laid eyes on our little girl.

I often wondered if Alison was hired as Nyla's nanny or Zachary's, because she tended to his needs just as often. The only things she wasn't doing was feeding him and putting him over her shoulder for his after-meal belch. Unfortunately, three had become two again, with the third upstairs loudly working on my damn nerves.

Zachary had purchased more suits in one of his latest shopping sprees. He was packing on the pounds in all the wrong places, and rather than invest in a gym membership to reverse his weight gain, he was content on spending money on a new wardrobe to cover his unappealing bulges. He was now twenty pounds heavier than when I married him, a small beer belly included. People assumed it was because he lived the happy life that being married to me provided, but I knew better. Better were the home cooked meals that no longer awaited his return from a hard day's work and travels. Zachary's love handles were no longer sexy, and the V-cut he once proudly displayed above his low-cut underwear was now purposely hidden under cotton sweats and a V-neck college t-shirt. His body was no longer that of the man who once dazzled on the basketball court during pick-up games.

It took us fifty-five minutes to tie the proverbial

29

knot, fifteen minutes to barely enjoy his subpar performance in bed that first night in the Dominican Republic, and months to finalize a freaking divorce that he was happy with. I didn't care either way. I just wanted him out of my life. Getting out of my life had only taken Zachary to the second level of our three-level home, thanks to his bitch-filled pleas, and a judge who acted like he knew how to separate stink from shit. Zachary was still waiting on the builders to finish his house in a Prince George's County neighborhood. That was the story he told and stuck to. We agreed he would live on the second floor—for Nyla's sake—but vacate the premise the moment his house was finished. A moment had turned into a year, and counting. I wish they would hurry the hell up. They've built battleships faster. Until then, Zachary was doing an excellent job getting on my last nerve. I would've been happy if Alison had moved in from her small basement apartment in the H Street Corridor, a revived NE Washington, D.C. neighborhood.

"Thank you," Zachary yelled back. The gratitude was obviously meant for Alison; his sarcastic tone was meant for me.

"Oh, go fuck yourself," I said in a low tone, for the sake of not causing another argument.

I enjoyed the momentary truce in the war of the McKnights that was now in its fifth day. Besides Nyla, I didn't know why I was hell-bent on not doing anything that would disturb this calm. I didn't want to waste my breath saying something I didn't mean, like "you're welcome". Frankly, I couldn't care any less if he dressed in garbage bags and had shoeboxes on his feet. I just wanted him to hurry up and get the hell out.

I stopped doing any of the things I used to do for Zachary while we were married, even after my long days as a lawyer at Porter and Blount Law Group. Some I did out of habit, but whether good or bad, they were easily broken. They were things I never allowed Alison to do, because I wanted to do for my husband. Well, he had lost that title—his doing—and he would no longer benefit from the privileges that came along with it. As far as I was concerned, he needed to be kissing Alison's ass. Thanks to her, by 8:00 a.m., his coffee had been poured and waited for him to add his cream and sugar. His dry cleaning had been bagged and placed at the back door to the garage for her Monday afternoon drop off. I would swing by the cleaners before my usual afternoon lunch, to help Alison out. I had other reasons that had nothing to do with Alison. Appearance was everything, and I was keeping up with the Joneses.

Brooklynn and Stetzon Jones had a marriage that gave Boris and Nicole a run for their money and the title of America's Couple. Their love for each other knew no bounds. They had a mutual respect for each other, even before he'd purposely ran into her in New York as she exited the elevators on the first floor of JP Morgan Chase. While Stetzon enjoyed success as the Vice President of Global Philanthropy, a thirty-five year old Brooklynn Jones was at the beginning of her second year as the newly appointed Chief Financial Officer. Since the day they met, they'd slowly become each other's best friend. Honesty and openness was their number one rule, each supported the other's accomplishments, and they lifted each other whenever failure befell either of them. They hadn't experienced a setback in years. Their public display of affection was the same in private affairs. Love had been in the air since the day their shoulders met.

I met Brooke Jones, nee Brooklynn Tait, when we walked into Dr. Newton's office, a professor at Alabama State University. We were there for different reasons. Brooke, a senior who had passed Professor Newton's chemistry classes with straight A's, was there to offer assistance to struggling students. I was probably one failed exam from failing that class, and I desperately needed the assistance she offered. I didn't remember Chemistry being that hard in high school, but that college stuff was a beast I had never met before. Two years after she'd met Stetzen—he was six years her senior—I was standing next to Brooke as her Maid of Honor, the coveted position I was given over her sister. I would've been fine had Brooke made a different decision, and from what I detected years ago at Brooke's third anniversary dinner, Andraya still had a chip on her shoulder. Two years after Brooke got hitched, she'd stood beside me in the same position, witnessing me make what had become my biggest mistake.

An hour after Zachary slammed the door behind him, I retreated to the master bedroom to ready for my day. After I turned on the shower and waited for the water to reach optimal temperature, I stood in the bathroom in front of the vanity on what used to be Zachary's side of the his-and-hers sink, washed the anti-wrinkle cream from my face that I'd applied just before bed—they did say prevention was better than cure—and massaged the Neutrogena wash into my face. Once inside the shower, I stood under the rainfall showerhead, folded my arms across my chest, and allowed the water to beat gently on my skin. In the silence, thoughts about the beautiful beginning of my relationship with Zachary and the painful end to my marriage slithered to the forefront of my mind. There were the nights I woke thinking he was still the man of my dreams. There were the times I reminded him I was lucky to have him in my life, only to be corrected that he was the lucky one. I didn't argue because I thought we were both telling the truth. Then the memory of that day forced away the smile on my face. Seeing Zachary everyday was the constant reminder I didn't need, and to have this invasion in the one place where I welcomed my solitude was unnerving. My chest swelled as I inhaled deeply. I exhaled and hoped the wounded feeling would escape along with that breath.

After my shower, with my natural short hair in a small ponytail, I applied a light color to my face, highlighted my cheeks, and glossed my lips. Satisfied with my enhanced beauty, I closed my eyes in thought. I thought about my current living arrangements and wondered when will it end. I thought about how I'd grown tired of pretending my marriage was solid, as if we were still committed to those vows we had proudly fumbled through, with smiles on our faces and tears in our eyes. I didn't get married to later become a part of any statistic. Thanks to Zachary, what I'd avoided had been made my reality.

$\mathcal{F}our$

$\mathcal{M}ichaela...$

"On what grounds?" my attorney, Charles Bibbins, asked as I sat in the lone leather chair in front of the large desk a little more than a year ago. A week after our initial phone conversation, we'd agreed to meet in his N.W. D.C. office. Attorney Bibbins came highly recommended by Suzette Chambers, my and Zachary's personal lawyer, and one of our closest friends. Suzette knew she would have to fully represent whomever retained her first, and couldn't be partial to any one of the two people she considered her friends. So, for the sake of our friendship, she'd made herself unavailable to us in that capacity.

"Irreconcilable differences."

I gave the generic response Hollywood provided when attempting to conceal the real reason, until the tabloids plastered their business on the front cover of the latest issue of Globe, In Touch, or Enquirer magazines. I sat back, crossed my legs, and waited for Attorney Bibbins to pry.

"Okay." He set his pen in the middle of his binder, clasped his hands on his desk, and leaned forward. His dark brown eyes stared into mine. "You'll have to give me more than that."

I stood to break his stare, walked to the back of his office, and gazed out the office window. I dug the right heel of my stiletto into the carpet as the memory of the moment surfaced. It burned my insides.

"He's fucking my mother," I revealed. I never turned to see his reaction. I offered no apologies for my bluntness. The cat was finally out the bag, and, apparently, so was my mother's.

I remember the moment like it was yesterday. I'd walked into my mother's living room, with Nyla in my arms, and saw my mother on top of my husband, riding as if she were on the final leg of the Tour de France. If you thought the image of your mother and father doing the nasty was one you never wanted burned on your brain, one of your mother and your husband was fifty times worse.

The cell phone vibrated and brought me back from

that dark, hurtful mind trip. I stood in the full-length mirror in the corner of the lavishly decorated room and adjusted a fitted gray sweater over my white shirt. The gray stripe pant was a perfect fit, even though I'd bought it without going to the dressing room. I'd chosen the outfit the night before and hung it on the inside of the walk-in closet door.

I walked across the room and grabbed the phone from the nightstand.

"Hello," I answered.

I stepped in my fuchsia pointed toe pumps—to add a splash of color to my ensemble—and waited for the caller to respond.

"You answered as if you had no idea who was calling," Brooke said in her usual soft, inviting voice that hadn't changed. "Did you delete me?"

"Like some of the simple bitches I know, you'll never have to worry about that," I replied. "I didn't look at the screen. Too damn busy trying to squeeze into these stilts."

I put the call on speaker, tossed the phone on the bed, and then grabbed one of my wigs from the closet. In front of the mirror, I adjusted the insta-hair on my head. It gave me a flawless do every time. The layered black hair extended just below my shoulders. The bang swept across my face and created a perfect frame. I loved going from plain Jane to beautiful Bianca. Just like make-up, a good wig can make magic happen.

"It's okay," Brooklynn offered. "We know nothing else gets your attention when you're getting fashionable. I hope you're getting ready for our lunch date. Are we still on?"

I paused.

"Of course, we are."

I'd had a conversation with Brooklynn a few days earlier as I made my way home from the office. It had been an exhausting week, and after an evening of exchanging more than just a few words with Zachary, I was already looking forward to lunch with my best friend. With her new position, which almost always had her on travel, we didn't get to spend as much time as we used to. My hectic schedule with my last case had not made our attempts to meet any easier. Needless to say, I was pleased to hear that her new position now had her traveling to D.C. twice a month.

"Noon, at the same spot?"

I grabbed the phone from the bed, and deactivated the speaker. "Yes. See you then."

I took one last glance over in the full-length mirror, grabbed my small white tote from the storage bench in front of the bed, and headed out the room.

"Alison," I called out as I descended the stairs, bypassing the second floor—which I never venture on unless the bastard wasn't there—and into the kitchen. I could hear small talk between her and Nyla. As I entered the kitchen, Alison paused. She stared at me from head to toe, and then nodded in approval. She smiled and then resumed her morning ritual of having breakfast with Nyla.

"Hot date?" Alison teased.

"How's mommy's baby?" I asked.

I smiled at Nyla, and purposely ignored Alison's mischievous inquest. I kissed Nyla on the top of her head, and then lowered my face for a returned smooch on my right cheek.

"You're not going to answer me?" Alison asked.

"The last hot date I had turned into a hot mess," I said. I took one-half of a bagel from Alison's plate. "I'm meeting Brooke for lunch."

"You know," Alison began. She stood from the stool she occupied next to Nyla and placed the plate in the dishwasher. She paused before she turned around. She held the small coffee mug as if she avoided smudging freshly manicured fingers. "It's been over a year and you haven't said much about what Zach did. It must be hard keeping it all in. You show that pretty face to the world five days a week, flashing that smile for your clients and colleagues to see. You've mastered the art of hiding the pain you don't want anyone to see. You come home every day to this beautiful jail, forced to see the face of the man who has caused your heart so much ache. You have to let someone know your reality." She took a sip from her cup and then peered into me.

I stood in the doorway between the kitchen and the dining room and quietly listened. My heartbeat tripled as I pondered a response. This was not on the short list of last things I wanted to talk about before heading out to meet Brooke, but here Alison was, trying to get me to travel down that road again, at the most inopportune time.

"My mother used to be my best friend," I began. "I thought she wanted the best for me, and when I did get what I thought was the best, she took it from me."

"What are you saying?" Alison stood close to me with Nyla now in her arms. "Your mother had something to do with your divorce?"

"She had everything to do with it," I said emphatically. I turned to face Alison. The look of concern she had when she began her questions had deepened. "I used to see her as a person, but that day she became the monster I grew to hate, just as much as I despise that fragment of a man I once proudly called my husband."

"What day?"

"The day I opened the door to my mother's house and saw her on top of my husband, riding him better than a too-short jockey on a thoroughbred."

Five

Kennedie...

It hurt to see the years I spent with my husband come to such an abrupt end. I believed Windsor loved me, and I never had to question the affection he had for our son. But, obviously, there was a part of him that yearned for something else, with someone else, and Selecia had confirmed that she was whom he yearned for. For a few weeks after her impromptu visit, I remained tight-lipped about what I knew to be true. Needless to say, those weeks were filled with nights where I literally slept awake. Windsor's attempts to question my insomnia-like nights were first ignored, but when my avoidance left him feeling unsatisfied, he became adamant. I appeased his concerns with work stories, and when I ran out of the truth, I turned to fiction, anything to keep my beloved husband from knowing what I had conjured.

While I plotted and planned, I drove myself crazy, but my crazy was not in vain. As Windsor carried on with his usual behavior, which included his situation with Selecia, I took care of business. My coworker, Madelyn Kyle, recommended Percy Valentine, one of the best divorce lawyers in D.C. Together they had nickeled and dimed her own philandering, now ex, husband during their process. I stayed away from the joint accounts I had with Windsor and had dug into my own personal savings to pay the retainer fee. I needed to plan way ahead. I knew the process was going to cause me to dig deep. This was not what I expected to do with my money. Shit happens. Since he hadn't said anything about Selecia's visit, I knew Windsor had no idea she had gone rogue, or maybe mum was his word until I decided to approach him. For some reason, I was certain what she did was not in any agreement they had. I was never good at pretending, but I deserved an Emmy for the performance I gave.

Armed with the knowledge of Windsor and Selecia's romantic rendezvous, and after weeks of agonizing, I decided I needed to confront my cheating ass husband. Of course, his response would not affect what I had already set in motion. I'd planned my interrogation carefully, and, unknowingly, he'd provided the perfect backdrop for my questioning.

Tuesday night—I guess that was my night—I came home from work to find Windsor already there. Earlier, I'd received his voice message that his mother would be picking up T.J. from school, and that I needed to come home after work. "No detours," he'd said. Under normal circumstances, I would've beamed with excitement as thoughts that Windsor had something romantic planned swirled about, but nothing I felt over the past weeks had been normal.

"I made your favorite," he yelled from the kitchen after I entered the house and closed the door behind me.

The combined aroma of freshly chopped onions, parsley, and olive oil greeted me. With a questioning side gaze at my surroundings, I walked past the large dining area where he'd set the dining room table for two. A bouquet of autumn rose and calla lilies made the perfect centerpiece. He'd pulled my favorite china, which was bequeathed to us from his great aunt.

I used to love coming home. It's where I always found love waiting. Home was where I found my peace of mind. But again, a sad feeling came over me, because what I'd walked into was a mimicry of what home used to be, where both Windsor and I pretended that what we had still existed there. Our love was now water under the bridge, thanks to Windsor. I stopped at the table and inhaled the fruity scent of the roses.

"And what exactly is my favorite?" I asked under a forced smile as I entered the kitchen. I figured he'd forgotten, just like he'd forgotten that he was supposed to love me and honor our vows.

"Apple glazed pork tenderloin," he answered without a doubt in his voice. "T.J is with my mother for the night, so it's just the two of us." By the two of us, he meant himself, what had been the best-kept secret that he's been screwing his boss's wife, and me. Hell, it hasn't been just the two of us in only God knows how long.

Windsor turned and smiled. The black half apron hugged his waist. *Hmmm,* I thought. I remember when that smile made me melt. I stared at his exposed chest, a momentary hypnosis by the sculpted physique that stood before me. In that instant, he resembled the man I loved, unapologetically. He was the man I'd aimed to please because I had every reason to believe he did the same. But weeks ago, his ugly truth showed up with a thunderous slap to my face.

I excused myself to wash and change into something more comfortable. I departed with a devilish smile, and I was certain his interpretation of my expression did not align with what I had in mind. After my quick shower—I needed to wash the day from me—I stood in the walk-in closet in the bedroom. Before I dressed, I stared at his clothes that hung on his side of the closet. I stared at his suits and imagined they all had remnants of her on them. I ran my fingers over the buttons of one of his laundered shirts, and supposed Selecia savored the many times she disrobed him. I imagined her staring into his eyes, licking her lips, ready to devour him, because, in her mind, he was all hers. There I was, putting myself through hell again. I banished the thoughts that assailed my mind and emerged from the room fully clothed. I looked rather homely in legging pants and a long sleeve tailored shirt. I was in no mood to dress sexy. I wanted to get dinner over with, and what better way to confront Windsor but on a full belly.

When I entered the kitchen, Windsor paused and examined my presentation. His eyes traveled from one end of my body to the next, and I could see the wishes and expectations leaving his eyes, along with his smile. I ignored his reaction and pressed my way toward the dining room table where dinner, candlelight, and wine awaited. I would've been amazed by his effort, but in the back of my mind the conversation with Selecia was on repeat. The smug on her face as she disclosed their secret affair flashed before me. I was unimpressed, knowing that the person who would occupy the seat across from me would be my ultimate betrayer.

While we dined, I pretended to enjoy his presence and what he'd prepared. Truth be told, both had left a bad taste in my mouth. I entertained his playful banter as I fought hard to suppress the urge to end the charade. He was putting on a good show because everything, as far as he knew, was normal. After dinner, he embarked on a long-winded soliloquy about his love for me. It was nothing but guilt talking. That was my best summation. While he talked, I drifted between the nonsense that spewed from his mouth and my own agenda. I wondered if this was a version of the same speech he told Selecia that had her slithering under him, in the late of night, probably on either of their office sofas.

"I'm such a lucky man," Windsor said.

He drank the last of his red wine from the tall flask and returned it to the table. *What was it that made you so lucky?* I thought. Was it because Selecia had ceased her moment, used her womanly wiles, and captured more than just his attention? Or, was it because his frolic with her had lasted this long, unbeknownst to me. Luck had been a lady, but as Selecia had pointed out with eloquence, she was that lady.

"I'm so happy to be spending the rest of my life with you," he professed.

Oh, the things men say when they don't know you have them

47

figured out, I thought. My grandmother always said knowledge was power. She has never lied. If only Windsor knew. His actions had made the lifespan of this marriage very short. The rest of his life, at least with me, was just a few moments from over. I took my time consuming what he'd prepared, not to savor it, but to digest the bullshit he fed me as a side dish. My mantra, when you have nothing good to say, nod and agree, was in full practice.

He sat back and enjoyed a moment's peace before he spoke again.

"Do you know how much I love you?" His question broke our silence and my patience.

"I have a pretty good idea," I said. I placed the fork to the side of the exquisite China and clasped my hands under my chin.

He smiled.

I stared across the table at him and watched his smile fade to nothing. Had he asked that question a few weeks earlier, when I was confident in his love, I would have shouted a favorable answer from that mountain top Martin Luther King, Jr. spoke about. But, like my grandmother has said many times over, when you know better, you do better. I was biding my time as I continued to digest Windsor's bullshit. Although he remained silent, his eyes held many questions.

"What about Selecia?" I asked. I showed no emotions as the question fell from my lips.

"Who?"

"Selecia Lassiter. Does she know how much you love me?" I took a sip from my wine glass. It was the last thing Windsor poured before he sat.

"My boss's wife?" he asked with no sign of nervousness in his words or his actions that followed.

"Your confession of your love for me, you realizing how lucky you are, or how happy you were to be spending the rest of your life with me, was it before or after she made sure your days had happy endings?"

"I don't know what you're talking about." He grabbed his wine glass and rose from his chair.

"Neither did I, until a couple weeks ago when T.J. and I came home to find your whore standing in the driveway."

"She wouldn't."

He sat, downed the last drops of wine, and then returned the empty goblet to the table.

"She wouldn't? I guess now you know what I'm talking about." I grabbed the wine bottle from the center of the table and walked to Windsor. "By the way, she would, and she did."

I poured his glass full, and then slammed the bottle

on the table. He jumped back in his seat and looked at me. His stare questioned my sanity.

"Your bitch," I continued with my face inches from his. I wanted him to see the words as they left my lips. "Your brave mistress just about came on herself in our driveway as she boldly revealed your romantic involvement." I stood behind him and slowly glided the palms of my hands down his chest. I brought my lips close to his ear to make sure every word penetrated his eardrum. "All those nights you were busy at work, you were busy screwing your little whore, trying to see how many walls you could get her to climb. The many nights our son and I stayed up waiting for you, you were preoccupied with her, trying to find out the depths of her lust."

The man, who spoke earlier with such ease, now stumbled over every justification he thought of. He stood and distanced himself from me to avoid the confrontation he brought to my front steps. He hiccupped on every question I asked him and, finally, his confession. He spoke with tears in his eyes, as if he were more hurt by his own philandering, and, in the end, he spoke what he thought were the magic words: "Can you forgive me?"

Six

Kennedie...

Forgive me, Father, for I have sinned. Talk about taking the easy way out, after you've finished doing all your dirt, as if your actions were supposed to just get swept under the rug. This wasn't some damn confessional, and I wasn't in the business of forgiving. What was it supposed to do, make all things good again? Hell, I ain't God. Still, I decided to give an ounce of consideration to Windsor's request. I tried to find it somewhere deep inside me but, in pondering my decision, everything else suffered. I prayed for sleep that didn't include dreams that were vivid reminders of what he did. My encounter with Selecia stalked me every time I closed my eyes, and images of the two of them together added to the nightmare. Thanks to my wild imagination, I filled in the gaps left by Selecia and Windsor's admission. Undoubtedly, I imagined the worst.

I couldn't concentrate on work. Colleagues questioned my walking dead-like existence, the fixed stares off into some distance, and the tears that sometimes came out of nowhere. I tried with all my might, but I just couldn't muster up the strength to grant Windsor's request. My grandmother would tell me to love my enemies and pray for those that showed hatred toward me, but I wasn't going to be the good wife and take the high road on this one. As the days passed, my hatred for Windsor grew. While he waited for his forgiveness, I became increasingly overwhelmed with anger. Tired of keeping it inside, I decided in one moment to release everything I felt.

After a determined stroll into the bedroom, I tossed my jacket on the bed and walked toward the walk-in closet. I stood on the other side of the bedroom with the closet doors wide open. Without a doubt, Windsor loved his image, and he took perfect care of what he spent his money on. I just wished he handled his marriage with the same care. Instead, he was cavalier and disregarded everything he stood to lose. I looked from one side of the closet to the other, trying to decide where to begin my destruction. Should I start with the suits on my left, with his shoes that were neatly displayed in the back, or his pants to the right? Or, should I just close my eyes and go Madea-crazy, making sure I damaged everything that stood in my path? I didn't stand there wondering why I wasn't enough for the man who had professed I was his everything. His decision to make bed with Selecia had nothing to do with anything I lacked. So, no, I was not going to swim in any pool of self-doubt. Instead, I pondered what happened to the man I loved. I felt so secure with his love, but my security was a false sense. I did not know Windsor had lost his love for me. What was he looking for that lead him to Selecia?

Windsor began his affair with Selecia Lassiter a few months after his start at Lassiter, Larson, and Beale, a very reputable architectural firm. He spent years splitting himself in half: one half my husband and the other half lover to his mistress. I grew bitter in my heart as I dealt with the crushing blow of Windsor's affair. Yes, my husband was remorseful, if that's what you want to call what he displayed. He wanted to start love over. Guess he never thought about the consequences of his extramarital endeavors. My anger had reached its boiling point, but I didn't know what to do. What I did know was that I didn't want to be reminded of his affair, his disregard of our vows. So, I gathered all of his t-shirts, underwear, and socks, headed down to the kitchen for a pair of scissors, and then went into destructive mode. I took the scissors and cut all that I had gathered in half, one half for the mistress and the other for myself. After all, only half of him belonged to me, and I was skeptical about that, too. Windsor's socks were cut in half for every time he stepped foot in his mistress's home, and since I didn't have an exact number, I thought of one that made sense. I cut his boxers for every time he had sex with her, and the t-shirts for every time he lay with her and came home with her on him. Though he claimed he was no longer splitting his love between the office slut and me, and pleaded for my forgiveness, I knew I couldn't trust him. I thought of the times they closed their eyes and felt their way in, out, and around each other. I thought about moments one had experienced the other's warm explosion. The thoughts made me sick to my stomach and heightened the madness. Since I didn't know what clothes he wore on their rendezvous, I played a game of Eeny, Meeny, Miney, Moe with his suits and commenced to cut the crotch from the ones I selected, and tore the jackets in half from the vent. When my destruction was a true representation of my anger, the same anger that failed to subside as I pulled, cut, and ripped, I pulled the bench to the center of the closet, sat, and then stared at the two piles of Windsor's clothes in the middle of the bedroom.

A glance at the image in the full-length mirror and I was introduced to someone who looked nothing like the poised, confident woman I was before Selecia forced me to face my husband's reality. Her hair was strewn about her head. Her fixed gaze made me accept the unimaginable anger in her eyes. With each breath, her shoulders rose and fell with ease, as if the burden she'd carried for so long was finally lifted. Her name was me. In the short time, Windsor had forced me to become this woman. I hated him for that. I stood, removed the hair from my face and, finally, I smiled.

All that was missing was a cigarette and a shot of liquor to celebrate this small, but meaningful, victory, but I didn't smoke, and I still needed to pick up my son from the daycare. I exited the closet, stepped over the two piles of discards, grabbed my jacket from the bed, and headed downstairs. I knew Windsor would be home soon enough to see the present I left for him in the bedroom, and I wished I could be there to take a snapshot of the look on that son-of-a-bitch's face. To me it was a beautiful surprise, but I doubt he would see it that way.

Seven

Michaela...

After I kissed my two-year-old daughter on her forehead, I grabbed the clothes for the cleaners, and headed out the door. I threw the gray laundry bag on the driver side of my truck, and hopped in as I waved goodbye to Nyla. She rested her head on Alison's shoulder instead of returning the favor.

As I drove, I reminisced on the conversation I had with Alison. She'd stood at the garage door with Nyla in her hand, still consumed by the disclosure of my husband's infidelity. She gasped at my mother's betrayal, and shook her head in disbelief as she struggled to find the words to explain her displeasure. I knew what I divulged wasn't breaking news. She admitted to overhearing my charge during one of the many unpleasant exchanges between

Zachary and me. I understood her pretense. She's never been one to burden herself with the affairs of others, especially without an invitation. Even then, she was reluctant to oblige. But this had weighed heavily on her mind. Alison meant well. The last year, she'd fixed her mouth to question my current living arrangement on more than one occasion, but instead of following through, she gave me the how-the-hell-did-you-end-up-with-that-trash glare. The question she never asked got a response that never came.

"What the hell is wrong with you?" I screamed into the windshield at the car that had just cut me off. *Where the hell are all these people going?* I repeated the same question in my head I often asked whenever I drove through D.C. streets during mid-morning hours. I'd come to the conclusion that D.C. didn't have rush hour, it had rush all day long. I contemplated driving in silence, but I needed a distraction from my thoughts and from the traffic. I cued the playlist I had been listening to for the last months. I ignored the snail pace traffic and focused on enjoying lunch with my best friend.

After the almost one-hour drive, I pulled into the parking garage next to Alba Osteria, Brooke's restaurant of choice. She loved eating Italian, and there was no better place to feast on an exquisite meal and listen to one of

Brooke's adventures. Alba Osteria wasn't a hidden gem, but a conspicuous establishment Brooke frequented for both business and pleasure. I didn't care which restaurant was the backdrop for our date, as long as I was with my best friend.

When I entered Alba Osteria, with its bright orange accented chairs and stools, I was able to see Brooke from where I stood. I thanked the hostess who greeted me, and started in Brooke's direction. She wasn't alone, but the female guest had her back toward the entrance. As I approached, Brooke's lips parted into a wide smile as she waved with excitement. Fiery red spirals framed her tanned oval face. She wore little make-up to embellish her natural beauty. Her pencil skirt and sleeveless printed top subtly flaunted her flawless figure. My eagerness to chat and chew with Brooke added to an unintended dismissal of the guest's presence. She stood to leave just as Brooke and I ended our embrace.

"Sorry, I'm late," I offered. I kissed Brooke on both cheeks, and then stood back to admire her. She looked amazing, but I didn't expect anything less from this fashionista. She always took pride in her appearance, and, unlike some people I knew, she didn't get comfortable in married life and let herself go. "A small errand, and traffic," I continued, and then turned to acknowledge her companion with an extended hand. I reneged the friendly gesture when our eyes met. She smiled, but my face froze in utter disgust as resentment came over me.

There's nothing like family. They could be several thorns in your backside or the pride in your life. One member at a time, my family became the former. A family would not be complete without them: the uncle who knew he couldn't hold his liquor but held his mouth opened under a spigot and got drunk at every family function; the older aunt who proudly flaunted the men she dated—usually half her age—because she thought it gave her a guest pass back into the twenty-something club; and the cousin who everyone watched with hawk-like eyes around their man, because her reputation of sleeping with anything that pissed standing up preceded her. I had ignored the memo that circulated about Patience.

Patience Baptiste was every bit the backstabbing whore everyone had pegged her to be. I was foolish to have even thought I was safe from her. I'd learned my lesson because I went against their better judgment and gave her the benefit of the doubt. Like the people she betrayed, I was thrown in her snake pit the moment she widened her eyes and salivated when I introduced her to Drew Butler. He was my boyfriend of nine months. To Patience, he was a new name to add to her mental bucket list. Patience believed she could get any man she wanted, even those who, at first, pretended they were out of her league. She had the power to change hearts and minds, and make a straight dick bend in her direction. If she lacked anything, it definitely wasn't confidence. I understood the effect she had on men who crossed her path while we strutted our stuff on campus. She's always had this natural obsession for taking anything that didn't belong to her, your man included. Our friendship and family ties led me to develop a false sense of security that she would never cross that line with me. I never thought my own boyfriend would allow himself to be seduced by Patience's essence.

"What is she doing here?" My question was cloaked in bitterness.

Patience had mastered the art of avoidance. Although we lived in the same area, she stayed the hell out of my way, heeding the warning I uttered violently years ago. I have not been able to talk, drink, or marry myself out of these feelings toward her. The moment I set eyes on Patience, I was reminded of the hatred that resided in the tomb of my stomach.

"Come on, Michaela," Brooke pleaded. "Let bygones be bygones."

Brooke attempted to keep the peace, although she was well versed in the sick history that involved Patience.

"Oh, I can let bygones be bygones, but what I can't

do is sit here and break bread with this backstabbing bitch," I said. I kept my eyes fixed on her.

"I was just leaving," Patience spoke. She attempted to break the stare-down between us. She'd cleaned up nicely, but cleaning up her outside did not expunge the past everyone knew so well.

"Please," I pulled one of the orange chairs from the table, and sat, "don't leave on my account. Continue to entertain us with your man and his dirt, assuming he is still your man." I permitted. "I'm sure that's what you were doing." I placed my large satchel bag on the back of the chair, and then looked at Brooke for confirmation. Brooke remained silent, which only affirmed my supposition.

I wanted Patience to open up her mouth and say the wrong thing. Considering my disdain for her, anything she says would be exactly that. She kept her peace. I was already fuming from the mere sight of her, and anything she said would've caused me to explode.

"Is there trouble in paradise?" I asked when Patience joined Brooke in silence. "I'll be honest with you. I expected havoc sooner. Drew ain't never been any good," I spoke in a dialect more familiar to Patience. "He's just a damn dog with money. I know he just started pissing on you, but he's only doing what he does best. I'm speaking from experience, thanks to you, so we both know you are not the first person he's done it to."

Patience stared at me. Brooke maintained her silence.

"What?" I continued. "You thought you were going to get this man and you were going to work miracles? You ain't Jesus, and he ain't water."

"I didn't come here for this," Patience finally spoke.

"Don't forget, you weren't invited," Brooke said, ending her roll as a spectator. "You invited yourself to that seat when you saw me here. You attempted to bait me in a conversation I had no interest in." Brooke adjusted her posture. "I told you I was meeting Michaela and you needed to leave before she got here, but you didn't listen. You sat back and folded your arms like a stubborn little girl, or like you have big balls, just like you're doing now." A waiter had not yet approached the table. They stood aback as they sensed the tension in our exchange. "So," Brooke continued, "since you're here, *this* is what you're going to get."

"Oh, now you're fighting her battles?"

Patience reached for the bag at her feet and stood. She had the audacity to act as if Brooke owed her something.

"Sit your ass down," Brooke ordered through clenched teeth. "If you were a halfway decent somebody, I would fight yours, too." Her eyes followed as Patience lowered to her seat. Patience sat back, and then crossed her legs. She held her bag in her lap. "You put the ho in home wrecker, and you are proud of it. You walk around like you did a good deed and you didn't get the thanks you deserved."

"I didn't wreck anyone's home. All I did was rattle the walls a bit," Patience sassed. A faint smile appeared on her face as if she had just scored a small victory. "Whatever happened after that was her doing." She nodded her head in my direction.

I needed to go to the river to pray, 'cause God knows Patience was about to make me lose the little religion I had. She was talking about me as if I were not even present. I sat as if I was unbothered by her nonchalant interpretation of her actions, but it slowly made my blood boil. I was able to calm myself after being bothered by Zachary this morning, then again after my conversation with Alison. Now, just the scent of Patience was causing an unpleasing, quiet eruption inside me.

"You're worse than Drew." Brooke spoke quietly. "You could've left him alone after you slept with him, but then you embarked on a relationship, as if you had no shame. He was leftovers, and leftovers belong in one place, the garbage. Your actions only proved that you belonged in there with him. You got this man back in your bed no sooner than Michaela tossed him out."

"You know what!" Patience interrupted again.

63

"I'm not done," Brooke cautioned. She was firm, and she spoke with more volume and base. "I know what Michaela and Drew had looked good from the outside, and that's the problem with you whores. You all want to steal the man, thinking he's going to leave his cloak of problems behind, and then when you find out that's not how the shit works, you want to wither and cry foul."

"But I thought..." Patience broke in.

"See." Brooke leaned in. Again, Patience's attempts to give any justifications for her behavior were quickly dismissed. I sat back, folded my arms, and watched Brooke do what she did best: fight my battles when I was tired of fighting. "That brain of yours has never operated as if it had all its screws. Oh, you thought what Drew did to Michaela were just things he needed to get out of his system? And then what, the magic in your pussy was going to make him act right?"

"Brooke!" Patience squealed.

I took a quick glance in Brooke's direction when she spoke language that doesn't usually come from her. Brooke's mouth didn't only speak gospel, but what she spoke was unexpected.

"We don't want an invitation to your goddamn pity party," Brooke continued. "You're going to dance all by yourself, and you won't be dancing here."

Patience expected this thrashing from me, but Brooke's attack took her by surprise. Brooke was right. Patience had no shame, and she was far from any feelings of guilt for what she did to me. When my mother told me to trust no man, she forgot to mention women shouldn't be trusted either. Patience wasn't just my cousin; she was also my best friend. Until I met Brooklynn in college, Patience was my go-to girl, my ride or die. I'd put a few guys she's dated in their proper place when they thought treating her like nothing was what she deserved. I fought for her when she was incapable of fighting for herself. She wasn't exactly the campus slut, but she was a close second. I reserved any judgment because we were blood. It was a hard lesson to learn, but Patience taught me blood could be as thin as water. Besides my mother, she was the one other person I trusted without any doubt. I ignored the naysayers, because nothing they said described the young woman I knew or grew up with, but then she eventually fulfilled their prophecy. Whenever your best friend suddenly stops talking to you, it's either because she slept with your man, or she was plotting to sleep with him. Patience, Drew, Zachary, and my mother, Whitney, all took turns deceiving me.

During our momentary silence, the waiter finally approached the table with three glasses of water. He placed a glass in front of each of us, and then introduced himself.

I removed the glass he placed in front of Patience and put it back on his server's tray.

"This is a table for two," I corrected. "She's leaving."

He looked at me with questioning eyes. Patience remained unmoved, already forgotten that the sight of her cramped my stomach. The expression on Brooke's face indicated that same nauseous feeling. This wasn't what Brooke and I had in mind when we agreed to this lunch date. We looked forward to a quiet afternoon, finishing a conversation that was started over the phone, and then make plans for our next meeting. Nothing we planned included the interruption that was Patience Baptiste. Patience had done a good job making sure our paths didn't cross, but here she was, willingly accepting this berating from Brooke and me. Patience's presence had spoiled our appetite, if nothing else.

"Still doing your wifely duties?" Patience asked. She stared at me with bravado, daring me to respond as the last word fell from her overly painted red lips. She had held on to the statement I made earlier to Brooke when I first embraced her. Patience had been waiting for the opportunity, and was ready to throw her daggers the first chance she got. She uncrossed her legs, sat up, and continued her stare.

"I'm not going to ask you nicely to stay the fuck out my business." Just like that, my voice went from quiet to loud.

"Ladies," Brooke interrupted. She looked around, eying the other occupants in the restaurant. Brooke didn't like confrontations. Even more, she wasn't fond of embarrassment either, which was why she'd kept her voice low as she ripped into Patience. "When I advised you to leave because Michaela was on her way, you hesitated. You were obviously looking for trouble."

"She didn't tell you, did she?" Patience asked. She ignored my directive. I could feel the pulse of my heartbeat rising in my chest.

What the hell is she about to say? I thought. My eyes narrowed. *She doesn't know about…? No, there's no way.* Brooke and I exchanged quick glances as Patience's question lingered. But Patience wasn't worried about a response. She was already poised to continue. She enjoyed the mystery her question created, and the angst that hung in the air.

"About Zachary?" Patience finally added.

Somewhat relieved, I exhaled and sat back in the chair.

"What about Zachary?" Brooke looked at Patience with evil eyes, and then turned her focus to me. "Everything is ok, isn't it?"

"Everything is just fine. I don't know what her problem is." I'd officially had enough of Patience. "As usual, she doesn't know what she's talking about."

"Nice try, Michaela." A mischievous smile appeared on Patience's face. "The only person who doesn't know what anyone is talking about is Brooke," she corrected. "You supposedly tell her everything, don't you?" She didn't wait for me to respond. "So maybe you just forgot to include how you've been pretending your marriage to Zachary is still perfect. Tell her that the woman you worshiped, your mother, my Aunt Whitney, has been screwing your husband since before the day you introduced them. Go ahead," she paused, "ask me how I know. And while you're at it, make sure you tell her how you front with that fake smile for her and the world to see, knowing everything you've been through and what you are going through is eating you up inside."

"I asked you to stay the fuck out my business."

The anger rose inside me like hot lava. I avoided looking at Brooke, but, from the corner of my eyes, I could see the concern in hers.

"While you were so busy holding grudges because of what I did with Drew, your splinter of a man, your husband, was inside your mother, trying hard to find her nonexistent walls. Seems to me your focus was on the wrong bitch."

Before I could catch myself, my palm had left an imprint on the right side of Patience's face. Her words had taken me too far over the edge. I stood, grabbed my bag from the chair, and headed toward the entrance in a quick escape.

"You just don't know how to quit while you're ahead." Brooke stood from her seat. "To say you are way out of line is a fucking understatement." Brooke was a few steps behind me when she yelled, "Michaela, wait!" She pleaded, but I ignored her appeal and continued my getaway.

"Just like my mother, yours can't hold water," Patience yelled. "Maybe you should've told your mother to stay the fuck out your business. Better yet, you should've made sure she stayed off your man."

Eight

Michaela...

If you don't keep your dirt under your skirt, it is sure to come out at the dinner table. Patience afforded herself yet another opportunity to twist the jagged edge knife she'd lodged in my back years ago. It was just like her not to let this moment pass her by, and she was willing to subject herself to the kind of berating she received. I wondered how long had she known. Of all the days, why had she chosen today to disclose this information?

It was clear it brought Patience immense pleasure to bring me pain, and this was just another attempt to do just that, as if the last time hadn't given her enough satisfaction. She smiled as she divulged my little secret to my best friend.

What was happening in my house and the dissolution of my marriage was not her business to broadcast to Brooke. I decided not to involve Brooke in the circumstances that led to my separation and eventual divorce from Zachary, which meant I had to deal with the sometimes-overwhelming emotions I experienced without her support. My intentions were to tell Brooke everything, but not until after Zachary moved his lying ass out of my house. He became my next mistake, and even bigger than the last one I made.

I remember when I couldn't turn my eyes from Zachary, but now I hated the mere sight of him. First it was Drew, now I had Zachary to thank for the new scars on my heart. I thought heaven had sent him into my life, but now I was pretty sure hell had everything to do with it. I wasn't a bad judge of character. They were masters of disguise and deception. At different times, both Drew and Zachary had entered my life under the same pretense.

I rushed from the restaurant, losing control with every hurried step. The overcast sky had finally fulfilled its promise to rain. I disregarded Brooke's appeal and focused on my desperate desire to abandon the embarrassing moment I allowed Patience to engage me in. I drove in silence. I ignored the traffic around me and allowed the events of the past to infiltrate my mind. My mind raced as fast as I drove, and I tried to control the tears that threatened to accompany every unedited scene.

In the driveway, I geared the car into park before it came to a complete stop, which caused my body to jerk forward, and then hurried inside the house in a pace that matched my exit from the restaurant. I attempted the impossible task of dodging raindrops, since I neglected to grab my umbrella from the seat. Inside the house, I removed my cell phone from my bag, tossed the bag on one of the two white chairs in the foyer, just beyond the mahogany French doors, and then headed toward the kitchen. I still had a hunger and thirst that needed to be satisfied, since the fiasco with Patience had interrupted plans for both. Unfortunately, I had to swallow her little pill on an empty stomach. I grabbed a bottle of Malbec from the wine display in the corner on the counter, and then grabbed a glass from the cabinet. I stared at both. I thought about pouring a glass full, but then I abandoned the idea, brought the bottle to my lips, and then tilted my head back. After a long drink, I returned the bottle to the counter, and, finally, I exhaled. This wasn't the life I had fallen in love with, and I was tired of feeling like I couldn't fix it. Patience was right. I was still busy pretending my broken home was still on solid foundation.

There are three sides to every story: my side, her side, and the lies that motherfucker told whenever he opened his damn mouth. Let my mother tell it, she wanted to tell me. I guess every time her nose was close to the tip of Zachary's pleasure stick, she had a change of heart. Either that, or she had concluded she didn't owe me an explanation, since she was in his life first. At least he was satisfying one of us. I still couldn't get any satisfaction. According to Zachary, he never wanted to hurt me. I guess I was supposed to rejoice and give thanks to the Lord that my husband had been screwing my mother. Oh, wait, I wasn't supposed to find out. They both enjoyed pulling the wool over my eyes. They had a grand time putting on airs, pretending that either of them gave a damn about my happiness or me.

I hated that hindsight was 20/20, and I didn't care about *If I knew then what I know now.* Then, I ignored the haunting thoughts that crept into my mind the day I finally introduced Zachary McKnight to Whitney Delgado. I was content that their introduction was not followed by her constant warnings that it wouldn't be long before this man hurt me, which she had done after she met Drew Butler. Drew's eventual affair with Patience lent credence to the fact that my mother was right with her prediction. Whitney had not given that same premonition when she met my future heartbreaker, Zachary.

The men I met after Drew never made it to my mother's front door. They weren't worth an introduction to her, and didn't need her approval, because what I had with any of them went nowhere really fast. Had I encountered them with expectations, they would have been perfect disappointments. But I had a different feeling about Zachary. He was different, and although the meeting and introduction had not happened the way I envisioned, it was time.

I'd walked in my mother's house a few moments before Zachary after he had gone back to the car for something he had forgotten. My mother had called me earlier that day to tell me she had some good news she wanted to share. Since I was already with Zachary, we made the short trip to her house together. I was excited.

Inside the house, Whitney stood in the living room with the phone close to her face. Nothing came from her mouth as she gazed at the screen. She lowered the phone and then stared at me with wide, suspecting eyes. Her chest rose and fell in a quick pace as she looked past me. I followed her eyes to the imposing figure that stood just inside her front door. She looked at him as if his face was familiar, but in their ensuing exchange, it was made clear they were complete strangers. Well, that was what they led me to believe. After a brief pause, Zachary's lips parted into his mesmerizing, seductive smile. He took a step in our direction. "Now I see where she gets it," he'd said. That was supposed to have given him some brownie points, but he didn't need to score. Zachary was already in, and by in, I was referring to my mother. She was proud that I was dating Lieutenant Zachary McKnight. As far as Whitney was concerned, no one compared to him, and even Drew Butler, a man who had both old and some new money, faded in comparison. Of course, Whitney and Zachary had been in cahoots to conceal their relationship.

There was something about the way the rain made me feel. It was God's way of washing away the impurities from the earth, yet people like Drew, Patience, Zachary, and Whitney had been spared. With closed eyes, I listened to the glossy beads of water being thrown against the living room window. Until then, the wind was calm, now it whispered secrets. I expected Brooke to show up at any time. I had not returned any of her calls, a passive expression of my desire to be alone, and I hadn't listened to any of the voice messages she left, as my phone indicated.

I suspected Zachary would walk through the door a few hours after I had my first sip of wine, unless a meeting with his detectives kept him at the station until late into the night. I was willing to take my chances. Until his arrival, I needed to occupy my time. Between sips of wine, while I paced from one side of the living room to the next, I rehearsed my approach to this impending conversation with Zachary. I slighted the images that both sent an unpleasing

---

chill down my spine and reminded me of the pain he caused. I tried not to be overwhelmed by the emotions all over again. Finally, I sat at the top of the stairs and enjoyed the quiet before my planned storm. I flirted with thoughts about what had transpired between Patience and me. With one hand fastened to the bottle of Malbec that had kept my company, I waited for Zachary to walk through the door. The aroma of grapes and dried herb had quieted the fury that built up inside me as I drove home, but I knew as soon as Zachary got home, his presence would revive them.

The last time I sat in this same position, I'd come home after that exhibition that starred Zachary and my mother. In that moment, the tears flowed like water through opened floodgates. Rage filled every vein in my body, and all I thought about was revenge. Nyla had her arms around my neck, and I couldn't explain to her why Mommy looked both sad and angry.

This time, there were no tears, and Nyla was at Alison's house as I requested in a text I sent on my way back from the restaurant. In a response, Alison asked if I was okay, but I ignored her inquiry, too. Although some time had passed since seeing my mother and Zachary, that was still the reason why I sat in the dark and waited.

"You don't have a heart, do you?" I spoke in a calm tone as he rounded the stairs. The door had closed behind him just a few minutes earlier.

"Damn," he said as he fell back a few steps. He grabbed the rail to stop his quick stumble. "Why the hell are you sitting here in the dark like someone who's gone crazy?" he added. In the silence that followed, the rapid thump of his heart was thunderous.

I stared at him through the darkness, and then took another drink from the bottle. Still gripped with both hands, it swung gently between my legs.

"I'm far from crazy." I finally answered his accusation. "Give me a few minutes, I'm sure I'll get there, and faster than you can blink or think of your next lie. My guess is I would've been in a much happier place had I gone crazy. I mean, there's always the plea of momentary insanity, right?" I smiled when he didn't respond.

"I never lied to you, you just didn't listen." He took several steps forward, but I stood to block him. I flicked the light switch to my right, and in the immediate brightness, Zachary and I stood with a concentrated gaze into each other, even though he was a few inches taller. He smiled as if he didn't take my stance seriously.

"You never lied?"

"No, I never lied," he repeated as the smile disappeared. He held a perplexed look as if he wondered what brought about this confrontation.

"Ok, then. What do you call them, half truths?"

"Listen, Michaela, are we really going to do this again? We went through this before you filed for divorce, during the whole fiasco, and then after, and here we are having this same discussion. It gets tired. I'm tired, and I'm sure you are, too. Whether or not you decide to finally listen, my story is not going to change." I waited for him to turn and head down the steps in the other direction, or make an attempt to get past me, but he did neither.

"Your story, huh! Don't you mean the shit you made up and then all the white lies you've added and continued to add? Fuck your story, Zachary. I bet you weren't tired when you were screwing my mother?"

"You know what? I'm done with this conversation," he said as he began his escape.

"Like hell you are. I've kept my peace long enough. In doing so, I live in pure misery. I had to see, hear, and smell your lying ass every day, as if I hadn't suffered enough. Throughout this entire relationship, this marriage, I put you first, you put you first, and even my mother put you first. Who looked out for me? Guess what? I'm done, Zachary. I didn't expect to compete with anyone, least of all, my mother. Of the billions of people in this world, you found your way into my mother. Maybe this was some boyhood game you and your coons decided to play, just to prove whose dick hung the lowest."

"Are you done?" Zachary asked. He was calm, but I expected that. Why should he be bothered? Everything has gone his way.

"Not even close," I said, tilting the bottle to my head again. He sat on the steps near my feet and waited for me to continue. "I found myself alone and filled with a surging hatred for you, the one place I never thought or hoped to be. I saw my hatred for Drew coming from a mile away, but not you."

"And what about your mother, do you hate her, too?" That was a dumb question. The hate I felt for Whitney paled in comparison. I didn't give Zachary the satisfaction of knowing what I held in my heart for her. I could find it in my heart to forgive her, but I couldn't forgive him, not even after hell has frozen over. I stared down at him with disdain. "I get it," he continued. "I hurt you, but only because I tried not to hurt you. If things had gone my way, what I had with Whitney would've ended without you finding out. That was not what your mother wanted. When you came over, I had no idea she had called you. Everything happened just the way your mother wanted it to. Nothing about that day was a mistake."

"What the hell are you talking about?"

"Do you think you just happened to walk in, and of

all places, your mother and I just happened to be getting it on in her living room? That was her plan, Michaela. That had always been her plan. I'm sure your schedule kept what happened from happening much sooner, but she was patient."

"But why would my mother do something intentional to hurt me?" I leaned against the wall and clutched the almost-empty bottle to my chest. One confusing thought after the other swirled in my mind like unrelated fragments in a category four hurricane. My mother and Zachary's awful betrayal gnawed at me as I tried to make sense of everything all over again.

"Why not?" Zachary interrupted. Without giving me a chance to respond, he continued, "Michaela, she hates you, that's why."

"Absurd!" I was silent again. I glanced at the remaining contents in the bottle, but I'd lost interest in finishing it. My face wrinkled as a disturbing thought surfaced. The images danced in my head. They were as frightening as the day, as if I were in that awful moment again.

"Then what's your explanation?" he asked, interrupting the vision that crept in. He kept his head down as he spoke. I stared into the back of his head but maintained my muted stance. *What has Whitney told him?* I thought. "I went to Whitney's house to cut her loose. It had been going on too long, and I started to hate myself for it. I no longer cared if she told you. It was obvious that telling you wouldn't have been satisfying enough, because I could've denied it. No, she wanted you to see. Every time you closed your eyes she wanted that image of us projected on your eyelids. She called you after I got there. I tried to leave, but her seduction began. Her tear-filled plea made me weak. She wanted one more night."

I sat on the step behind Zachary, tilted the bottle to my lips, finally emptying what was left.

"One more night," I repeated. "Right."

"Look, I'm not going to cry foul. I knew what I was doing. I didn't know I was a part of some plan to hurt you. I knew it was wrong."

"Wrong?" I laughed. "Wrong is when you put your right shoe on your left foot. You're acting like you accidentally stepped in shit. You slept with my mother, and not once, not twice, not three times. What you did was...was." I paused and took the deep breath I desperately needed. "What you did ended our marriage, Zachary. What you did betrayed my trust in you, in love, in us." He sat in silence. "Did she tell you what I did?"

"She only said you took something from her, and what you got was exactly what you deserved."

Finally, he stood.

As he made his way past me, without my objection, and headed to the second level to what we had deemed his quarters, I held my eyes to keep the tears from escaping. I'd fought so hard to suppress the very memory that had surfaced, and had actually won. After a few false starts, I met the perfect man, give or take a shortcoming or two, had what others perceived a perfect marriage, a beautiful child, and a home. As I stood there, it became obvious Whitney had held on to my nightmare and what she lost because of it.

"Zachary," I called out. Despite how forthcoming he was as we spoke, I hadn't forgotten the reason why I had sat in wait.

"Yes."

I turned my head in his direction, though he was no longer in sight. "You have until Friday to get the hell out my house."

Nine

Kennedie...

Windsor broke so much. He started with the promises he made and ended with my heart, and both came with its share of pain. If I didn't choose me, he would have broken so much more, as if what he'd done wasn't enough. Yet, he somehow thought what he did was worthy of my forgiveness. Some of his behaviors had changed, but he had been a master at hiding his infidelity before. I would be a fool to think it would be easy for him to give up whatever he had with Selecia. The time they spent together had given her the confidence to stand before me, profess their love, and condemn my marriage to him.

I loved my little guy, although he looked so much like his father. His smile was infectious, and his laugh warmed my heart. He sat in the back in his car seat after I picked him up from his preschool. He was in his own world, as always. I caught myself smiling on the inside as I stared at his image in the rearview mirror. For the moment, I was focused on the effortless joy in my baby's face. The destruction that awaited Windsor at the house, his behavior that triggered my actions, and our interaction that would start as soon as I got home were put out of my mind, and I reveled in the temporary happiness my son afforded. Halfway home, T.J. fell asleep. The drive home was his rocking chair to dreamland. His sometimes-incoherent banter as he drifted to sleep was his own lullaby.

By now Windsor should have gotten past the initial shock. He should have answered all the questions that swirled in his mind: *Can you believe she did this shit?* Yes. *Has she gone crazy?* Yes. I suspected he paced the foyer as he waited for me to walk through the door so he could attack me with the one question he thought only I could answer: Why? After all, I was supposed to be working on forgiving him, giving him the second chance he's waited for. Well, I was sidetracked.

The still of the car after I entered the driveway immediately brought T.J. from his slumber. It was almost as if he had an internal clock. Once a stumbling T.J. and I were inside the house, I was greeted with silence. I listened for signs of Windsor's presence, something to gauge how he might be feeling about what awaited him in the bedroom, not that I gave a damn. I could have checked the garage for Windsor's car, but that would have shown a level of concern that didn't exist. I sat T.J. in the kitchen and placed a glass of milk—his drink of choice—in front of him. When he was finished, he grabbed his tablet and sat on the bottom of the stairs in the living room where he usually occupied himself until his father came home. I ignored the card and the bouquet of flowers—White Peonies—that were left on the island in the kitchen. "Thanks for the roses," I said out loud, "but there isn't a flower in the world that would make me forgive you, baby."

If Windsor had made a run to the flower shop every time he thought about going to bed with Selecia, then maybe we wouldn't be in this situation now. Maybe I wouldn't have gone ham and reduced his articles from his wardrobe into little pieces of cloth. His little gesture was too little, and way too late. I kissed T.J. on the top of his head as I made my way upstairs and into the eerie silence.

Windsor looked at me the moment I appeared in the bedroom door. The decor mimicked a display found in Arhaus, my favorite furnishing store, including the upholstered queen bed and the sheepskin wool rug. Everything was in place where I left them earlier, except Windsor was now present. He sat on the bed and returned to a fixed stare at the piles of clothes that were on the floor. His suit jacket hung on the post next to him.

"I guess this means we're even," Windsor said, breaking the silence between us.

Some people just don't know how to filter their thoughts before they spew bullshit. I held my response as I walked in, removed my jacket and tossed it on the bed. I thought about his assumption.

"Satisfied, yes, but I'll wait patiently for my turn to get even." I stood in front of him and then continued. "You don't honestly believe shredding a few pieces of clothing makes us even? Have you forgotten what you did? Trust me, whatever you're feeling at this moment is nothing compared to what I've felt over the last month. And it can't hold a candle to what I felt that evening your side-chick took it upon herself to downgrade my status from happily married to miserably trying to figure out my husband's displeasure."

"I didn't forget, but if this is your way of reminding me, thanks," he said.

Windsor stood and returned the eyeglasses he'd held in his hand to his face as he walked to the window across the room. His plaid tie hung loosely in front of his partially buttoned white shirt, which he had removed from his pants. Again, we were both silent. My actions had nothing to do with reminding him. I'm sure they created enough memorable moments to last a lifetime, so he hasn't forgotten. Maybe it was supposed to have been only one time, but what happened that first time had left an indelible impression, enough for him to keep going back. I guess you could say Selecia Lassiter had that comeback.

"No need to thank me," I answered as I walked to the window and stood next to Windsor. "This is my pleasure," I said. I looked back at the piles of clothes behind us.

"I asked you to forgive me."

"And what about what I asked you for, huh? Was our marriage just pomp and circumstance, a sideshow to disguise who you really are?" I asked. I looked at him with violent eyes. "Funny how we don't always get the things we ask for. I've decided forgiving you isn't possible." I gazed into the side of his face with intent.

"What's so impossible about that?" He kept his focus forward.

"If you must ask, forgiving you would mean I've accepted the things that drove you to her. It would mean I believed you when you said your intentions weren't to hurt me. Well," I said as I turned from him and headed toward the door, "I don't care about your reasons, and regardless of what you intended, you did hurt me."

"Kennedie, I'm sorry."

87

"I think it's a little too late for 'I'm sorry,' Windsor." I turned to find him staring at me. Pity filled his eyes, but there was no room left in my heart for compassion. He should have thought about this very moment when he decided sleeping with his boss's wife was worth the risk of losing his own. "You're only sorry because you got caught." I paused to collect my thoughts.

"Actually, I didn't..." Windsor began, but a sharp glance at him stopped him mid-sentence.

"Were you going to say you didn't get caught?" I didn't need him to answer. I already knew those exact words were on the tip of his tongue. "You are absolutely right, Windsor. Getting caught was never what you set out to do. Your little bitch told. When you get a chance, thank her for pulling the wool from my eyes." I turned and continued my departure. I expected him to say something that would stop me in my tracks, and he didn't disappoint my expectation.

"You need to focus!" he yelled.

I spun to face Windsor again.

"On what?" I asked sharply.

"On what we have."

I laughed.

"On what we have?" I repeated. "There is no 'we,' Windsor. 'We' don't have. I have. I have a man who has been lying and pretending. I have a man who convinced me that who was sleeping next to me was the person I fell in love with, knowing he is not you. What I have is a man who can't commit, at least not to me. I have a man who, when he had to choose between his home and a piece of ass, the piece of ass won, many times over."

"We can fix this," he pleaded. "It's not too late."

"Stop it, Windsor. Just stop. Again, there is no 'we'. 'We' didn't have late dinners and conversations over glasses of Merlot, Chardonnay, or whatever expensive wine you decided was apropos to toast the fact that you were successful in hiding your transgressions. 'We' can't fix this. 'We' didn't break us, and, to be frank, I don't have time to devote to fixing something that I didn't break."

"I love you, Kennedie."

"You love me?" I repeated. I laughed and hoped he felt lower than dirt, because what he did made him exactly that in my eyes. "What do you expect those three little words to do now, save our marriage, save us? They never stopped you from your little secret rendezvous. And I bet you said the same thing to Selecia."

"But..."

"Windsor, stop," I interrupted. "Stop throwing empty words at me, just because they sound like what you think I need to hear. They used to make my heart sing, but now every time I think about you, about your betrayal, my heart weeps."

"We can go back."

"To what?" I yelled. The only thing Windsor was doing was wasting my time, and making me mad while he did. "You want us to go back to the day before you decided she was worth throwing away everything we had? I don't want us to continue into a love-hate relationship where you're trying to convince yourself you love me, and I'm trying to stifle my undying hatred for you."

I stormed out of the bedroom and left Windsor frozen in disbelief. Nothing had gone as he expected. He was supposed to come home and I was supposed to forgive him, give him another chance to right his wrong. You give second chances to little boys in high school, not to a grown-ass married man who understood that every decision had consequences. Did he expect to cheat? Probably not. Grandma always said a man doesn't turn into a dog overnight. Windsor had been raising his hind leg and pissing on fire hydrants since he was knee-high to a grasshopper. Did he expect to get caught? No, and if he did, he knew exactly what words he would use to talk his way back into starting over. He'll ask for forgiveness, and the love I have for him would dismiss all the reasons why he wasn't worthy. We would continue as if nothing happened. He should have built a box around Selecia and force her to stay in a sidepiece's place. She had her talons in my husband, and then showed up at my house with her big announcement, as if there was nothing I could do about it.

I walked downstairs. T.J. still sat at the bottom step, seemingly unbothered by the commotion that had just transpired. I headed into the kitchen and removed the folded brown envelope from my purse, which I had left on the back counter. Windsor halted my return to the bedroom when I turned to find him standing in my direct path. T.J. stood in the distance behind him, his nose still buried in the IPad.

"Here," I said. I slapped the envelope against his chest and then stepped around him.

"What's this?" he asked as he tore the envelope.

"You can read," I said, and continued my exit. I left Windsor standing in the kitchen as he unfolded the contents he removed from the envelope.

$\mathcal{T}_{en}$

Kennedie...

February 14. While everyone was busy making this a night to remember, I would give anything to wipe the day clean from the calendar, and from my memory. I didn't know then, but this was the date, a few years ago, that I'd made my biggest mistake. Because of him, Valentine's Day will never be the same. In the beginning, way before we said, "I do," that day began with flowers, cards, and candy, and that all happened before breakfast was served in bed. Those evenings usually ended in Windsor's arms, slow dancing on rose petals after enjoying his garlic-marinated steak by candlelight. He knew his way around the kitchen. Tonight wasn't going to be a repeat of the past.

I sat in the turquoise-colored accent chair with a glass of wine to wash down the bitterness I was sure would enter my mouth, my shredder, and my collection of Valentine's Day cards Windsor had given me over the years. I had treasured them because they reminded me of the beauty in the man I married. I read each card, including his own little personal touch, "Love, Windsor." I guess he couldn't bring himself to sign what would have been an appropriate description of his true identities: Liar, Adulterer, or Fraud. There were the cards that promised to always love me, the few that loved the way I smiled and moved, and let's not forget those that said he loved the trust and openness between us. *Trust and openness*, I thought. *What a bunch of bullshit!* Only one of us could be trusted, and the only things he had been opening lately were the legs that belonged to Selecia Lassiter, with his face between them. Then there were the anniversary cards that pledged undying love for me, and the desire to grow old with me. As I read, I fed them to the shredder, and then sipped my wine as the lies he'd carefully chosen were disintegrated.

I sat in the chair with my legs crossed at the ankles, my knees cradled in my arms, seething with anger as thoughts about the dose of deception I was handed a few months ago swam through my mind. *There goes our happy home*, I thought. I stared at the imprint on my ring finger and was reminded that my happiness was the result of his false pretenses, and his happiness he found whenever he ran to the arms of Selecia Lassiter.

I wish I could've called my mother, Natalie, but like many of the other wishes that included her—wishing she were here, or wishing she gave a damn—that never came true. That woman had never shown interest in my pleasures, and she couldn't give two fucks about my pains. Hell, I'm still waiting for her to show up at my wedding. Maybe she'll be happy about my failed marriage and celebrate. At least I would've known she gave a damn about something that involved me.

I picked up the phone I set on the coffee table. I thought about calling Kiana. She's been my best friend since high school, but I figured she was probably on her back, with her heels toward the ceiling, making sure her neighbors knew Alec's name, and rightfully so. She was still enjoying the promised bliss of marriage. Hopefully, she doesn't find out even that promise was meant to be broken. I dialed the number that belonged to the woman with the voice who could sweet-talk a man from a ledge.

"Happy Valentine's Day, my beautiful child," my grandmother answered.

"Ma-Grand," I said. I called her the name I gave her when I realized my mother's disappearance from my life was permanent.

I paused and thought about the nights I went to sleep hoping my mother would soon realize her mistake, but soon never came. I had to come to the sad reality that her mistake had already been labeled and shipped south.

"I'm sitting here, trying to find some semblance of happy in this day and, so far, I'm not having any luck," I continued.

"And how much does this have to do with...?"

"Please, don't say his name," I pleaded. "He's worse than maggot meat. I never thought the man I loved would've done what he did. He made me see him in a different light, and it's rather unflattering."

"Is that what you think about him?"

"Honestly," I began. I sat back in the chair and, without much effort, ran my fingers through my hair. "To keep myself from being disgusted, I try not to think about him at all."

"You didn't think he was perfect, did you?"

"You're talking like perfect doesn't exist. Isn't that what you said about Grandfather?" I stood and began a leisured walk to the kitchen and the glass of Bordeaux I poured earlier, though I craved something much stronger.

"I hate to break this to you, but they didn't make them all like your grandfather then, and they sure as hell aren't all made like him now," my grandmother said. She sounded disappointed, as if she wanted to apologize for my pain. "Luck was on my side when I met your grandfather; I can't say the same about my friends I saw smiled or cried their way through vows."

"Who are you talking about?" I grabbed the wine glass and paused before I took a sip.

"That's not important. Let's just say I know a lot of 'I dos' that have ended because they no longer did. Just like you, they chose the one bad apple from the bunch."

I guess the same fortune that had befallen my grandmother's friends had landed in my lap. I, too, thought it was luck that brought Windsor my way, now luck was laughing in my face.

"To be fair, I was never looking for perfect. If I stumbled across it, fine. I was prepared to deal with his minor imperfections, but there's no way I can overlook what he's done to me, and to my son."

I took a small sip from the glass, moved the wine glass in a small circle motion, and watched the red liquid waltz against the curves. I felt a small tear gather in the corner of my eye and began its tickling trail down the side of my face. I placed the glass on the small table next to me, and then quickly wiped away this trace of hurt.

"This really hurts, Ma-Grand."

"It won't hurt for too long, Sweetheart." My grandmother paused. I matched her silence and wondered what could have gotten her attention. Just as I was about to breach the silence, she spoke. "You don't think you can forgive him?"

Those were the very last words I expected to hear from my grandmother's mouth. By no stretch of the imagination did she have a soft spot for any man who engaged in extra-marital affairs, breaking promises made to both woman and God. That Windsor wasn't one of her favorite persons wasn't a secret, and she wasn't afraid to tell him he was only liked because he made me happy.

"Now, you know what the bible says about forgiveness." Truth is, my grandmother knew the bible very well, so I wasn't about tell her anything she hadn't heard before.

"Kennedie!" she shouted.

"Without the shedding of blood, there is no forgiveness," I began. "So, unless you are interested in having future conversations with me on the other side of freedom..."

"Kennedie!" my grandmother interrupted again, but I disregarded her interference.

"So, I guess we'll both sit and wait for hell to freeze over."

Again, my grandmother and I were both silent. In that momentary quiet, my mind shifted to moments of Windsor and me. I thought about the time we made what was supposed to have been our first meal together, and the takeout we ended up feeding each other because our lovemaking had befouled our preparation. I remembered the nights we sat by candlelight and toasted the life we lived. I thought about the nights Windsor's hands gently held me at the nape of my neck as we danced to the silence of the night, and then the soft of his lips in the same spot. When the thoughts ended, I flung my hand and waited to hear the glass crash against the white wall and the abstract pattern created by the red liquid. I stared out the window and into the night that looked just as lonely as me.

Eleven

Michaela...

August 4

It happened again. This time he said it, those awful words I never wanted to hear from him: I love you. Why does love have me feeling like this? I hate him! I hate him! I hate him! Why does he do this to me? Why can't he stop? Why won't he stop? Why won't she make him stop? Why won't love make him stop? I screamed at the top of my lungs, hoping someone would hear me, and that didn't stop him. I know he sees the cold emptiness in my eyes. I closed them, wishing the pain away, hoping to escape his invasion. Each deep, intense thrust brought me back to the painful reality that included him. I see the pleasure, the satisfaction in his eyes. When he was finished with his violation, he apologized. He always apologizes. He's sorry. He just can't help himself. But what good is his apology when he constantly repeats his offense. I want to sleep. I close my eyes and I see him. I feel him, although he's not here. I no longer sleep to dream. When I do sleep, I have nightmares that are of him. So, I'm lying here, again, on the bare mattress, just as I did last night, and two nights before that, staring at the door, waiting for the shadow of his feet to disturb the light from the hallway that's creeping in my room, just in case he hasn't had enough. He needs more of me. The sheets are in a corner of the room. They smell like him. They have remnants of him. Tomorrow I'll hide them in the bottom of the trash, just like I have done the others. I would give anything to know what normal sleep feels like. Hell, I would give anything to just feel normal. Everything is hurting. It's either him or me, but one of us has to go.

It was the feeling that I had been asleep too long that had me sitting up in bed in a panic, trying to slow the pounding in my chest. After finally winning the battle, I partook in a labored walk to the bathroom. After a long shower and some time in front of the bathroom mirror, I emerged looking better than I felt. A stumble down the lane of painful memories was to blame for the kind of night I had. The night before, I sat on the corner of the king size bed with my childhood journal in one hand and a cocktail glass in the other. I needed something to numb me to the emotions that the revisit would stir up. The diary was hidden in a shoebox under my least-favorite pair, in the back of the closet, where Zachary would never make the mistake of finding it. My shoe collection was just a reminder that I spent too much money on styling my feet, which he was always reminding me. I didn't pay much attention to his reminder. I read each line etched in the journal in anger, bringing back the hurt I felt as a scared and helpless thirteen-year old. My mother didn't believe me, she didn't help me, and he wouldn't stop hurting me.

I thought about the hateful words that came from my mother's mouth. *What you got was exactly what you deserved.* Those words rung in my ear every night since Zachary repeated them a week ago, and that made the hurt that much worse. The thirteen-year old girl who had lain helpless under the weight of her brother had grown into a woman in her thirties whose mother still felt that she deserved his assault. Until now, she had kept that sentiment to herself. *What she lost?* What she lost was incomparable to what he took from me. I lost my virginity to…my brother, someone I loved before his actions fueled the abhorrence I now felt for him. It was years before I could trust another man, let alone let them get close enough to touch me. Even my relationship with my own father suffered as a result. I remember the watershed moment I experienced when Drew rested his hand on my heart. As if I could still feel that moment, the sensation from his warm hand on my chest had jolted me back to the present. I dabbed the tears that dripped from the corner of my eyes to keep them from soiling the page of the already-tattered diary.

I stood at the corner of the bed—the same corner I sat and read the night before—and eyed the journal I set on the pillow next to me just before I fell asleep. I resisted the urge to read one more entry, agreeing with the thought that one bad trip definitely did not deserve another. I returned the diary to the box, under the beige crystal back pumps, covered it, and then began yet another sluggish stroll to the back of the closet.

I've never experienced so much contemplation at any other time in my life. The part of me that had accepted the reality of what was wanted to sweep my marriage to Zachary, my horrible childhood experiences, and my mother under the rug and forget that any of it ever happened. Until a week ago, that's exactly what I'd done. Once again, Patience was the beginning of the resurrection of a series of unfortunate events. And now, my mother had opened Pandora's box, where I had successfully locked away every frightful, haunting image that made my teenage years a living hell.

I spent four years on Dr. Maitlyn Benjamin's overused leather couch. I had gone to her feeling like I was already dead, and there were nights I felt like I was ready to make that a reality. I needed her to revive me, though death was probably a better feeling than what I felt living in the reality that my brother created. If I wasn't dead, I felt broken. Most of the times I fell asleep to Dr. Benjamin's soothing voice that delivered questions that hung in the air until they eventually fizzled away. It was during those moments that I usually slept without seeing his lifeless eyes staring down at me just before he collapsed. I was angry with my mother for failing to protect me, mad at Isaiah for raping me, and disappointed that I was too damn tired to plunge the knife into him one more time.

Finally in the kitchen, I read the message Alison scribed on the post-it she stuck to the top of the Keurig. *Didn't want to wake you. Took the kiddo for a walk.* If only she knew, waking me was the last thing she needed to worry about. Only the fact that she was a winter baby could explain why Nyla was such a fan of the cold. Me, I longed for a taste of the unseasonably warm weather that gave us a taste of spring in December. Accepting that my wish coming true was a long shot, I welcomed my morning dose of coffee. I poured a cup from the brew Alison made, and attempted to enjoy the bouquet of hazelnut, vanilla, and almond. Coffee was the best part of waking up. I ignored the phone on the counter that beckoned me to make the one call I avoided all week. The thoughts in my head, the same ones that were the interruption of everything, wouldn't let me enjoy my coffee the way I did before all hell broke loose.

Finally, I gave in to the urge. I grabbed the phone and keyed in Whitney's number. With each ring, my heart pounded in my chest. After a deep breath, I whispered a short prayer, took a long sip from my mug, and braced myself for the voice of evil to echo in my ear.

"Who is this?" Whitney answered.

The hatred she held for me resonated in her salutation. *How could I not have known?* I thought. Already, I regretted entering this rhythm-less dance with the devil reincarnate.

"You've been waiting to pour salt in my wounds," I began.

I didn't need to give an introduction. She knew exactly who I was. She may have attempted to erase me from her memory, just as I had her, but I was certain she hadn't deleted me from her phone. She may have saved my number under some fictitious name that cursed my existence, but she had me saved.

"What the hell are you talking about?" Her tone was dismissive, as if I were the interruption she'd long avoided. "Whatever it is that you want, this is not a good time. You asked me to forget you even exist, and I think I've given you exactly that. So, I'll ask again, what the hell are you talking about?"

"Are you satisfied? Have you honored his memory?"

There was silence between us, and then she spoke.

"So, I see the bastard finally told you. I wondered what he was waiting for." Her words were enveloped in satisfaction.

"The only bastard I know was your sick-ass son," I interrupted. "He raped me. You want to talk about people getting what they deserved? He got what he deserved."

My retort was the right hook she didn't see coming. Still, Whitney was unshaken.

"I thought Zach would've said something sooner, since you've kept this little secret from him. Actually, I was hoping he had. We could've had this heart to heart a long time ago. I almost got tired of waiting."

"Heart to heart?" I repeated her words. Clearly she couldn't have been talking about a conversation that included her. "Only one of us on this phone has a heart. You are wicked and calculating, and I can't find the words right now to describe what you have beating in your chest."

"Listen to you," Whitney interrupted. Amusement was evident in her voice. "Pretending as if you know me so well."

"Why didn't you tell him why I did it?"

"You're not good at asking the tough questions, Chaela," she asserted with another hint of cheer in her tone.

I squirmed at the sound of the moniker I'd abandoned. It was the name my brother Isaiah would call me, and no matter who said it now, it was his voice I heard. It always brought back the sordid past, and this time was no different.

"I thought about how much it would pain you to divulge that experience, and it made me smile," she continued after a long pause. The words she chose served their purpose. They provoked a deserved response.

"You're such an evil bitch!" I roared.

"I had time to practice!" she yelled back.

I turned and slammed the mug on the marble counter behind me. Coffee and fragments of ceramic added to the décor of the kitchen space.

"And it definitely made you perfect it. Why didn't you tell him you did nothing to stop Isaiah from raping me?" I ignored the mess I made. "You thought that bit of information that you chose to keep to yourself would magnify how terrible you were at being a mother?"

"I did the best I could with the kids your sorry-ass father and God gave me."

If I didn't know better, I would've thought my ears had deceived me. Even if she wasn't fully aware, Whitney placed the blame for her second-rate parenting skills on my father, Duncan Bridges, and God.

As far as I knew, my father was a faithful and strong man, and nothing could break him. But that day, he lost his son, his daughter was long gone, and he didn't even know it. The fact that I had blamed him for my hurt and had distanced myself from the affection I received from him made the situation worse. When he found out my mother knew what Isaiah was doing to me but never sought help for neither him nor I, it caused the end to their marriage. They had been married since before Isaiah was born, but since my father couldn't save his children, there was no point in saving his marriage.

"I told you what was happening," I said, "but you did nothing. You buried my face near your armpits and uttered 'everything will be all right'. That's what you always told me. Surprise, Mother! Everything was not all right. But now I know those words had nothing to do with me. That was your vow to him."

"Yes!" she yelled, proud that I had finally figured her out. "I wanted justice."

"Justice or vengeance?"

"Whatever! I wanted you to pay for what you did."

"And since you couldn't get away with murder…." I paused.

"Like you did?" Whitney added.

Every breath I took held hatred for him.

"What about him? What about what he did to me? He shouldn't have paid for what he did to me?"

"He was your brother. He didn't have to pay with his life."

"And I was his sister," I snapped. "Neither of those titles mattered to him. Don't go getting sentimental. I told you what he was doing. I gave you the opportunity to save me, to save him. What was I supposed to do, continue to be subjected to his abuse until you were ready to deal with the reality that your goddamn son was a rapist?"

"Still…" she interrupted.

"Still?" I stood in the kitchen in disbelief. "I yelled for my mother, but you weren't there, so I took matters into my own hands. I did the only thing I knew to make him stop. If you are going to blame me for taking your son away from you, I hope you're sharing the blame. You killed him, too."

Finally, I breathed, and then turned to find Alison just inside the kitchen. She stood aghast, with a penetrated stare directly into me. Her eyes held the tears I was too angry to let flow. I was so engaged in this quarrel with Whitney that I wasn't cognizant of anything else happening around me. Until then, this was a secret I'd kept from Alison, too. It wasn't that I didn't trust her, but it wasn't information she needed in order for us to build the friendship we had. She walked closer. She failed to soften the concerned expression on her face. She pulled me in close, and I offered no resistance. As her arms tightened around me, I ended the conversation with Whitney, placed the phone on the counter, and then collapsed my head on Alison's shoulder.

"Everything is going to be all right," she said as our bodies swayed.

Alison's raspy voice rung in my ear. The same words that came from my mother years earlier sounded so much different. I now know Whitney's reassurance had nothing to do with me. Unlike my mother, I believed Alison. The reality that Whitney refused to deal with, my reality, had led to the destruction of so many: a dead son who obviously had problems and needed help, a teenage girl who only therapy and time could fix, and a marriage that was already on the rocks.

"You can't keep inviting people into your life who mean you no good." Alison's voice had a quiet calm. I knew Alison cared because she's said it often enough. With her arms around me, and my head safely on her shoulder, I felt her compassion. "You can't choose your mother, but you can choose to stop letting people hurt you. You know what they say about hurt people, and your mother has some healing to do."

Alison disclosed so many truths in what she said. I had

given Whitney another opportunity to hurt me, and there was no hesitation in her willingness to take advantage of it. Just as I was a broken teenager, Whitney was broken, too. There were still unresolved feelings about my father and the marriage that never worked. She hadn't gotten over being abandoned by her own father, the man we only heard about but have never met. Everything she felt was compounded by the fact that the son that had caused the strain in the relationship between Whitney and her father, and their eventual split, had been taken away by the daughter she secretly wished she had buried alive. All the men she loved had left her for one reason or another. Still, that was no excuse for harboring this hatred for me all these years.

$\mathcal{T}$welve

Michaela...

I always walked away with the same feeling after one of my talks with Alison, and the last time was no different. I needed a shoulder to cry on, but what she gave me was so much more. I'd kept so much inside. It was how I survived until I went spilling my guts to Dr. Benjamin. Although she declared her office a judgment-free zone, I still heard Isaiah's voice in my head, telling me what he did to me was my fault, as if I had walked into his room and offered up myself to him. Until Patience's babble, I had dealt with Zach and Whitney's ultimate betrayal, and made it through my divorce, losing only a few tears and a couple of sleepless nights.

Whitney had the audacity to show up on the first day

of the proceedings. She'd sat front and center to watch my happiness fade, and to relish in the fact that my marriage to Zachary had suffered the same fate as her marriage to my father. I could only imagine the silent jubilation that took place on her insides. She would jump for joy if she could, except there was the demanded silence in the court. She'd already had her starring role in everything that had transpired, but I made damn sure she wasn't going to get her opportunity for a reprise. She'd sat until I had my attorney ask the judge to have her ass escorted out. Although I would've liked the support of my best friend Brooke, I'd decided to keep her out of the loop. I hadn't spoken to or seen her since our lunch disaster, the one railroaded by Patience's mischiefs. I ignored her attempts to reach me, and I kept breaking silent promises to return her call, even after hearing the pleas in her messages.

If you asked me, Alison wrote the book on everything from love to loss, and anything that happened between. She'd prepared Nyla and me my favorite—salmon with brown sugar glaze, stuffed artichoke, and rice. After dinner, while Nyla engaged in child's play in her room, Alison and I sat on the floor in the living room, in front of the couch, and partook in a nightcap. For a woman her size—she wasn't too much taller than me—she had no problem throwing back shots. That's how we had decided to take the edge off. She must've been honing this little talent at home where she wouldn't be judged. Trust me. With my extra-curricular activities, I was in no position to cast the first or last stone. Sure she indulged—a glass or two of wine while she prepared dinner—but I had no idea she embraced the hard stuff. A half bottle in and I began to speak my entire truth, which I had hid behind for too long.

I had been estranged from my family ever since the incident. They had damn near given me a concrete cross to carry to my own crucifixion. They hated me, and treated me as if the ground I walked on was poisoned. No one wanted anything to do with me, because I had taken away their beloved Isaiah from them. And, of course, my mother had her own motives why she pretended to care. I had the physical and emotional scars, but it was better for them to believe his shit didn't stink than to believe he did what I had accused him of doing.

Maybe it would've been more compelling had I laid under his bloody, lifeless body until my mother and the police came, instead of sitting in a far corner in my room with my rapist's blood on my hands, and the black handle knife at my feet. Two months after losing it at my brother's funeral, where I stood to see his casket lowered into the ground—it was only then I was certain he could never hurt me again—my father asked for a divorce. To say my father was upset would be an understatement. Not only did my mother not believe me, but she had also kept my complaints a secret from him. I believed her when she said everything would be ok, so I didn't think I needed to plead my case to my father. While I cursed and hated my father for not protecting me, and even distanced myself from him emotionally, he hated my mother for not giving him the opportunity to save his son and protect his daughter. He left me with the woman who, unbeknownst to me, carried an unprovoked hatred for me.

"You know, I never liked that woman, your mother," Alison said. Her statement lacked emotion, which was understandable, considering the person she spoke about. "I only tolerated her because, unfortunately, she had the prestigious title of being your mother and Nyla's grandmother, though undeserving." Alison became silent. She tilted her head back on the couch and stared into the high ceiling. "There was just something about her I didn't trust."

"Well," I interjected, "now we all know what that was, don't we?" I smiled and then poured another shot for each of us.

"Whenever I saw her, I got this unsettling feeling, the shivers, like someone had just walked over my grave."

I turned my head in Alison's direction as she

referenced the centuries old expression and allowed my eyes to question her. She angled her head toward me when she felt my stare.

"What?" she asked. "I'm just saying." She smiled and then returned her focus to the ceiling. "That bitch had a strange disposition." Alison reached for her shot glass from the coffee table and raised it to the heavens. "Cheers," she said. She brought the miniature glass to her lips and threw her head back. She placed the empty glass on the coffee table and poured it full.

"Hey, that bitch is my mother." I covered my mouth to stifle the laughter that attempted to escape. "But I can't blame you for calling a spade a spade." I took the shot that I'd set on the table.

"Or in your mother's case, a bitch a bitch." I looked at Alison sideways. "What?" she asked. She shrugged her shoulders, smiled, and emptied the glass. "You said it. I call 'em like I see 'em, and now I see your mother for exactly what she is."

Alison and I sat in front of the ivory velvet couch with the empty shot glasses still in our hands, and our legs stretched out in front of us. We sat in a long silence. Unless we wanted to wake the next morning feeling as if we'd opened and closed the local bar, we needed to quit while we were ahead. Thoughts of my life flashed in my head and the list of persons who had betrayed my love and my trust had increased by one. *After what Isaiah did to me I thought I had experienced the worst. Then Drew happened. His involvement with Patience had cut deep, because I was just starting to trust men again and, even worse, Patience was family. Zachary, the man who had perpetrated my Knight in Shining Armor, had me ready to dismiss the hatred I once held for love. How could the same man who had changed my reaction to men and love cause me to hate the idea of both all over again? And finally, Whitney had allowed years of hatred to finally manifest itself in her secret affair with my husband.*

I thought about Nyla, who went to sleep as soon as I tucked her in. I wanted to apologize to her for what her father's greed and carelessness, and her grandmother's wickedness, created for her. The man whose face she saw every evening, who kissed her forehead every night while she slept, now only saw her a couple nights a week and every other weekend, which was the agreement we decided to follow once he was out the house. Being a single parent was never what I envisioned when we decided to bring our child into the world. I'd become my own mother. Co-parenting from a distant was never a part of the deal.

I wasn't sure where Alison traveled in her mind during our silence, or what thoughts swirled in her head, but what they were caused Alison to let out a deep breath.

"You want to know what becomes of the broken

hearted?" she asked. She sounded defeated, as if the memory of her journey had just pulled the happy rug from under her feet.

Her question was unexpected. It wasn't something I've thought about, but considering the mood and the conversation, I decided to be amused by her explanation.

"What?" I responded. I turned my face toward her.

"Me."

"You, Alison? Get out of here!" I tapped her shoulder in play, and then smiled as I leaned to pour another shot. The bottle was now half empty, and I was more relaxed than when we first sat. Alison maintained a poker face.

"He didn't even wait for the ink from the judge's signature to dry before he was gallivanting about with her glued to his side. And that's not even the craziest thing."

I looked at Alison as if she'd introduced a cliffhanger that had me sitting on edge of my seat.

"You mean, it gets crazier than your just-crowned ex-husband already jet setting with his mistress?"

"He took her on the trip we had been planning for our ten-year anniversary. I never wished bad on anyone, but I..." Alison paused and then abandoned her thought. "She was business, that's what he said when I approached him about my suspicions. I was his wife, but all the treatment I got from him had me feeling like I was his sidepiece, even though I knew that two-bit tramp couldn't walk a block in my shoes, much less a mile."

"Oh, Alison, I'm sorry."

"Why? I'm not," she corrected. "While I was busy giving myself reasons why I should try to make my marriage work, he gave me one reason why it wouldn't, and that reason was Janee Cunningham."

Interested in Alison's story, I sat up. "Same script, different cast."

"Conrad and his dick was like a blind man and his walking stick, feeling his way through every jezebel in his path. Until Janee, he was able to keep his affairs very private, but whatever she did made him holler."

A drunken man tells no tale, and the truth was rolling from Alison's alcohol-soaked tongue with little effort. She'd kept this side of her hidden, and it was my fault. I learned as much about her as she did about me. Alison lost more than sleep and a few dollars during her ugly divorce from Conrad DeCosta. While battling her husband's nasty behavior in the courtroom, at home when no one was there to witness her tears, she mourned the loss of her unborn son. Her ex-husband had no clue his antics and the stress had caused such a devastating loss, and Alison hadn't planned on telling him. Conrad was a shark known for kicking others while they were down. Any sign of vulnerability would've caused him to be cruder.

Our night ended with both of us falling asleep on the floor in front of the couch, and that was where Sunday morning and Nyla found us. Oblivious to the night that Aunt Alison—that's what Nyla called her—and I had, Nyla snuggled between us and laid her head on my chest. Thinking about what Alison shared about the fate of her pregnancy, I wrapped my arms around Nyla, closed my eyes, and then exhaled. One thing I could say about my baby girl is that I never knew love like that.

Thirteen

Kennedie...

Windsor stood in the living room of the house we once called a home. When I tell you love didn't live here anymore, that's exactly what I mean. My grandmother taught me to never hate, but of all her lessons, that was the one I chose to disobey. I hated Windsor, and I had a laundry list of damn good reasons. His untamed brown hair danced in the light breeze from the ceiling fan as he turned toward me. He sported a white long sleeve shirt, khaki pants, and brown shoes. He kept his facial hair cut low, and he smelled God awfully good. Those were just a few of the things about him that I fell in love with. Then the image of him and her entered my mind, and I was soon reminded of the reason why he was standing in my living room, and the reason why hate was the only feeling I now had for him. He stared at the papers on the coffee table. They were in the same place he left them weeks earlier when he refused to sign and had walked out. Then he vowed not to set foot in the house. Until now, he'd kept his word. He even sent his brothers to pick up a few items he needed to hold him over.

Windsor looked at me and then at the papers as if he needed further instructions. I thought I had made myself clear when I called him a few weeks earlier. If he hadn't pulled a disappearing act, we could've gotten this over with already. Instead, he avoided me as if I didn't exist, and I was going to somehow forget about what I needed him to do. He even avoided our son.

"So, this is how you're going to end it?" he asked.

"Ending this was your doing. I didn't need words because your actions spoke loudly enough. You just made going along with it a hell of a lot easier for me. What the hell did you think was going to happen?"

"Well," he started his response.

"Don't say anything," I interrupted. I wasn't about to listen to the load of crap I knew he was fixing to tell, because I'd heard enough bullshit from him to last several lifetimes. Furthermore, he had already wasted enough of my damn time. "Let me answer that question for you. You didn't think I would throw away the eight years we've been together, although that is what you did. Or maybe you thought I wouldn't want T.J. growing up in a broken home like I did. Well, your actions caused this. Don't you worry about T.J., he will be just fine."

"So that's it?"

"Please don't stand there and ask me if 'that's it' one more time. That was it when, with no warning, my husband stopped reacting to me. That was it when I spent days and nights trying to figure out what the hell I did or didn't do to cause my husband to go astray. That was it when I would lay awake at night trying to keep thoughts from driving my ass crazy. You're damn right, that's it. Sign the papers and get the hell out, Windsor. You've hurt me, and you don't get to hurt me again. You don't get to see me cry for you again. What guarantee do I have that you won't do it again, especially when I didn't expect you to betray me in the first place?"

"Besides my word, nothing. But..."

"And so far, I'm zero for one in taking your fucking word," I interrupted. "You know, when the thought that you might be cheating entered my mind, I thought, no, Windsor wouldn't be able to live with himself, so he would never do anything like that to me."

I felt the tears in my eyes, and I thought I'd cried enough over this bastard. Three months of thinking, and just about as long crying, and I still had more tears left to cry. I pressed my hands to my eyes and hoped the tears would subside.

"You lost your job, and you didn't tell me. You slept with Selecia Lassiter, your boss's wife, and, of course, you kept that your fucking secret. If it were not for her husband, I wouldn't have known she had been maintaining your salary. And to think you had this bitch, with her husband next to her, smiling in my face and kissing my cheeks at last year's Christmas party, cooing about us being such a beautiful couple. Of course she thought you were beautiful. What else was she supposed to think while she was screwing your brains out? She had your balls in her hands and your dick in her mouth every time our backs were turned. Sign the damn papers, Windsor, and get the hell out of my house!" I yelled.

He sat on the couch, looked up at me, and then began his signature.

"Where's my son?" he asked. He dropped the pen on the documents and stood up. I didn't answer. "Where's my son, Kennedie?" he repeated a few octaves louder.

"Oh, you couldn't be asking about the son you've abandoned." I sat on the other couch across from him, folded my arms, and stared at him.

"Oh, so you want to play games?"

"No, Windsor, that would be you. That's exactly

what you're doing now. I'm giving you freedom to do whatever the hell you want, with whomever the hell you please, without worrying about little ol' me."

I guess Windsor thought his yell would have me running and hiding behind the couch, peeping my head from behind to see if he was going to explode. He knew I wasn't afraid of his bark or his bite. I had nothing to fear but fear itself, and I wasn't even afraid of that. I'm not sure what Windsor was used to, but I wasn't a replica of some stupid bitch who would retreat under her shell because she felt threatened by his widened brown eyes and stare. He was nothing but a Chihuahua in Pit-bull's clothing.

"You think I wanted my son here to witness this? I refuse to let him see, this early, that men like you exist." My finger was a few inches from his face when I spoke my last words. I turned and began to walk toward the front door. Windsor followed closely behind. I could feel him breathing on my neck. I held the door open and wished he would hurry his deceiving ass out of my house.

He walked pensively toward the exit that eagerly awaited him. He stopped on the other side of the threshold and turned.

"I'll give you what you want, but get this, my son isn't a part of any deal. So don't think for one damn minute you can stop me from having a relationship with him."

I stared at him fearlessly, unflustered, and then slammed the door without saying "thank you" or "fuck you"; the latter was closer to being spoken. He wasn't worth my pleasantry or my dismissal.

"You shouldn't have done this!" he yelled from the other side of the shut door. I didn't give a damn what else he had to say.

I could create a list of things I shouldn't have done when it came to Windsor Oliver. I shouldn't have said yes after he'd waltz his way into my life. I shouldn't have said yes to his Hollywood fairytale proposal. I shouldn't have ignored that strange feeling that we were two wrongs that didn't make one right as I glided down the aisle with that manufactured smile. I shouldn't have stopped my birth control pills because he was ready to be a father. Basically, I shouldn't have mixed pleasure with business, then I wouldn't be standing here, regretting nearly everything that came with meeting and eventually marrying Windsor Oliver.

Fourteen

Kennedie...

Before the thump from the slammed door faded, I grabbed my cell phone from the couch and scrolled to Trent Ashby's number. Each ring heightened the thrill that surged through me. Windsor had left, pouting and stomping his feet like a little boy who had lost a bet in a marble game, but I was dancing on high clouds. Windsor had always been a cautious man. He had to be in order to keep his affair with Selecia Lassiter from the tongues of those who knew them, and me. Windsor had a lot to lose, so I was certain he was blindsided by her decision to taunt me with their indiscretion. Selecia was more concerned about her own potential gains. Not knowing if I was the kind of woman to fight for her husband

and save her marriage, she'd posted up at my house on that cold evening at the start of the new year, hoping I would hand my husband over to her on a silver platter. To his dismay, that was exactly what I decided to do, give him the freedom to sling his dick and swing freely. I hadn't gone digging into Selecia's claim that her own marriage was nothing but an arrangement that allowed her to engage in such behaviors without consequences. She couldn't have been so bold, if it were not. Or maybe she'd banked on that exact thought. Unfortunately for Windsor, he wasn't getting off so easily.

You shouldn't have done this, I thought. I repeated Windsor's last words in my head. Rather than rant about what I shouldn't have done, he should've been paying more attention to what he should have. He should have read before he signed. I guess he wasn't taught to read the small print, or that the devil was in the details. I wanted to shout from the mountaintop but, for now, I had to settle with sharing my excitement with Trent. I sat on the couch and settled in for a long conversation.

"Finally," Trent answered in the same deep-toned voice that demanded my attention a few weeks earlier. "I was getting tired of waiting."

"Well, hello to you, too," I said.

I smiled.

"Oh, I thought I said that." He cleared his throat. "Hello, beautiful," he announced. He sounded demure, which we both knew he wasn't.

"I told you I wasn't going to reach out to you until I got what I needed. So, that was me being a woman of my word."

"What did he do?"

"Exactly what I told you he would. He was too busy arguing to check anything. Nothing like a hotheaded man."

"So, he signed?" Trent asked with a hint of disbelief.

"Sealed and delivered," I added. "I'm meeting with my lawyer in a week, and I hope everything goes this easily."

"Good. Remember to tell them exactly what I've told you. Everything must match exactly what is on the separation decree."

"What if Windsor's lawyers have questions?"

"And they will," Trent assured. I sighed. "But don't worry, the judge will ask him three questions: Is it his signature on the document? Did he sign the documents under duress? And, was he given the opportunity to read before he signed? And I told you, this judge owes me."

"Ok."

I hoped Trent could deliver on his promises. I guess it couldn't hurt to just wait the year and then file for my divorce, and that is what I was willing to do, until I met

Trent and he offered his services.

"If I wanted to take you to dinner, how long would I have to wait?" Trent asked.

I hoped he wasn't thinking my heart needed a hero. I was more than prepared to handle the emotions that came along with this process. I had made the mistake of mixing business with pleasure and, as you could see, that hadn't worked in my favor.

"I have been thinking about you," Trent continued, breaking the long pause between us. "I know you're dealing with a situation, but I'm sure you could use a friend."

I had more than enough friends to turn to, if I needed them. Still, I knew exactly what Trent meant.

"Are you available next Monday evening?" *What the hell are you doing, Kennedie,* I thought. I wanted to pull back the words.

"For you, always," he answered quickly.

"Okay. Figure out where we're going and send me the details. And, Trent."

"Yes."

"This is a not a date," I clarified.

"You can call it whatever you want."

"I'm serious."

"I know you are. I'm looking forward to our non-date date. Hopefully, I will hear from you before then."

"I can't make any promises," I said before saying goodbye.

We both chuckled before we hung up.

Talk about help from a most unlikely source. This was my first time at the rodeo, so to speak. What I found in my research had left me feeling more than a little disappointed. I didn't need a year to be certain a divorce from Windsor was what I really wanted. If they hoped minds would change and people would find their way back into each other, hope had been lost on my situation. I was one-hundred-and-fifty percent sure. Making things right wasn't an option for Windsor, even if I had led him to believe it was. My mind was made up, and God better have a compelling argument why I should change my mind.

I'd walked through the metal detectors at D.C. Superior Court and stood in the middle of the long hallway. I looked lost, and rightfully so, because I was. I could've just played follow the leader—the chorale of lawyers and women ahead of me—cause it seemed all roads led to divorce court. It was as if the wedding was a sham, the honeymoon was a bust, and people were heading straight to the judge to undo what used to be a dream. I could've asked one of the two guards who stood to my right telling stories about their weekend, but I was almost certain I would be their next topic of conversation after they'd assisted. Hell, how else were they going to pass the time?

"How much longer do you plan on standing there?" The deep boom in his voice demanded my attention.

"Excuse me?"

When I turned, I expected to find someone who looked a lot older than the man who stood before me. I gazed at him from his spit-shine oxfords to the top of his fade cut. He wasn't unbelievably sexy—I stared at a fully clothed figure—but what oozed from him was enough to at least allow myself to be entertained.

"What I mean is, can I direct you somewhere?"

He'd smiled, slid his tongue from one corner of his top lip to the other, and then repeated that same seductive gesture on his bottom lip. His come-hither smile and eyes that'll have you floating to the bedroom impressed me. His unblemished copper-brown complexion reminded me of the clay hills of Georgia. Rather than being nasty about him approaching a married woman, I'd decided to play nice. My grandmother was right. You can catch more bees with honey than with vinegar.

"I appreciate your offer to assist, but I think I'm fine. Thank you," I said. I turned away from him, prepared to wander until I found my destination.

"Are you happy?" he'd asked.

He smiled when I turned back in his direction, and

then he waited as if he knew I would respond.

"Is that the pick-up line you lean on whenever you see a girl you think might give you an ounce of her time?" I asked with a subdued attitude. "That certainly can't be your best?"

"Not with every woman," he said, an obvious—subtle, if I were wet behind the ears—attempt to correct me. "Only those who proudly admit they are spoken for."

"And that is your conclusion based on…"

"I see you're married," he said, interrupting my statement. He nodded toward my left hand and at the only other thing that reminded me I was bound to that man.

"Oh, that. Consequence of momentary stupidity," I'd explained.

Not sure why I even put it back on, but I forgot to remove this sign of devotion to my marriage. I removed the white gold diamond ring and tossed it in my bag. My next stop would be to find one of those ladies who gave cash for diamonds. Windsor did spend a pretty penny on it.

"Did you feel that way before you sauntered down the aisle, probably to a song you spent months selecting, or was it after he stepped out on a beautiful woman such as yourself?"

I didn't know this handsome stranger, yet he talked as if he knew my story. He made all the right assumptions because, unfortunately, what happened was a familiar occurrence, and normal to men who perpetrated this crime.

"Thank you, but my looks don't preclude me from being cheated on, and it's not something death takes into consideration, either."

Trent Ashby worked as a clerk at the court. He'd been both willing and forthcoming after I explained exactly what it was that had me standing in the middle of the hallway looking like I'd lost my best friend. In a way, I had. Something about him made me feel I could trust him. I'd followed his order to meet him to discuss exactly what he could do to expedite my process. Over caramel macchiato and cappuccino at a nearby Starbucks, I presented an abridged version of my five-year marriage to Windsor and the violation that precipitated my actions. I gave my all to Windsor, and while Trent could look at me in one moment and declare I did not deserve what Windsor did to me, Windsor didn't have the good sense to come to the same conclusion. Asking for my forgiveness was his pitiful attempt to save this marriage. I knew I could never trust him again, and I never imagined myself living with a man I didn't trust, even if I loved him.

Trent was ready to help. He had one of the judges in his back pocket and he could cash in a few favors. I never asked him the name of the judge—I knew that would be revealed in time—but before I could ask what the judge had done, he cautioned me not to. I didn't understand why he would waste a favor on me. After leaving Starbucks, I was back in court. This time, I knew exactly where I was going, and walked as if I was on familiar grounds to gather the necessary paperwork to serve his ass.

Fifteen

Michaela...

Val, né Percy Valentine, stood in the hall against the wall in front of my office. He assumed his familiar stance—head down, feet apart, with an awkward stare, as if he were about to break into a horrible rendition of *Can You Stand The Rain*—until I acknowledged him. It would've been so much easier to knock and then announce his presence, but since he loved to play his little game, I always found myself ready to indulge him. He'd been a much-needed distraction during my divorce from Zachary. In his office, over drinks from his personal stash, we laughed about the joys and pains—mostly pains—of our respective lives. He's seen a once composed me unravel. It's funny how we are so selective in the parts of us we show to the people we love, even to those who have known us the longest. For the most part, Val and I were passengers in the same boat.

"Good morning, Val," I greeted after I glanced over the computer screen at his imposing figure.

He smiled, peeled himself from the wall, and started in my direction.

"Hello, beautiful stranger!"

My fingers moved in a feverish pitch across the keyboard, but I kept my focus on Val as he moseyed in the office. He didn't bother to close the door behind him. It was still early. I had woken up long before my alarm sounded, and rather than lying in bed with the wonders of the world swirling in my head, I decided to get an early start to what I hoped would be a productive day. I had been in my office a little under two hours. I had busied myself in the still of the early morning before Val made his presence known.

"I'm not a stranger," I said. I returned my concentration to the screen.

"But you must admit, you are beautiful."

In just a few strides, Val stood over me. He waited for the blush I tried to suppress to expose the fact that he was able to trigger that reaction in me. He flashed a victorious smile as if he had finally succeeded in provoking such effect.

Val was a stalwart man. His handsome face and

innocent smile made everyone overlook his flirtatious demeanor. I imagined he'd been a class clown, though he's never claimed that superlative. We had been friends for a few years and, let me tell you, that man had me at "hello." The married, devoted woman I was had tactfully placed him in the friend zone, which still gave Val a place in my life that not many men could claim. His baritone voice had overwhelming confidence, and a confident man was always number one in my book.

The fit of his blue suit was impeccable. He wore my favorite white polka dot tie I gifted him two Christmases ago, and he smelled damn good.

"Coffee, no sugar, and a drop of cream," he announced as he placed the large ceramic mug on the desk in front of me. "Just like you like it," he added.

Usually I would let him enjoy being the lone star in his delivery of these playful comments, but I had the urge to join in.

"You don't know how I like it." I smiled. I reached for my mug, sipped, and then lounged back in the chair. There was some truth to my declaration. I preferred the flavors I enjoyed at home, but that was not a legitimate reason to dismiss his sweet gesture.

My retort rendered Val speechless, and that was unlike him. There was not much you could say to Val that would make him a momentary mute. Usually he had a quick comeback, but this time everything escaped him. He sat in one of the two button-tufted burgundy leather chairs in front of the large antique desk. He sat back, got comfortable, and then, as if something had just jogged his memory, he sat erect. I took another sip of the coffee and then maintained a puzzled stare directly at him.

I stood and walked to join Val on the other side of the desk, sat on the arm of the chair he occupied, and then crossed my legs at the knee. Val's wants and his desires were in a tug of war. With his eyes, he desired to trace my legs from the smallness of my ankles to the semi-thickness of my thighs, but he wanted to respect the professional discourse that precipitated his visit. I promise I was not thinking about Val when I pulled the black silhouette dress from the closet, or when I slid my feet into the sleek red pump that added three-and-a-half inches to my already tall frame. I thought the crisscross strap at the back of the dress was a little too revealing for the office, so I concealed it under a fitted red blazer. I purposely bought it too small to zip or button. My breast had maintained their size since Nyla, so there was much to be desired, and Val had been waiting for his chance.

"Ok," I said, "What's on your mind, Val?"

"Huh?" He answered as if I'd interrupted a distant thought. "Oh." He exhaled. "I need a favor… and let me be transparent, it isn't a small favor."

"That's nothing new. Your favors are never small." I rose from the chair, took another quick taste of coffee, and then placed the mug on the desk. "You know I'm going to need details before I even consider saying yes." I turned to face him, folded my arms across my chest, and rested my bottom against the desk.

"Fair enough. I need you to take this Oliver case," he said, without hesitation. "I know what you are going to say," he added as if he expected my refusal. I maintained silence, and, with a slight nod, I permitted Val to speak on my behalf. "Michaela, you're a divorce lawyer and, might I add, a damn good one. It's about time you get back to normal. How long are you going to work behind the scenes?"

"Was that supposed to be a panty dropper?" I smiled, but he didn't seem amused by my remark.

"Come on, Michaela. I'm serious," Val said as he stood.

"Another month, give or take a day or two," I said as the smile disappeared from my face. I returned to my seat and refocused on my computer screen.

I wasn't a behind-the-scenes kind of woman. I relished opposing a disgruntled husband or wife—though most of my clients were women—who operated as if the money was already in the bag. I had no heart for the heartless man, dedicated and persistent to drag the woman, to whom they'd once professed their love, through the mud. I had no mercy on them or their pockets, but I needed the mental break.

I pulled the chair closer to the desk and looked up at Val. He towered over me after he abandoned the chair he once occupied. I tried to focus. I concentrated less on his cocoa-brown eyes that maintained a fixed stare into me, or the curly dark hair that framed his thin, pink lips.

"Michaela, this is not you. What happened to your fire, your passion, that appetite that had you walking in the courtroom with unfaltering bravado? Did you let him take that away from you, too?"

"Listen, Val," I continued, "you were there. You saw how emotionally spent I was during my own divorce. I'm no longer on the outside looking in."

"Which makes you the perfect person for this case," he cut in. "You are exactly what she needs. Trust me when I tell you."

"Why, did the husband sleep with his mother-in-law, too?"

"His boss's wife," Val answered.

"Oh, he's a classy hoe." I smiled and lounged back in the chair. "So, when do I meet Mrs. Oliver?" I hoped I was right in my assumption.

"Are you saying 'yes'?"

"Do I have a choice?"

"I just like you to think you do." He turned and started toward the door. He was just as confident in his exit as he was when he first walked in.

"Am I going to walk in here one morning and she's sitting in one of these chairs, or are you going to answer my question?"

Val checked the time on his watch. "She'll be here at 2:30," he said just before he walked out.

"Val," I called out. I got up from the chair and ran to the door; well, my version of running, since I had on heels. "Why can't you do it?"

"I can," he said. He turned and closed the distance between us. "I told you, you are what she needs," he continued with his face inches from mine. He might have been too close for anyone else's comfort, but he was Percy Valentine. "Jacqui will bring you the files we've created on Mrs. Kennedie Oliver."

"Thank you for the coffee," I said, turning away from him. "Next time, I'll take mine without the side of extra work. Thanks." I smiled and headed back inside my office.

Sixteen

Michaela...

There really was no rest for the weary. They say the best way to get over your problems at home is to become so involved in work that you forget home existed. I can't tell you who *they* are, but I didn't agree with them. Home now only consisted of me, Alison, and Nyla, and that was all I needed. Still, Val made sure work was exactly where my focus went. After Jacqui appeared in my office with the file bearing the name of my new client, I poured a cup of coffee and assumed my usual position at the far end of the large conference table. I grasped the warm mug with both hands, rested my elbows on the table, and attempted to become familiar with my client's profile.

Kennedie Leanna Spencer-Oliver, I thought. The limited

details Val had provided had not included her name. I stared down at the pages inside the red folder. *Thirty-five years old.*

"Oh, still young. Couldn't have been married that long before insanity and the reality of marriage kicked in."

One child. Operating Room Manager.

"And she makes her own money. Men are never satisfied." I didn't have to wonder about his offense, since Val had made that known. As I turned the page, his charge jumped at me.

Marriage Infidelity.

"Go figure. I wonder if Zach knows him. After all, all dogs know each other," I said in a soft whisper.

That's a name that hadn't bittered my mouth in some time, and I didn't miss the taste. It has been peaceful not having to breathe the same air as Zachary. I drove myself crazy because I'd made the unselfish decision to put my daughter first. Although it was Zachary's indiscretion that had me purchasing a one-way ticket to split city, I still fought an internal battle. I felt I was the cause of my own hurt. I broke my family apart, when I could have chosen to keep us together. Would I have reacted differently if the other woman weren't my mother? I don't know. What I do know is that two people I'd loved had bamboozled me. Two people who claimed their love would never cause me pain had broken that promise, among other things.

"Michaela," Jacqui interrupted. I was deaf to the soft knocks on the door as I concentrated on the contents in Ms. Spencer-Oliver's file.

"Hey, Jacqui," I greeted. "Come on in." I raised my head from my read to find her standing just inside the office. She'd preempted the invitation as she had done so many times before.

"I'm sorry to interrupt you, but you have a visitor," Jacqui ended her apology—although it wasn't necessary—with a smile.

As always, a smile escorted every word that fell from her mouth. I've always said she was the best person to deliver bad news. I'm not sure what, if anything, she hid behind her smile, but she always appeared as if all was well in her world. For all we knew, everything was. With Jacqui, her personal life was off limits to anyone she worked with. She's sung that hymn since the first day she stepped her size nine in this firm and had everyone at bay who tried to snoop. I was fine with our level of interaction and never made it my business to find out more than what she told.

I looked at my watch and thought, *maybe time had slipped by and I hadn't noticed.* It had only been a few hours since I'd spoken to Val, and not much time had passed since Jacqui and her smile walked out of my office after she'd placed the client's folder in my hand.

"But I have a few more hours before..." I discarded my statement. Ready or not, the show would have to go on.

I've never been unprepared for a meeting with a client, and I wasn't going to start now. I knew I only had a little time, but it was still enough to appear as if I knew something about the woman I would be representing in court.

"No," Jacqui interrupted after she observed the anxiety in my face. "Ms. Brooklynn Jones is here."

Relieved, I said, "Thank you, Jacqui," and began to close the folder in front of me.

Just as I readied to head to the front to meet my best friend, she entered the office. Jacqui and Brooke exchanged pleasant stares as Jacqui turned to leave.

"I figured it would be quite difficult for you to ignore me here," Brooke announced when she heard the door closed behind her and she was confident we were alone in the office. "Especially since I showed up to an empty house this morning."

Brooke stood at the other end of the table. As always, she looked amazing. Thanks to her frequent visits to the salon, she'd managed to maintain her perfect tan in the dead of winter. I'd joked she didn't have the kind of black I had, and she'd implied her honorary status meant she was safe. Her naturally curly, red hair was blown straight. I thought that style was a better fit for her. A hodgepodge of well-tailored garments completed her look for her surprised visit.

"You look great." I smiled.

As much as I had been avoiding Brooke, I was happy to see her. And despite her present attitude, there was no doubt the feeling was mutual.

I closed the folder and stood, ready to engage in our usual greet.

"Girl, save it." Brooke's command stopped my approach. "You ignored my phone calls like I was some nuisance calling to borrow money. I was concerned about you. You acted as if my messages didn't dignify a response, but you want to walk up to me with arms opened wide, as if we had a slumber party last night and exchanged stories about a boy. The least you could've done was acknowledge you had received the messages."

"You're absolutely right." I quickly accepted my wrong. There was no need in beleaguering the point that the way I had treated her was unfair and underserving.

Brooke ignored the fact that I had already conceded.

"You need to stop behaving as if I did something to you and tell me what is going on," she continued.

Brooke set her bag on the table, pulled the chair, and sat. She had given me the go-ahead to rationalize my behavior, but it made no sense to even waste time on any justification. Moreover, I'd already admitted my fault. Still, she stared into me with disappointment in her eyes.

"This isn't easy, Brooke."

"I'm not saying it is, whatever *it* is. But I'm sure going through it alone made it harder than it was supposed to be. We said we would always be there for each other, but how can I hold true to that promise, if you don't let me know when I'm needed?" Brooke protested.

I paused, and then took a deep breath. The haunting image of Whitney and Zachary began its invasion. I hadn't been able to rid myself of the scene that now served as a constant reminder that my ex-husband was no damn good, and my mother was even worse.

"How does one even begin to tell someone that their husband cheated on them?"

"Newsflash," Brooke interrupted. "You wouldn't be the only woman on this earth who has had an unfaithful husband."

"How do you swallow your pride and fix your mouth to tell them that the other woman, the enabler, was your own mother?" I folded my arms across my chest. "Zach's infidelity was the last thing I expected. I wasn't prepared, but are we ever?"

It's been weeks since events I'd hid from Brooke

147

were revealed, thanks to my malicious cousin. Since then, embarrassment kept me from facing or even talking to Brooke. I hadn't made myself available for our usual lunch dates, and I knew it was only a matter of time before she took matters into her own hands and force me to face the music. Sooner or later I expected her to show up unannounced, although work was the last place I expected to see her. Near or far, Brooke had always been my remedy.

"I'm not just anyone, Michaela. The last time I checked, I was your best friend, unless that has changed within the last few weeks. We've known each other for almost half our lives. If you can't tell me something like that, who can you tell?"

"No one," I sat in the chair next to Brooke. I didn't bother to look at her. "And that's exactly what I decided to do. I didn't want to be judged by you or anyone for my failed marriage."

"Judge you?" Brooke placed her hand on mine and, finally, our eyes met. "I don't know about anyone else, but I would never judge you for something Zachary and your mother did. You took away my opportunity to support you, as I always have and will. There isn't a judgment zone in our relationship, Michaela."

Her eyes became warm and comforting. Finally! Those were the eyes that had always greeted me, not the cold ones that scolded me the moment she walked through the door.

"A skank doesn't care about how they're related to you. Patience taught you that lesson first," Brooke continued. "They could be your worst enemy or your mother. If they want your man, nothing will stop them from getting him."

"I look at you and Stetzen and your perfect marriage, and here I am. I can't even get past the five-year test."

I removed my hand from under Brooke's and sat back. Brooke and Stetzen had either mastered the art of handling their affairs privately, or they were very good at wearing the mask they wanted everyone to see. But I knew Brooklynn Jones, and she wasn't about keeping up appearance. What you saw was what was.

"And what if I tell you Stetzen and I have our own share of problems?" Brooke asked.

"I would say you were creating stories to make me feel better." I smiled and then became serious soon after.

"You know my mantra: tell the truth and shame the devil. Now, haven't I always told you the truth?" Brooke questioned, not expecting a response.

Brooke stood, walked to the back of the office, and gazed out the large office window. Regardless of what was said, I knew better than to accept what she'd hinted at as having one ounce of truth to it. I knew Brooke well enough to know that while she didn't wear her heart on her sleeve, she's never been one to kiss and not tell.

"You and Stetzen, the poster couple for a successful marriage?" I laughed, dismayed by Brooke's supposed admission.

Brooke turned her attention from the window. She smiled.

"We're not the couple anyone should aspire to be. Each couple must find what makes them happy and work every day at duplicating it," Brooke explained as she became serious. "It's not always the easiest thing to do, but no one said marriage was easy. Anyone who thought the hard work ended once the rings were on their fingers was in for one hell of a surprise.

"Stetz and I are happy, but we have our problems, too. We argue about the family he wants and how I was laser-focused on my career, so I stopped taking the pills. But," she said. She let out a loud breath. She looked at me with wide eyes as if she were about to confess something I didn't already know. "He doesn't know I've replaced the pills with the depo shot." She lowered her head when the last words fell from her mouth.

My eyes widened to match hers, and my mouth fell open at her shameful admission. From the outside looking in, we can't assume everything is all rosy. Brooke was guilty of the same crime she accused me of perpetrating. She, too, had her issues, but had kept them private for her and her husband to work through. Those issues included that bold lie she happily told him.

"What the hell, Brooke!" I was stunned at my reaction, but it was legitimate. Brooke had declared there wasn't anything she hid from Stetzen, and since I knew nothing to prove otherwise, I accepted that as her truth, until now.

"He doesn't see me taking the pills daily like I did before, so this deception was easy." When she raised her head, the guilt in her eyes was profound. She wasn't proud of what she'd done, which explained why she'd kept her dishonesty to herself, but she was already too far in.

"What does Stetzen think?" I asked, changing my tone.

"He thinks we just need to keep trying. We've even discussed adopting, if all else fails." She gazed at her feet, feeling as if she'd committed the ultimate betrayal. "My God, I hate lying to him, but a newborn would stop so much progress right now."

"Would you rather he or she were born ready to enter high school?" I joked in an attempt to change the mood.

Brooke smiled.

"Is that possible?"

"Come here, girl," I requested. I extended my hand and, finally, we embraced. "I love you."

"I love you, too," Brooke responded as she tightened her arms around me.

"I know it must be hard sleeping next to the person you love, knowing you've been lying to him."

"It is," Brooke acknowledged as she began to separate from me. "I'll tell you this, I've had my share of tossing and turning, but…"

"No," I quickly added. "Let me finish. I certainly wasn't saying that to make you feel bad about what you're doing. I know your career comes first. I'm just saying, what you're doing is what men have been doing for years, and it doesn't bother their conscience one bit. It doesn't make it right, but do what you have to do."

"Thank you for being empathetic."

"That's not empathy. That's me keeping it real with my sister."

"Listen," Brooke began. She held my hands and stared in my eyes. "I understand your desire to keep certain aspects of your marriage to yourself, but you shouldn't, and neither should I. God knows, if Stetzen and I ever find ourselves in divorce court, I want my best friend there with me."

"Oh, please!" I pulled my hands from her grip and stepped away from my best friend. "Stetzen knows he has a good woman. He's not about to do anything to lose you. And you are not going to do anything to lose him either."

"You know sometimes men get this momentary case of stupid, and all of a sudden the good they have becomes second to the opened legs in front of them." Brooke laughed as she grabbed her bag from the table.

"Girl, you are preaching to the choir director," I said as I joined her in laughter. And just like that, the mood in the office changed. Oh, the love I have for my best friend.

"Listen." Brooke became serious. "We're not done. If you want, I can have my flight rescheduled, and I can make dinner reservations."

"Let's do just that. I have to meet a new client in a few. Just send me the information."

"I'll see you this evening," Brooke confirmed as she pulled the door open.

As I stepped out to escort the stylish Brooklynn Jones to her car, the phone buzzed.

"Ms. McKnight," Jacqui's voice sounded over the intercom.

"I need to get that. I will see you tonight." I gave Brooke departing pecks on both cheeks and then rushed to the back of the office to answer. "Yes, Jacqui."

"Mrs. Kennedie Spencer is here. She's aware you are finishing up with another client." Jacqui whispered as if Ms. Spencer stood directly in front of her.

"Thank you, Jacqui. I'll be out to meet her momentarily."

After I hung up, I sat behind the desk and collected my thoughts. I was already looking forward to dinner with Brooke and, this time, without any interruptions. The previous time, Patience, her revelation about my marriage, and what had occurred between Zachary and Whitney were unnecessary interludes. I still had much I hadn't shared with Brooke. Since she trusted me enough to reveal the secret she'd kept from her husband, I needed to return the favor.

Seventeen

Kennedie...

I thought February would never end. I stepped into March feeling like an almost-free woman. I was looking forward to that day when I would no longer be known as Mrs. Kennedie Oliver. Unlike Tina Turner, I wasn't interested in keeping Windsor's name or anything that belonged to him. Hell, changing T.J.'s last name wasn't too far down the list of things I needed to do to erase any connection to Windsor. I woke with excitement as I thought about what I had planned for this day: drop T.J. off at school, treat myself to lunch, meet with my attorney, and then enjoy some alone time with my little man.

Before T.J. began asking questions, because I knew they were coming, I sat him down to explain why he hadn't seen his father around like before. I tried to keep the explanation simple, but simplicity only begot more questions. I tried to remain stoic in my reasoning. T.J. was both a precocious and a very perceptive boy, even for his age. He read through and questioned everything.

"But Tobias' mommy and daddy aren't together, and he says his mommy hates his daddy." He'd held a downward stair and twisted his fingers as he spoke.

"That's not a nice thing for Tobias' mommy to say," I explained, although I was certain her sentiment was justified and well deserved. "I don't hate your daddy."

Okay, that was a small lie, but T.J. didn't need to know that. Truth is, I wanted Windsor to suffocate on the air he breathed. If what they say is true, that God doesn't like ugly, then I needed Him to have his way with Windsor. I knew God wasn't in the business of answering prayers to harm people, but I figured I would try my luck, though vengeance was His. I pledged to never show my true feelings about the piece-of-trash I would forever be linked to because of the son we shared. I agreed to let T.J. form his own impression of the bastard. I used to love Windsor. I gave my heart to him under the false pretense that he would never hurt me like others before him. His promise to protect me, to never cause me pain, was broken the second he laid eyes on Selecia Lassiter, his Delilah. The hate for him that consumed me was what his actions created.

After I dropped T.J. off at school, I returned home and prepared a hefty breakfast—oatmeal with strawberries, blueberries, a boiled egg, and two strips of bacon—that would've made my grandma proud, since she thinks I survived on coffee alone. Normally, I would grab coffee and toast as I headed out to work, but, this morning, I had nothing but time. I sat at the island and enjoyed the quiet until the ring from the cell phone interrupted. I peaked at the screen at the number I didn't recognize and reverted my attention back to my breakfast. Since the ringing continued, I pressed the green phone icon to accept the call, and then placed the call on speaker.

"Ms. Spencer speaking," I answered stating my maiden name, and then waited for an introduction from the caller.

"So, you've already changed your name?" The devil's familiar voice sounded through the speakers. It was Windsor. He was a lot calmer now than he was when he'd stormed out the house the last time we spoke.

"Shouldn't I? No other part of you belongs to me, so why should I keep the name?"

"You know, you're a piece of work, Kennedie," he snickered.

"Am I, Windsor?" I was already cursing myself for indulging him. "I need you to get off my phone with your crap. I have been nothing but a wife to you and a mother to my child, and those titles were important to me. You..." I paused. This man wasn't going to cause me to lose my mind. I inhaled and then let out a long breath. "What do you want with me?"

"You know what!" he exhaled.

"What, Windsor?" I was tired of men like Windsor getting upset because they were forced to lie in the bed they made. And I felt the same about the women who coddled them. They danced around their fragile egos that weren't there when they were out there behaving as if anything they had was worth losing. And now that the reality of their consequences has set in, they want to sit in front of you with their thumbs in their mouths and tears in their eyes. Windsor had lost any right to display hurt, because none of what he felt now was felt when he was climaxing with his other woman.

"Let me tell you what I know," I continued. Talking to Windsor caused me to lose my appetite. I pushed the bowl away from me and stood. I walked out of the kitchen and started upstairs to the bedroom. I figured I could prepare my clothes for my appointment while I lent an ear to his foolishness. "I know you messed up, and that's putting lightly what you did to me. Yes, you thought you could smooth things over with your half-ass apology and your lukewarm *I love you*. I know you thought I was going to sweep your one mistake—that I know of—under the rug, and we would just carry on like you hadn't been fucking me over for only God knows how long."

"Where's my son?" he asked as if he hadn't heard any of what was just said.

"Are you asking about the same son you turned your back on weeks ago?" I waited for Windsor to respond with some offensive rhetoric, but my silence was equally matched. "Well," I continued, "he's certainly not here waiting on you to show up."

"I hope you're not over there trying to play my son against me."

"I'm trying to rid myself of you, Windsor. Discussing you would be the antithesis." I laughed. "You honestly think I have nothing better to do with my time than to sit around with my four-year-old son and feed words to him so he could hate you? I don't have to do that. I've learned that kids will hate you in their own time, and for their own reasons. They don't forget anything." I placed the phone on speaker, tossed it on the bed, and then walked into the closet. I browsed each section of the walk-in closet and settled on a crimson pencil skirt, a navy-blue tank, and a blue fitted blazer to complete the conservative look. I had already determined anything Windsor had to say was unimportant, so I paid little attention to the murmur that came from the phone.

In front of the floor length mirror, I held the chosen garments against my body, and then nodded in approval. "I do plan on discussing you plenty with my attorney," I continued as I made my way back into the room.

"Why do you keep referring to him as *your* son?" Windsor asked.

I lay the garments on the bed and then picked up the phone. I wanted to make sure nothing I said was distorted because I spoke from a distant.

"I can refer to my son however I want. If I remember correctly, the only thing you did in the delivery room, before you passed out, was breathe."

"Look, Kennedie, just make sure you hear me when I tell you, leave our son out of this, or else..."

"Or else what, Windsor?" I interrupted. "Are you going to take him? And then what? Is your little girlfriend going to keep padding your pockets so you can take care of him?" I chuckled. "I want to see you even try," I added through clenched teeth. "When I'm finished dragging your ass through the court system, you're going wish you'd never met me, let alone asked me to marry you; the same wish I make, even as we speak."

I waited for Windsor's response but got nothing. For the first time, I had left him flabbergasted. This was unbelievable. The irreverent Windsor Oliver was left wordless. I removed the phone from my ear, glanced at the screen, and then realized the call had gone dead. Windsor had hung up. I ignored Windsor's abrupt end to our conversation and continued with my morning as I had planned. I shrugged my shoulders, smiled, set the phone on the nightstand, and started toward the bathroom. I couldn't get back the time I'd wasted listening to Windsor's senseless rhetoric.

After I showered, I took my time getting dolled up for my meeting with my attorney. I applied some concealer to hide the mark my mother left on my face. The imperfection was a birthmark, that was my explanation to anyone who inquired, even to my grandmother, but she knew I was not born that way. I can't remember exactly what I did to deserve this mark from the beast—it didn't take much for me to feel her wrath—but it was there. I carefully brushed some contour on my cheeks and jawline, slimmed an already slim nose, and then puckered my lips to smooth on a light coat of flesh-tone lip-gloss.

On the balls of my feet, in front of the antique-framed mirror, I twisted and turned, and then smiled at the well-dressed woman who smiled and winked back at me. I didn't have much I could thank my mother for, so I silently thanked God for the way my body looked in the skirt. I removed the scarf from around my head and allowed the brown highlighted mane to fall into place and into a newly styled bob. I needed a new look, a break from the long, straight trademark, and this was what Elena, my hairdresser since before my marriage, decided I needed. Finally, I stepped into a pair of blossom print pointed toe pumps and glanced at my image one last time before I retrieved my phone from the nightstand.

Eighteen

Kennedie...

As I headed out the door, I checked my phone and noticed the two missed calls and voicemail message that were received while I showered. I listened, but decided to respond to the message later. In the car, I tossed the phone inside my bag, and then dialed my grandmother's number on the dash.

"Hello, beautiful lady!" I greeted when my grandmother's voice sounded over the Bluetooth inside the car.

"So, you're ignoring your grandmother now?"

I heard the smile in Geraldine's voice, and I loved it. It always warmed my heart to speak to her. She was always in good spirits.

"I could never ignore my favorite lady." I checked the rearview mirror and then pulled into the street.

"Doesn't sound like you're at work, and I know you don't run the streets. Where are you heading?"

"I have that meeting with the attorney today."

"Finally cutting the loser free?"

"Finally!" I repeated.

"Good," Geraldine spoke after a long pause.

Geraldine was definitely one of my favorite people. Regardless of how she felt about Windsor—and she had her reservations—she stayed neutral, for my sake. I was happy, and that was all that mattered to her.

When they first met, she spoke her impressions of Windsor in a masked way. Only my grandmother and I knew what she meant when she grabbed our small dog, slowly glided her hand down the length of his spine, stared at me and said, "This dog has fleas."

After that moment, I attempted to see Windsor through Geraldine's eyes. I saw the worrisome expression on her face when I declared Windsor to be the love of my life. Maybe she was clairvoyant. Maybe she saw something in him that my love had obscured. Instead of heeding her warning, I proceeded without caution. I should've kept her proclamation in the back of my mind. Instead, I ignored the naysayers, the ones who firmly believed that forever doesn't always last and predicted the end of their new relationship solely on the previous one. I ignored my grandmother's prophecy, too.

"I knew it wouldn't be too long before he did something to make you see the error of your ways," Geraldine added. "Your mistake wasn't only in falling in love with this man, but you married him, too."

"To no objections from you or anyone else who just sat there and watched me make that big mistake."

I glanced in the side-view mirror before pulling to the side of the two-lane highway to give room to the ambulance whose siren blared loudly behind me.

"I didn't have anything nice to say, so I kept my mouth shut. I learned that lesson the hard way. I figured I would watch to see your happiness fade, hoping that it wouldn't, or wait for the sheep to show you the wolf he really was. It always happens. The charade can only be played for so long."

"Looks like everyone pled the fifth during the ceremony."

"I can't speak for everyone," Geraldine quickly rebutted, "but I know I certainly did. You wanted to be Mrs. Windsor Oliver. The day you claimed him to be the love of your life was the day I decided nothing said would have changed your mind."

"Shows how much I knew about anything."

"Well," Geraldine sympathized, "you believed in the love he gave. What else were you supposed to do?" She paused.

In our silence, I glanced at the time. It was just before noon. I had time to sit and enjoy lunch and still get to my appointment on time. Thoughts of having lunch with my sister, Dana, vanished just as soon as they entered my mind. It had been a while since we last sat and talked, but she came with so much. First, the bill would be my responsibility, even if she had extended the invitation. I swear that heifer always dined on a budget. Unfortunately, it was my budget. And, I would feel obligated to fill her in on everything that happened. I didn't have the energy for an abbreviated trip down the lane of memories or the time to answer the many questions I know she would have. Dana was a chip off the old block that was Natalie Lamar, but she was my sister.

"Have you spoken to your mother?" Geraldine spoke just as the contemplations fizzled.

If she was trying to change my mood—and I didn't think that was her intent—she was successful. The mere mention of evil's moniker instantly soured the banter between my grandmother and me.

"Now why would I do that?" The feelings I harbored

for Natalie Lamar were no secret to my grandmother. Natalie's vile mistreatment had left me embittered. "You know I haven't spoken to that woman since the day she slapped that one-way ticket to your house in my hand. Remember, my last attempt to right her wrong blew up in my face because, like so many, she didn't want to be reminded of the hurt she caused, as if it was a picnic in the park for me." My grandmother remained hushed, and then she let out a long sigh. "Are you okay?" I asked. Her silence and response caused concern.

"I spoke to her earlier this morning, Kennedie. She's not doing too well." Her voice was soft and melancholy, and she hadn't sounded like that in some time.

"I didn't know you were still reaching out to her. That woman has given you her ass to kiss so many times, most times just because the wind changed direction. Yes, she always came back with some lame excuse, but only to later repeat her attack. I've watched you hold your breath and bite your tongue because you didn't want to enrage an already furious monster. God knows if I were you, I would've given up on her a long time ago."

"Then she needs to be thanking God I am not you." My grandmother paused. "Everyone else has already turned their backs on her. She can't afford to add me to her list of deserters. Regardless of what she's done, she is my child."

"Well, we can't choose where evil comes from."

On the dashboard, a call came in from Trent. Instead of pressing ignore, I allowed it to go to voicemail. I already had plans on returning his call later.

"Kennedie, she's your mother."

"She's my curse," I retorted. I'd denounced that relationship after I realized exactly what it wasn't.

Images of being raised—or tormented—by a woman who despised even the fact that I was breathing hurried through my mind. I thought about Natalie about as often as she thought of me, never. I didn't know then, but she did me a favor when she decided to ship me off to a place I knew so little about. She never wanted to be my mother. With reluctance, she'd held the title, and during that time, she was the great pretender. I don't know why she wasted so much time when she could've made both our lives easier sooner. She pretended she loved me, until I became the butt of her misguided anger. Nothing infuriated her more than the simple fact that I was in her presence. That was the only thing I had done to be the target of her bitterness, and I didn't give birth to myself. Even her care was bogus. But she was very convincing. When she was tired of putting on airs, she'd boldly spoken her truth.

"Natalie is my mother, yes, but only by default," I continued. "The only thing she has done is give mothers a bad name."

"Still," Geraldine pleaded. She was adamant, as if she had forgotten everything my mother put me through, the conversations we had even after Natalie forbade me to call her.

"What about those she deserted?" I blurted. "She dug a ditch around her own feet, and now she wants those she backstabbed and neglected to come to her rescue. I'm not going to ask if she's ok. I don't have the time to pretend to care."

"I think it's about time you forgive her."

"Thank God we can all think for ourselves." I stared at the display screen in the dash as the words my grandmother spoke floated through my mind. "Now that life has its hands firmly around her neck, she wants forgiveness? How convenient! She wasted her wishes on wishing I were never born. Let's hope she doesn't waste dreams and prayers on hearing the words *I forgive you* from me."

I've heard my grandmother's speeches on forgiveness and, regardless to whom she spoke, they always ended the same. She believed there is no peace without forgiveness. Well, I didn't disagree with her, because she was absolutely right. I needed my peace, so I forgave Natalie a long time ago. If I hadn't, I would've allowed the misery I lived in as a child to turn me into a bitter woman. I probably wouldn't have had a child of my own, or I might have mistreated him just as she did me. What I won't do is forget the many nights I went to sleep thinking about my mother's disregard of my existence. I still think about the time she looked me squared in my face and told me she'd already given me the gift of life and not to expect anything for my sixth birthday. Well, none of the birthdays that followed her hateful statement were ever acknowledged. I guess she kept that promise.

"The bible says..." Geraldine began.

"I know what the bible says," I snapped. She gasped, and it was then that I realized what I had done. Still, I offered no apologies.

Bringing up Natalie's name had already worked my nerve—something I didn't need this morning—and had soured my mood. I was not up for a Sunday school lesson. My reaction wasn't to what my grandmother said, but to my mother's thinking she could use Geraldine as the means to forgiveness from someone to the person she'd pledged her hatred.

"The bible says to honor thy mother and father," I continued, "but it doesn't say I have to honor someone who squirmed at the very thought that I came from her."

"Don't be evil, Kennedie. You only get one mother."

"How unfortunate! As bad luck would have it, I got

stuck with Natalie Lamar. I guess life played a big joke on everyone."

I laughed at the very things about my mother that once caused me great pain. I was at peace with how she treated me because I hadn't become the person her resentment could have created. As much as she wished and hoped I failed at life, I prayed harder that I would live to see the disappointment in her face my success would create.

Nineteen

Kennedie...

I hadn't paid much attention to the snail pace traffic I found myself in until the silence between my grandmother and I afforded me the opportunity. I didn't have the energy to curse something I could not control. Long ago, I'd accepted this was the new normal for D.C. living. I would've been concerned had I gotten in the car and had the road to myself, but no one sat still in D.C. I left early to give myself the extra time, because I knew the drive across the city to Porter and Blount in Northwest wasn't going to be a walk in the park.

People have been coming to the DMV in droves. I've lived in D.C. long enough to watch the once proclaimed Chocolate City—and rightfully so— slowly transition to the Mocha City, all because of gentrification. Build it and they will come, they say, and they were definitely coming.

"Kennedie, your mother is dying." Finally, Geraldine broke the silence. Her voice was filled with urgency.

"We all are, some of us a bit slower than others, but we all have our expiration date," I said, unaffected by my grandmother's declaration. "If these are her last days, she'll have to get her peace and her sympathy from someone else, 'cause she damn sure won't be getting any from me. Those wells have gone dry."

"My God!" Geraldine said after a long pause. "Who have you become?"

"When it comes to your daughter, I am who I have always been. Maybe she should start a list, make sure my name is at the bottom, go on an apology tour, and let's just hope God calls her home before she gets to me."

"Kennedie!" my grandmother shouted.

"So, say I forgive her, and then what, she gets to die with a clear conscience? Like hell, she will."

I'm not sure what my grandmother thought I was going to say. Based on her reaction, what she received was below her expectations. As far as Natalie was concerned, my soft spot was as hard as a rock.

When I woke, I smiled as I pondered the adventures the day had in store for me. When people spoke of the day that the Lord has made, I believed they were talking about this very day. I'd held T.J.'s hand and smiled in the crisp morning breeze as I walked him to his classroom. He'd kissed my cheek and barely whispered *I love you,* probably because his preschool crush, Abigail Lawson, stood a few feet away, not giving any of her attention to him. I'd managed to maintain my composure while I entertained Windsor after I came home. The sound of my grandmother's voice as I began my journey to southwest D.C. had been music to my ears. But everything was ruined when Natalie's name fell from Geraldine's mouth, sending my mood into a tailspin.

"I'm going to pray for you," Geraldine offered.

I didn't need prayer. I needed her to let this attempt rest.

"What are you praying for, and who are you praying to?" I asked. "'Cause I know we all don't pray to the same God." I smiled. "Oh, and when you are done praying for me, make sure you pray a little harder for your daughter, she's the one who's knocking on death's door."

"You're going to hell, girl."

"You don't get to decide," I answered. "And if I am, it looks like Natalie will beat me there."

I waited for a response from Geraldine but was met with absolute silence. I would be lying if I said I didn't mean for what I said to come out the way it did, but I meant *every* word. If Geraldine wasn't upset before, I knew she was upset now. She'd raised me to be compassionate but, when it came to Natalie Lamar, everything my grandmother taught me went out the window.

I was dismissed rather horridly as I heard the disdain in my grandmother's voice, not toward me, but to my indifference to Natalie.

Finally, I came face-to-face with D.C.'s second worst nightmare, parking. After I made my fourth trip around the block, I lucked up and found a space directly in front of the glass front mini skyscraper that, at night, added to the District's version of a skyline. Another newly erect multi-million-dollar building, and no one thought about a parking garage. I pulled into the space vacated by a midnight-black Audi. The driver smiled and nodded, obvious flirtatious gestures, but he appeared ten years too young, and I was in no mood to entertain anyone with breast milk still on his breath. Still, I returned the politeness as he disappeared into the cockpit. He stared into his rearview mirror as he slowly drove off.

As much as it pained me to admit it, the conversation with my grandmother had left me somewhat rattled. It's a funny thing about memories, as much as you try to forget them, they will always remember you. I geared the car to park and waited until I returned to a version of my composed self.

*T*wenty

Michaela...

"Ms. Spencer-Oliver!" Val exclaimed. He approached her with his hand stretched toward her. "I'm Percy Valentine. It's nice to finally put a face to the voice."

I chuckled inside because, although I heard the words Val spoke, I was more familiar with the thoughts that churned in his head. What he said was slang for "your face is as beautiful as your voice." Val wouldn't have been wrong had he shouted his thoughts from a mountaintop. Ms. Spencer-Oliver flaunted a layered bob that glistened as if she spent the right amount of time in a beauty shop chair. Stylish big-rimmed glasses framed her face as she stared at Val with slanted chestnut eyes. She was dressed with the purpose to impress. Her crimson pencil skirt hung to the curve of her hips. Her smooth shapely legs gave her above average height.

I knew Val well, and as subtle as he thought his gesture to be, he could never hide his flirts. The hint he tried to disguise was a dead giveaway. Val was right. Beauty had not skipped a beat, as far as Ms. Spencer-Oliver was concerned. She stood, extended her hand to Val, and wrapped her long manicured fingers around his hand.

"Thank you, Mr. Valentine," she spoke, finally relaxing her pursed full lips, which were the right shade of rose. "And, please, I prefer Ms. Spencer, if it's not too much trouble, or just Kennedie." Then, she engaged in a slight bend to retrieve her small handbag from the couch in the opened waiting area.

I stood next to Val and waited to be introduced. From our conversation earlier that morning, it appeared Val hadn't said much to Ms. Spencer about the level of my involvement in her process.

As we walked to my car after Val's birthday celebration at his estate a week into the new year, Val disclosed the acquisition of his new client. Val's landscape had always been a distraction. I often found myself admiring the way his pathway snaked between the carpet-like green grass from his back patio. I appreciated the coziness of his outdoor lounge area in a far corner in the immense back yard, with the granite top fire pit. The gazebo he had built after he'd agreed to host his sister's wedding ceremony was massive and attractive, and stood in the middle of the backyard.

"You remember Madelyn?" Val asked as we walked along the stoned pathway.

"As in your on-again, off-again girlfriend, Madelyn Kyle? I've lost track. I don't know where you guys stand these days. Are you guys on, or off again?" I joked. I'd shoved him playfully on his arm.

"Are you going to let me tell you about the client, or am I going to have to deal with your sarcasm?" Val asked, his words encased in attitude. He had abandoned our slow stroll for quick a pause.

Madelyn had always been a sensitive subject. Since her divorce, Madelyn had made it clear she was just fine with their friends-with-benefits relationship, but Val was getting to the point where he wanted more than the occasional hookups whenever the mood was right. Against what they had both agreed, Val had put his heart in it. He knew going in, this wasn't something he could do. This wasn't the first time he'd found himself in this position, and, just like the last time, he'd sworn to himself he wouldn't have the same problem. He'd been wrong again.

"Geesh, sorry. Please proceed."

In the unusually warm January night, Val and I spent a

good part of the next hour talking about his first conversation with his new client. He had come highly recommended by Madelyn—the same Madelyn he had his clap-on, clap-off relationship with—since together they had broken her ex-husband's bank, including his offshore accounts, thanks to some skillful maneuvering and backdoor deals. His client was not only still distraught that her husband of nearly five years had cheated on her, and with his boss's wife, but she was upset that the woman had been bold enough to show up at her house to break the news to her, between the insults and snide remarks. Val didn't know the barefaced perpetrator when his client mentioned the name, but the name of her husband, Garen Lassiter, was very familiar to him.

Garen and Val had met a couple of years earlier at the Congressional Black Caucus Black and White Gala, but the woman on Mr. Lassiter's arm was not introduced as his wife, and her name was something other than Selecia Lassiter. Val had paused and rubbed his chin as he thought about that first encounter with Mr. Lassiter. What he'd learned about Selecia Lassiter's adulterous affair had caused a bit of confusion to swirl about.

"Ms. Spencer," Val said, bringing my attention back to the present. He'd decided to address her using her preferred name. "Let me introduce Ms. Michaela McKnight," he began. With a broad smile, I proceeded with the same general greeting Val and Ms. Spencer had a few minutes before. In unison, Ms. Spencer and I extended hands and, with a firm handshake, we both smiled. "Ms. McKnight will be the attorney on your case. I'll be here solely to advise," Val added.

Her smell of jasmine and violet leaves was a familiar scent, since it was the last thing I'd put on before walking out the house this morning. The bouquet complimented her sophistication and womanliness.

"Kennedie," Ms. Spencer said. She nodded in approval. "Shall we get started?"

"Sure, we can," I answered and pointed Kennedie in the direction of my office. "And, I won't mind if you call me Michaela. Everyone else does."

"It's a pleasure to meet you."

Kennedie smiled.

As we walked, with Val following closely on her right, Kennedie turned to him. "Please don't do that again," she cautioned in a whisper, though loud enough for me to hear.

Heeding her warning, Val discontinued his escort. He meant no harm. He's just an honest flirt who gives a compliment when it's deserved.

A few moments later, I offered Kennedie a seat at the conference table after we entered the office and closed the door behind us. She perused the office. She examined the mahogany bookshelf that spanned the length of one sidewall in the same area as the table. The items and volumes of law books were gifts from my law professors, Brooke, and Zachary. Kennedie carefully read the framed certificate and letters from my sorority, my Doctor of Jurisprudence degree from Georgetown University, and my letter of acknowledgment from the Mayor of D.C. that were strategically placed around the window on the wall behind my desk. She even made it her business to read the framed letter from my grandmother, the one she'd written when I was first accepted into law school. I did not object to Kennedie's inspection. Considering all that I had been through, I had every reason to be proud of my accomplishments.

"Do you think I'm qualified?" I asked. I stood behind Kennedie and watched her preview my credentials.

"I've never done this before, so I'm not quite sure what to expect." She kept her attention on the framed letter.

"Well, this is why you have me," I said with a wide reassuring smile. "I…"

"Mr. Valentine said you were just who I needed," she interrupted. She turned to face me. "I never asked for a reason why he felt that way, but do you mind?" She walked in my direction and finally took the seat I'd offered earlier.

"I don't mind at all. I have both the professional and personal experience to get you through this."

"Personal experience?" Her eyes furrowed.

"We'll get to that later," I said. I pulled the seat from the table and sat across from her. I took a moment to examine her.

Kennedie's face had an uncanny familiarity. It was the same face that stared back at me a few years ago. It wore the disappointment that the man she thought would be her everything, turned out to be her nothing. She had eyes that had no more tears. They shared the known sentiment that she had trusted too much and, as a result, had given deception the opportunity to sneak up and slap her with reality. They held a lingering question: Why is it that the person who was supposed to love you always succeeded at perfecting hurting you? She knew love hurt, but she had looked into his eyes and he felt right. Now, because of him, she knows his swears and promises were but in-the-moment speeches, ignoble deeds perpetrated by the man behind the mask.

"Now," I continued, "depending on the type of man your husband is, he might play dirty or he might decide to go down without a fight. Either way, we'll be prepared for anything he and his attorney throws at us."

"I wish I could say he would make this as easy as

possible for both of us, but he's as spiteful as they come. I suggest we pray for the best, and expect the worst from him."

I didn't mind playing fair, but I was also always ready to take the gloves off and take it to the streets whenever a husband and his attorney decides they wanted to hit below the belt or go ten rounds to a knockout. I didn't know Mr. Oliver. From Kennedie's statement, I already had in my mind how I was going to approach him. I was already looking forward to our own encounter.

"So," I said, I pulled a legal pad and a black pen from the holder in the center of the desk, "tell me what happened with you and Mr. Oliver." After I realized I hadn't offered Kennedie anything to drink, I paused, and then slowly rested the pen on the pad. "Can I offer you some coffee or tea?"

"You can, but I'd prefer something a little stronger, if you want me to take this trip."

She smiled.

I tried to stifle my reaction to what Kennedie desired. I stood ready to grant her request. In the back of the office, in a corner behind a smaller bookshelf, I pulled a bottle from a very limited stash on a counter, a glass from a shelf below, and then some ice from the dorm-size refrigerator. After I poured the drink, I slid it in front of Kennedie. She asked me to join her, but I respectfully declined, citing the need to be sober as she dictated the troubles in her marriage.

With her hands around the short glass of whiskey—on the rocks, as she requested—Kennedie discussed the sweet and the sour of her marriage.

$\mathcal{T}$wenty-one

$\mathcal{M}$ichaela...

It was no holds barred for Kennedie when she began to speak about her husband's infidelity. She spoke as if she repeated memorized lines from her tell-all book. I needed a smoke—and I've never smoked—and that drink I'd refused earlier as I listened to the intimate details of her now defunct marriage to Windsor. She was a smorgasbord of emotions, and I went on an emotional rollercoaster with her. She smiled as she talked about their first encounter. She remembered how he'd solicited her attention, his calculated advances, his fairy-tail proposal, and the extravagant wedding he thought she deserved. Too bad he didn't think she deserved his respect.

Kennedie cringed as she described her husband's

mediocre bedroom skills, which she never complained to him about. She loved him and love trumped all. He should've thought she deserved good sex, too. The tears came when she began to disclose how she'd come home to find her husband's mistress—his boss's wife—posed in her yard, ready to gloat and sing her own praises for the position she held in her husband's life, and many times that position included her on both hands and knees. It was the same woman who had bestowed upon Kennedie and Windsor what seemed a genuine greeting all while knowing she was screwing him—and he was returning the favor—under her nose. Selecia Lassiter—Kennedie had spoken her name with such repugnance—had satisfied her yearnings for Windsor, and she'd made no apologies for quenching her thirst. The unsuspecting spouses had proudly paraded through the sea of partygoers with the adulterers grasping to them because they were both the perfect catch.

"I held my chest and head high whenever I walked with my husband." Kennedie lingered in thought before she spoke again. "And that was how I appeared at the company's gala. After all, I had married the smart, sexy, and handsome Windsor Oliver."

"And he's no longer any of those things?"

"He's nasty and greedy, that's what he is." She took a drink from the short cocktail glass. Kennedie exhaled as if she had finally accepted that part of Windsor that was always there but hidden behind his crafted persona. She dabbed the inside corner of her eyes with her middle finger. "Little did I know, the taste of him hadn't faded from her lips, and her tongue still had that leather texture created by his man juices."

"So what do you want?" I tried to keep the inside smile from appearing on my face.

I placed the black pen on the binder, removed the wire rimmed reading glasses from my face, and waited for Kennedie to respond.

"Out." Kennedie's reply was without hesitation. She sat back in the chair and crossed her legs. "And the sooner I have him out of my life, the better."

"Let me be more clear." I placed the reading glasses on the binder next to the pen and stood. After a few strides, I pivoted to face her. "Look, you know your husband..."

"Obviously, I didn't know my *ex-husband* at all," Kennedie amended. "Might as well get used to calling him what he will be, right?"

"I know we haven't discussed the assets that you and your *ex-husband* have amassed, but are you willing to go fifty-fifty, or do you want it all? We can get it all."

"No, I definitely do not want it all. Anything I gave birth to," she instructed, obviously referring to her son, "is mine. I want anything with my name on it. Everything else we can split fifty-fifty. I don't want to be greedy."

"No, be greedy." I paced back to the table and stood behind the chair. So often I've seen women take the high road only to be thrown the nastiest curve ball. "I am so sick of men like your husband. It's men like him that keep women second-guessing the men they meet. We see them as wolves in sheep's clothing, and we anticipate their fuck-ups because we know it's inevitable."

"I'm not faulting Windsor for every man's infidelity, or any woman's apprehension when she meets what seems to be a good man. We are too damn quick to give men titles they haven't earned. Some men truly are too good to be true. Unfortunately, we are usually married, have put our careers on hold to focus on his dreams, and have had a child before we realize we have been conned. We're often neck-deep in shit before we start to smell it, and by then you've come home to be confronted by this bold bitch, as if you stole *her* man."

"And still you only want what's yours."

"Yes! Nothing more, nothing less."

Kennedie was nothing like me during my initial meeting with my attorney. I was infuriated. A few months earlier, with my daughter on my side, I'd walked into my mother's house and was greeted by the most unimaginable scene. My mother was mounted on top of my then-husband Zachary, and she looked like she was having the time of her life. She'd turned and smiled, and then she collapsed her body on top of his. After he recognized the face of his audience, in a panic, he tossed her from him and stood. My daughter was the only thing that kept me from going bat-crazy. I felt betrayed. There was no way in hell I was going to walk into Attorney Bibbins' office as if everything was hunky dory. Hell hath no fury than a woman who had witnessed her husband screwing her mother. I had declared war and, unless he surrendered—which I knew Zachary wasn't going to do—my team was poised to take away what little dignity he thought he would have left.

"Aren't you mad?" I asked. I sat and pulled the chair closer to the table.

The pain in her eyes was profound. Although a few tears had made their way to the surface, Kennedie was still too composed as she discussed her husband's transgression.

"I'm not mad, I'm hurt," she explained. "See, there's a difference. Mad would've had me locked up behind bars…"

"And they don't even serve alcohol," I interrupted.

Kennedie smiled.

"Exactly," she concurred. "And with a manslaughter charge, what good would that do me or my son?"

We sat in silence as if one waited for permission from

the other to speak. It baffled me how seemingly good women find themselves in the arms of selfish, narcissistic, and manipulating men. Men like Windsor and Zachary should be forced to wear a sign warning you of the type of person they are and the dangers you'd encounter. At least you'd know what you were getting yourself into, and it would be your fault if they still had you at hello. But that would rob them of the mystique of sneaking behind your back and the pleasure of watching you drown in self-doubt, blaming yourself for their greed. You go from feeling like love had finally found you, to looking at what love has done to you. Finally, you have to accept that, once again, love made a fool of you.

"She was emboldened to do so," I began, slicing the silence.

"And you say this because?"

Kennedie abandoned the drink, sat back in the chair, and then folded her arms low across the bottom of her belly.

I knew when Kennedie spoke moments earlier she'd referred to her own blindness and sacrifices. This was déjà vu: boy meets girl, girl puts her life on hold, boy makes a name for himself, boy pisses all over girl, with no apologies.

"Like most men," I explained, "Windsor's heart is below his waist, dangling between his legs. Once Selecia felt him inside her, she believed that was her permission to claim him as hers. Confronting you was the next logical thing to do. If she was satisfied with the small piece of him she was getting, and I'm not making any assumptions here," I touched Kennedie's hand and smiled, "she would've continued their secret affair, and you wouldn't have known shit about it. The only time women like Selecia go running at the mouth is when they want wife status. That's what she wanted, and she needed you out of the way in order for her to get it."

"And she can have him." Kennedie sat up, grabbed her glass, and emptied what remained of the whiskey I poured at the start of our conversation. "If she thinks he won't do to her what he did to me, then I wish them the best. Funny, I actually thought I deserved him. They are perfect for each other."

Kennedie and I sat and talked, first as a lawyer advising her client, and then as two women bonded by their husbands' unfaithfulness. It was probably hard for Val to stay away, but he did exactly that. Still, I knew as soon as the door closed behind Kennedie, he and all his handsomeness would be standing in my office requesting the intimate details. Thanks to Val, I had come from behind the scenes at the perfect time. He was right. I was exactly what Kennedie needed.

Just as I expected, Val had timed Kennedie's

departure perfectly. He sat in my office in one of the chairs in front of the desk when I walked in. He damn near frightened me. I was greeted by his voice before he turned around and revealed himself to me.

"So…"

Val's charm was never turned off.

"Man, I know you like a book," I said as I closed the office door and approached him.

"Perhaps you do," he agreed as he stood. "So I don't need to ask you how this afternoon went. You should've already been talking."

Before I responded, I reached for my cell phone, which was on my desk, vibrating. It displayed a message from Brooke.

Dinner reservation.

The Hamiliton

7:30pm.

See you soon.

"This has to be quick. I have dinner in a couple hours." I said. I acknowledged Brooke's message and then placed the phone on the corner of the desk.

"Hot date?" he asked, almost in a whisper. He didn't hide his jealousy well.

"Yes, with a hot chick named Brooklynn Jones." I laughed, and then I turned to find Val smiling. "As a matter of fact, I think you know her."

"Speaking of Brooke, what's her story?"

"She doesn't have a story, Val. She has a life. Still busy, still married, still not interested."

"Wow." He ran his hand from his dark curly hair, over his face, and paused just below his thin lips. "Is that how you're going to shoot me down every time I ask about your best friend?"

"Every time you ask, so either get used to it…"

"Or?" Val interrupted.

"Or stop asking." I walked to the opposite side of my desk and sat. "Am I no longer enough?" I asked. I smiled, crossed my legs, and then looked at Val with inviting eyes. He stared at me as he attempted to assess my seriousness.

"If I didn't know better…"

"You'd think I was serious?" I finished his response. "I'm glad you do know me better." I uncrossed my legs and stood. I walked back to the other side of the desk where Val posed with his hands in his pants pockets. He appeared uncomfortable, and that was not like him. "Of course I'm not serious, Val. Come on. I've told you. I know you too well."

"Anyway," he said. He turned to check the seat behind him, and then sat. "About Ms. Spencer," he added.

I leaned on the edge of the desk as I fed Val the information he waited for with little patience. I thanked him for pulling me back on the frontline. I admitted I did miss strutting my stuff in the courtroom, and laughing in the face of defeated husbands who believed gender and money predisposed them to the thought that they were above the law, or any level of self-respect.

I wanted Kennedie to go for gold, leave Windsor with not even a pot to piss in, but that persuasion fell flat. True, she probably didn't need the money, and he probably wasn't worth the trouble, but I was disappointed. She robbed me of the satisfaction of seeing another bastard leave the courtroom happy that he was allowed to keep the shirt on his back.

Twenty-two

Kennedie...

I expected trials and tribulations, and even the bumps along the road. I thought we would acknowledge the interruption, smooth the rough edges, fix the patches, and then continue on our path to happily ever after. But happily ever after had slipped through my grasp, and I had Windsor and his accomplice to thank. Things happened so fast. I went to sleep one night and enjoyed sweet dreams of the man I loved, and then woke in a bed of lies to the nightmarish reality that this same man only masqueraded as a man who was devoted only to me.

I spent the better part of the afternoon reliving my years with Windsor. Not including the second-rate sex, the years were good until Selecia made her chess move to crown him her King. She had been given reasons to bolster the relationship with my husband. Most sidepieces knew their place and, for the most part, that's where they stayed. They took what they got whenever they could get it. Then there were the ones who felt they deserved the spotlight, and were brave-hearted and unashamed to do so. Selecia Lassiter was one of the latter.

I wish I could say I saw this coming, but I was blindsided by Windsor's infidelity. I might've been more amenable to forgiving Windsor, but after Selecia made it her business to confront me, I knew she had no intentions of leaving Windsor alone. She'd stood at my house as if she wore the diamond ring Windsor had placed on my finger and I had intruded on her marriage. She had balls. Although her reason to speak the truth had come from a place of selfish ambitions, at least I knew. How foolish of me to think my husband was all mine. This is what the truth feels like.

The same traffic that nauseously accompanied me on my drive to Porter and Blount Law Group had awaited my departure. My preoccupation with the circumstances that lead to the demise of my marriage kept my mind from the snail-pace flow of traffic I found myself in. I dove with the sound of a light evening breeze whistling past the small opening in the window. Moments later, I arrived on the quiet street and then turned into my driveway. I geared the car to park and exited, and began my approach toward the door. A slammed car door distracted me as I neared the front door. When I turned, two uniformed officers advanced toward me. They walked in unison as if they were on a drill practice.

"Are you Mrs. Kennedie Oliver?" the female officer asked as the two officers approached.

"Officer...." I leaned in for a closer look at the nametag.

"I'm Officer Banks, this is my partner, Officer Paxton," she announced. She turned her head slightly to acknowledge the stoic Hispanic officer who'd stood to her right. "Are you Ms. Kennedie Oliver?" Officer Banks continued.

"Not for too much longer."

I smiled.

"And is this your house?" Officer Banks added.

"No, but after Massa and the Lady dies, I'll have the house and, finally, my freedom, according to his will," I teased, and then folded my arms. "Of course, this is *my* house. Now that we've gotten the introductions and small talk out of the way, I have a few questions of my own. Let's start with why do I have two officers standing in my yard?"

I looked across the street and there she was, posted up like a regular member of the 227 squad, except her crew was spread up and down Wagner Road in the Paradise Heights subdivision. I wasn't certain if her wave was simply to say *hi* or if she wanted to make sure I knew she was there to bear witness to anything that should transpire. With Alaine Glassin, you could never tell. She was head of the Association, so she had no problem making everybody's business her own. Married with all three of her children away at boarding school and college, and a husband who spent a better part of each month on business trips, she had all the time in the world to waste. She was front and center when Shereese's husband's clothes came flying from their second-floor bedroom window. Alaine had stood and watched him collect each piece one by one from the perfectly manicured lawn under Shereese's watchful gaze from the same window that spat out each garment. Alaine had watched as he tossed the clothes in the back of his Accord, slammed the door, and sped off, and then she spread the news like wildfire.

With reservation, I waved back just to be polite. I knew as soon as she was back in the privacy of her house, she would be on the phone talking to anyone who would listen to her interpretation of the confrontation that was happening outside my front door.

"Well, Ms. Oliver," Officer Paxton stalled.

"Is my son okay?" I interrupted his hesitation.

"Ms. Oliver," Officer Paxton continued.

"Spencer," I interrupted. "My name is Kennedie Spencer."

"Okay, Ms. Spencer," Officer Paxton corrected. He exchanged a quick glance with his partner. "Tanner is fine. He's with..."

"Ms. Spencer," Officer Banks cut in. She shot Officer Paxton a look as if he were about to reveal a secret. "There was a complaint filed against you this morning, that you have been abusing your son. Now, out of precaution, we have to remove him from your home until an investigation is completed."

"Who has my son?" I asked Officer Paxton. "And what the hell are you talking about?" I turned to Officer Banks. I stared at her in disbelief. "He was fine when I took him to school this morning. Now, where is my damn son?" I repeated.

We stood in silence as I waited for someone to let me in on the sick joke being played; it couldn't be anything else. Anger built inside as the time slowly ticked by.

"Tanner is with his father," Officer Banks spoke. She looked at her watch. "He'll be here shortly to collect a few of the child's belongings. Why don't you put some of his things in an overnight bag?"

"Like hell I will," I snapped.

"And then..." she persisted, ignoring my defiance.

"And then?" I interjected and turned to finally enter my house. "My son isn't going anywhere."

"You don't have a choice, Ms. Spencer." Officer Paxton finally got his voice back.

"Like hell I don't." I turned back to face the two officers.

"Ms. Spencer!" Officer Banks called out in a stern voice.

"This is the most absurd thing I've ever heard. Everyday I'm saving the lives of total strangers. I've seen everything from the almost dead to the barely alive, and you think I would come home and harm my son? Oh, and Mr. Oliver will not be leaving here with my son."

I opened the door and slammed it behind me, leaving the officers to entertain themselves. I stood in the foyer, dumbfounded by what had occurred. I couldn't sit by and wait for Windsor to show up and leave with my son, after the boldface lie he told. I've never laid a hand on my son, and Windsor knew that. I reached in my bag for the cell phone and dropped the bag right where I stood. I dialed Windsor's number but reached his voicemail. This is what he does when he knows he's done wrong, and he was dead-ass wrong. I hung up without leaving a message and then dialed Trent's number. I walked toward the kitchen as the phone rang. I needed something to calm my nerve. As Trent's voice sounded, the doorbell rang. I ended the call and rushed toward the front door. When I pulled the door opened, Officer Banks stood with her left hand close to her weapon; the other held onto her radio. Her uniform and jacket hid whatever weight she carried. Her hair was pulled into a tight ponytail, and her face appeared more serious than it did during our earlier encounter. Officer Paxton stood a few feet in the distance.

"Ms. Spencer," she began. She paused as if she were waiting for an acknowledgment, which never came, "your husband will be here in a moment. As I explained earlier, he has to retrieve a few items for your son."

"And like I explained to you earlier, officer, that man is not setting foot in my house," I clarified.

"He won't have to, if you prepare the child's bag like I asked," Officer Banks scolded.

"And," I added, ignoring her explanation, "like I said in plain English, he's not leaving here with my son."

"Unfortunately, Ms. Spencer, you don't have a choice," Officer Banks reiterated.

"I've never laid a finger on T.J. I've never even raised my voice at him. This is beyond ridiculous."

"Someone will be able to determine the validity in your claim and that of Mr. Oliver. But for now, we have to remove the child from what is reported to be an unsafe environment."

"According to that lying son-of-a bitch."

As Officer Banks began yet another explanation of her duties, I focused on Windsor's car as he pulled up. Officer Paxton approached him as he exited the car and began to walk in my direction. T.J. sat in the back seat.

"Mommy," T.J. bawled, but he sat there as if he obeyed his father's last directive.

I felt helpless as I listened to my son's cries, but I couldn't rescue him. I stepped aside as Windsor walked in. As soon as he passed, I slammed the door, leaving both Officer Banks and Paxton on the other side. Windsor turned when he heard the thud.

"What the hell are you doing?" He walked toward the door. The penetrating glare on my face dared him to take one step closer to me. "Open the damn door, Kennedie," he insisted, but Windsor's bark has never frightened me. "Have you lost your mind?"

"We're about to find out just how much of mind I've actually lost."

"Kennedie, open the door, or else."

"Or else what?" I shouted. I stood firm and stared at Windsor with daring eyes. I ignored his command. "You bastard. This is a new low, even for a son-of-a-bitch like you. You know damn well I've never done anything to harm my son."

"Only thing I know is that I'm concerned about *our* son's safety, and I won't be here to protect him," he said as he abandoned his charge toward the door and turned in the direction of the stairs. "You threw me out, remember."

"I didn't throw your ass out, but I should have. You stormed out like a child who had gotten in trouble for something he didn't do," I asserted. I walked up the stairs behind him. "You can drop the act now, Windsor. Officer Banks can't hear your lies."

The bangs on the door, which started the moment it closed, became louder. The doorbell rang nonstop. I ignored both. I supposed any moment now, the door will come tumbling down in a forced entry.

"You haven't spent five minutes with him since you stormed out of here, and you want to talk about his safety and protecting him? You are beyond ridiculous." I continued to lash out at Windsor. I followed behind him as he walked in and out of T.J.'s bedroom, closet, and bathroom. "Where were you when he wanted to know where his daddy was? Who do think answered his questions? And even then, I still defended you."

Windsor ignored my questions.

"Who protects him from this emotional pain you've caused, all because I bruised your galaxy-size ego? Did you

203

see his face in that car? He was terrified."

"Is this where I'm supposed thank you, Kennedie?" Windsor paused. "You wanted your divorce and you're getting it," he said. He started down the stairs with T.J.'s bag over his shoulder. "But you will not get my son. I told you, he's not a part of any deal."

"So, let me make sure I get this right, 'cause maybe, I don't know, I'm the crazy one here. You fucked up and I'm supposed to apologize for my reaction?" I lingered at the top of the stairs and scowled down at him. "This is retaliation. You always seem to forget it was your engagements that have us where we are. This is what you meant when you hollered I shouldn't have done this."

"Not quite, but it seems to be playing out that way," he said with pride.

"Just how do you plan on proving what you claimed I did? I guess now you're going to fabricate the signs of the abuse, just like you did this false allegation." Windsor remained silent as he headed down the stairs and to the front door. His quiet was on purpose. "Let me tell you something," I furthered. I pulled on his arm and forced him to face me. "I don't know what your plans are, nor do I care, but if anything happens to my son, you'll live the rest of your life wondering about the nightmare you're living in. You'll forever be looking over your shoulders, wondering when I'm coming to disrupt your little existence. You know I'll move heaven and earth for my son, but you also know I'll live under the damn jail for him, too."

Windsor smiled, the only response to my threat, but he knew I would risk hell and jail for anything that I gave birth to. When he opened the door, both Officers Banks and Paxton stood just outside. Officer Banks stared at me, but I ignored her and focused on a third officer who'd stood at Windsor's car, with T.J. still in the back.

"Like I said," Windsor began as he stepped outside between the two officers, "I have to make sure my son is protected." He insisted on keeping up the charade. He had the two officers' ears, or so he believed. "I will not be here to protect him, and my son is my priority."

I grimaced at Windsor from the corners of my eyes as the bullshit fell effortless from his mouth. Hatred replaced the blood that surged through every vessel in my body. Never in my wildest nightmare did I ever think I would look at Windsor and feel anything other than love. He resembled someone other than the handsome man to whom I once pledged my love.

"Can I please say goodbye to my son?" I asked. I cut my eyes at Windsor. I wish looks did actually kill.

I was done playing Windsor's game. I couldn't wait to see how he intended on getting this charge to stick. In my mind, I was already lining up my team to make sure Windsor got the exact trouble he was looking for.

Officer Banks nodded to the third officer who then opened the back door to Windsor's car. T.J. jumped out and ran across the lawn. As I stooped, he jumped into my arms. His breath was heavy. His heart was fast.

"Mommy, I want to stay with you," T.J. said, catching his breath.

I tightened my arms around him. Letting him go was the last thing I wanted to do. Based on their silence, I was certain both officers gawked down at me, ready to counter my next move.

"You'll be back in a few days," I whispered. I looked up at Officer Banks who gave a subtle nod of approval. She gave me the reassurance I needed; an acknowledgment that Windsor's charge was made of glass. "Mommy just needs to take care of some business, and Daddy is helping her out. You'll be back home and in your own bed before you know it."

"You promise?" T.J. asked. He lifted his head from my shoulder. His sad, glossy eyes made my heart melt, and tears I'd been able to hold back finally fell from my eyes.

I stared over at Windsor. He stood at his car on the driver side. He seemed impatient in his wait. The disdain I held for this man had swelled, especially after he'd selfishly exposed my son to this trauma. Officer Paxton grabbed T.J.'s hand and escorted him to the car. Although I knew I would see him sooner than Windsor thought, I couldn't watch the car pull off.

"Ms. Spencer," Officer Banks said. She held a business card in her hand. "If you have any questions, please do not hesitate to give me a call." She began a slow, backward walk toward their squad car. "I've been here before. If this divorce is not what he wants, he'll pull every stunt to make sure this is the hardest thing you've ever had to do. He will probably make sure you hurt both financially and emotionally, starting with your son."

I was quieted by Officer Banks' remarks. They were probably just as much a confession as they were a warning. Officer Banks had probably just broken some police code, but she was human, a woman.

"Have a good evening, Ms. Spencer," Officer Banks offered as she and her partner entered the squad car simultaneously.

Not sure how good an evening she expected me to have after the things that unfolded. Although I appreciated her sentiments, her words lingered without an acknowledgment. After all, she had been a part of the interruption that greeted me when I reached home. When I entered the house and closed the door, I leaned against it, tilted my head to the high ceiling, and allowed the tears to fall again.

*T*wenty-three

Kennedie...

I should've chased behind Windsor's car like an escaped patient from the psyche ward at St. Elizabeth's, but that would've given Windsor the ammunition he needed. I didn't think any sane woman would've sat idly by and watched her unstable—cause he really was—soon to be ex-husband run off with her child without exhibiting some degree of crazy. Instead, I was losing my damn mind, pacing the hickory brown hardwood floor in the living room. The dark wood ceiling screamed at me, beckoning me to do something, but the thoughts that swirled in my head were distractions.

I needed help figuring out my next step. I grabbed the phone from the couch to dial Trent's number. I noticed the number of messages displayed on the screen. I'd left my cell phone on silent since just before my meeting with Michaela. I had one message from my grandmother. She either called to inquire about the meeting, or she wanted to get further under my skin by attempting to force me to acknowledge Natalie. The message from T.J.'s teacher, Ms. Donahue, informed me of the allegation Windsor made, and that he was walking out the door with Tanner as she was leaving the message. It was my fault. I hadn't alerted them about the impending divorce, or to give them any directions, but I also didn't think Windsor would stoop to this new low. Shame on me for putting this past him. The other three messages were from Trent. He'd called back after I'd hung up on him. From the list of missed calls, I dialed Trent's number. I slowed my pace across the room as I waited for him to answer.

"The bastard has my son," I seethed as soon as I heard Trent's soothing voice on the other end.

"What do you mean? Kennedie, who has your son?"

The concern in his voice was palpable. For a fleeting moment, I wondered if he had the same worry for everyone, or was this reaction specifically for me.

"The audacity of him to accuse me of abuse, pull my son out of school, and they let him leave here with my damn son." Finally, I stopped pacing and braced myself against the back of the brown leather chaise sectional.

"Have you ever...?"

"What?" I fumed. "Of course not. Discipline yes, any damn time it's necessary, but I've never abused my son."

"Good. Calm down."

"Calm down? I just told you Windsor has my son, and you're telling me to calm down. That's impossible right now. I know he's scared. I want my son back."

"Kennedie, I heard what you said, but I need you to calm down so you can hear what I have to say. Now, you said they let him leave. Who are you talking about?"

"The two officers who stood guard at my door when I came home, listening to Windsor's lies."

"Do you remember their names?"

I hesitated. I wasn't sure why Trent needed that information, but I wasn't about to question him. I gave him the names of officers C. Paxton and S. Banks. I remembered the initials I saw on their nameplates. I told Trent there was a third officer who stood in the distance next to Windsor's car, but I did not get his name.

"Now what?"

"Let me worry about that," he cautioned. He paused, probably anticipating a rebuttal. "What are you about to do?" he continued.

I certainly wasn't going to just sit here while Windsor

had my son out there, filling his head with God knows what.

"I'm going to find my son," I yelled as the small bead of tear fell down my face.

"No, you're not."

"Say what?"

"You're going to wait for the phone to ring an hour from now. In the meantime, do something to occupy the time. Run a bath, finish a bottle of your favorite wine, do whatever you need to pass the time, just don't leave, and do not call that man."

I was silent.

"Kennedie!" Trent called out.

"Okay."

After I hung up, I walked to the other side of the sectional. I placed the phone on the couch to my right and stared at the screen. The saved image of a happily smiling T.J., with eyes of innocence and bravery, glared back at me. As the picture faded to black, I exhaled and caught the tears that fell from both eyes.

Minutes after I agreed to follow the orders of this perfect stranger, restlessness and anticipation set in. So many things floated through my mind: *Why had I crossed paths with Trent Ashby? What did he want in exchange for his help? What was this familiarity about him that I couldn't rest my finger on? What the hell was Windsor doing with my son?* I shook my head to relieve myself of the disturbing thoughts, and then stood to walk to the kitchen. I grabbed the phone from the couch so I wouldn't have to rush back when it rang, if it rang.

I couldn't steady my hand as I poured a large tumbler of pinot noir. A flood of thoughts consumed my mind, including Trent's words, *Do whatever to pass the time.* That was easier said than done. I couldn't think of anything that could distract me from the fact that I wouldn't be able to hug my son or kiss his forehead before bed. T.J. was with a brainless psycho who had his mind set on vengeance, as if I were the one who'd stepped out on him. I rested against the counter and took a mouthful of the red fluid. I allowed the rich taste of black plums and wild violets to calm my racing mind and help me sit still until this incoming phone call that Trent spoke about.

Twenty-four

Michaela...

"Is everything okay?" I greeted in a long embrace that ended with a peck on either cheek.

I stood next to Brooke as she neared the end of a contentious phone call. She rolled her eyes to the corner and shook her head as she provided nonchalant responses to the questions posed by the person on the other side. She hated to give attention to an unimportant task, and the exchange seemed no different. Although her style was simple—skinny-fit black jeans, black and white scoop neck blouse, and an open front black jacket—she still could be the perpetrator of a few murders, if looks could kill. And she'd probably walk away scot-free in her yellow leather pumps. Her hair flowed in a gentle breeze, but that little disturbance did not disrupt her flawless appearance.

"Everything is fine," she assured as we headed inside The Hamilton, as the gold letters above its entrance proudly announced. I followed in apprehension. "That was Stetzen. He's just getting the message I left him about tonight."

"And he's upset?"

"At first, yes. It's you, so he understands," Brooke explained.

"Or he pretends he understands," I extended. I wondered why she didn't wait to be seated by the hostess.

"Oh, we're over here," she said. She pointed to a table to our right. It wasn't the most private location, but we've never needed privacy to discuss anything we wanted.

"Guess you taught him well."

"You are a non-negotiable," Brooke said. She looked at me and smiled. "And he knew that, even before he met you."

"Like I said, you've trained him well." I looked at Brooke with side eyes as I slid into the chair to her right. "Sorry I'm late," I offered.

"What happened?" She began browsing her menu.

"Val," I answered. I grabbed the menu that was placed on top of the place setting. Well-versed in Val's shenanigans, Brooke shook her head.

"Christmas in April," Brooke whispered. Her mouth was hidden behind her menu. She gazed up at whomever stood behind me.

"Mrs. McKnight, good evening," he announced.

I turned to examine the man who spoke my name. His sound was unfamiliar.

"Judge Ashby!" He spoke with honeyed voice. It was unlike the orotund and unemotional tone that often directed me, and many others, from his bench. "How are you?"

"All is well." He lowered his head closer to my ear and, sotto-voce, he continued, "In case you haven't realized, this isn't the courtroom, Ms. McKnight." He returned to an erect stance. I made a conscious decision not to correct his formality, his insistence on addressing me as Ms. McKnight, although he cautioned me about doing the same. "You can call me Donald. I know you've wanted to shout it a few times in court." He smiled.

The judge was almost all right. A few times during contentious moments in the courtroom I've wanted to call him a few things, but Donald wasn't one of them. I maintained decorum and argued my way into favorable decisions for those I represented.

"Well, Donald," I said with some reluctance, "I'm just ending a great day with an evening out with my best friend."

"Mrs. Jones," Brooklynn announced, as she extended her hand, "but you can call me Brooke." She lowered her eyes, smiled, and then refocused on his fine-looking face.

I knew exactly where her eyes went. She's always been a crotch-watcher, and marriage didn't take that obsession from her. Judge Ashby grabbed the tips of Brooklynn's fingers and nodded his head in pleasure.

His presence was distracting. His salt and pepper grey hair glistened under fluorescent lights. Dazzling grey eyes and a bright white smile made him irresistible, even to those who had reasons to resist. He lacked nothing in the height department, and his broad shoulders and soft, large hands made him beautifully powerful.

"A pleasure to meet you, Mrs. Jones." He released Brooklynn's fingers and then rested his hand on my shoulder. "You ladies enjoy your evening."

"Thank you." I looked up at his imposing figure. He turned and then continued his promenade to the rear of the restaurant. "Give my regards to Chloe," I added.

"I certainly will, Ms. McKnight," Judge Ashby agreed as he continued his walk.

Brooklynn sat back.

"Thank you Donald," she teased. "Looks like someone has it for the man in black." She leaned forward.

"And by someone, I mean you."

"The man is married, Brooke, and to a woman who wouldn't hesitate to snap you in half, if you looked too long in his direction." I closed my menu and sat back.

"Please! When have you let a little competition steer you away from any man you want?" Brooklynn finally grabbed the oddly shaped decanter that had been filled prior to my arrival and began to fill her glass.

"First of all, I left Dominic and Giselle in the very distant past. Hell, that was a battle I shouldn't have fought." Dominic and Giselle were people I should've avoided in college. I was ready for love. Giselle helped me realize I wasn't going to find that in someone like Dominic Mitchell.

"And second?" Brooklynn added.

"Second, since you insist, he's practically old enough be my father."

"And if the woman I saw him walk in here with is the Mrs. Chloe you wanted him to give your regards, she's practically old enough to be his daughter." Brooke tilted her head and looked at me from the corners of her eyes.

"Maybe she wears her age well. Maybe she is his daughter." If what Brooklynn stated about the appearance of the woman who'd accompanied Judge Ashby was right, I could say for sure, she wasn't Mrs. Chloe Ashby. The woman could very well be the judge's daughter, but I didn't know enough about the family to neither confirm nor deny.

"Hmm, maybe," Brooklynn agreed. She wore the look of a skeptic.

"Why don't you go after him?"

"First of all," Brooke mocked. She waved her left hand in my face as if I had temporary amnesia about her marital status. "I'm married."

I grabbed the wine flute. After I sipped, I closed my eyes to enjoy the bouquet that wrapped around my tongue.

"I ordered your favorite," Brooklynn suggested. She wrapped her manicured fingers around her glass and tasted.

"And what is that?" I asked, unable to identify the deliciousness that danced in my mouth.

"Cabernet Sauvignon."

"Girl, this is your favorite."

We laughed.

That is exactly why I loved my best friend. Until that day, I avoided Brooke and had missed those moments with her. We've been through a lot since we met. We've watched each other entertain pretend love. We've kept each other's secrets, nurtured foolish hearts, and witnessed love and happiness we found in the men we espoused. Unfortunately for me, love and happiness had turned into hate, accompanied by misery and, eventually, my divorce from Zack. Until Brooke's impromptu visit to the office, I'd kept my split from Zachary from her. There wasn't anyone on this earth who I trusted more than I trusted Brooklynn Jones. And yes, that included the bastard that eventually put a ring on my finger.

"Pardon me, ladies," the waiter announced as he approached. He reintroduced himself. Apparently, I missed his first introduction. He memorized our order and refilled our wine glasses before he headed to the kitchen. While they prepared our meals, he returned a few times to check on our comfort. He kept our water glasses filled, even though we only took small sips.

Over Tuna Tartar, the tantalizing aroma of Lamb steak, and the sizzling presentation of Berkshire pork, Brooklynn and I laughed as we reminisced about our emotional past, and then those things that kept us awake at night.

"You know what?" Brooklynn asked. She sliced a bit of the lamb.

"What?" I took another sip of wine, and then held the glass as I waited for her to expose her thoughts.

"I keep waiting for Patience to walk through that door and turn this date upside down."

"She wouldn't dare. I'm sure she hasn't forgotten what happened that last time. Just a glimpse of our faces and she'll quickly abandon any thoughts of bringing her easy ass up in here."

We sat back and laughed, but our laughter was short-lived.

"So, your mother had her world rocked by Zachary?" Brooklynn asked as she addressed the big-ass elephant in the room. "I mean, I have a hard time believing any mother, your mother, would do something like that."

"But that's exactly why she did it, because she is my mother." My explanation was simple, but it was the truth.

"But why?"

"That's easy. Ms. Whitney isn't my biggest fan. The woman hates me."

"Your mother hates you?" she questioned. "She's one of the nicest persons I've ever met."

I sat back and allowed Brooke's words to penetrate my mind. I once held that same belief about my mother. I once thought she could do no wrong. I once thought she'd take a bullet for me, and then I came to the painful realization that she would sidestep a bullet and watch me succumb to my injury, all with a smile on her face.

I readied to tell my best friend the one other secret I kept from her all this time. I exhaled quietly. I decided to take a soft approach.

"When I was thirteen years old, my brother was murdered."

"Really! By whom?"

I leaned toward the table and said, in a feathered voiced, "I killed him."

Brooklynn laughed.

"Are you trying to impress me, Michaela?" she chuckled again, and then returned her attention to the meal in front of her. "You don't even like to kill ants."

She shook her head.

"You think I would lie about being a murderer? There are some people who would claim that to be their fame, but not me."

"What are you talking about, Michaela? I thought I knew you."

"You do know me," I countered. "Who you don't know is the thirteen-year-old who begged for her mother to save her. Who you don't know is the little girl who had to stab to death the only brother she had, who she once loved, in order to save herself. Yes, my brother, Isaiah, raped me."

"My gosh!" Brooklynn placed her napkin on the table, stood, and then walked to the opposite side. With a hug and a tight squeeze, she whispered, "I'm so sorry you had to go through that."

"Thanks," I said as she made her way back to the other side of the table. It seemed everyone in our section of the restaurant had their eyes on us. "I've dealt with that.

What I now have to deal with is the fact that my mother held this hatred and her desire for revenge for so many years."

"And her idea of revenge was...?" Brooklynn postponed her question. She stared into me as she waited for me to interject.

"Making sure I walked in on her and Zachary in a moment of unbridled passion." I managed to smile although even the mere thought of what transpired between Whitney and Zach hurt my soul. "Actually, they were just fucking like wildebeests." That my mother had admitted her detestation had lessened the blow. Imagine if someone who actually loved me had betrayed me.

"I don't even have words right now?" Brooklynn declared.

"Believe me, I understand."

And I did understand. There was nothing Brooke could've said that would've bettered what I endured as a scared teen, and then as a woman who had to embrace the unfathomable truth that in the pit of my mother's stomach lived immeasurable hatred that had only festered with time. In one fell swoop, everything I wanted, everything I had, was taken from me. I lost love, my husband, trust, and my mother. Whitney and Zach made me lose the very things I had been living for.

Under the silence that befell us, Brooklynn and I

finished our meal. We declined dessert but welcomed another bottle of Brooklynn's favorite, Cabernet Sauvignon. Judge Ashby had ended his night, but not before introducing Chloe to Brooklynn, and bidding us a good night. Chloe Ashby had always been a classic woman, and tonight she presented herself as nothing less. I'm not sure who Brooklynn saw walking in with the Judge. Judge Ashby rested his palm in the small of her back as they walked out.

"So, speaking of things I haven't told anyone," Brooklynn spoke, breaking the long silence. "I lied."

"I know. You said you've been lying to Stetzen about the pill." Brooke looked at me with puzzled eyes. "I get it. He was ready to proudly display the baby on board sign, except that you aren't on board."

"That is true, but the reason for not wanting a child has nothing to do with my career."

"Then what is it?"

"I don't deserve a child," Brooklynn insisted. Her eyes became filled with regret, accompanied with a pool of tears that lingered at her bottom eyelid.

"Of course you do," I assured. "Any woman who wants and can have children deserves them. Stop punishing yourself because you decided to delay starting a family. Granted, it is without your husband's consent, but still."

"No, you don't understand." She began to

rummage through her purse. Moments later, she unfolded a protected document she'd stored in a section of her purse, and placed it in front of me. I gawked at the Rorschach-like picture on the table. "His name is DeMarco. I named him, even though I never held him; even though I never got to experience love at first sight."

"What happened?"

I abandoned the rest of my wine as I listened to Brooke's emotional account. A seventeen-year-old mother-to-be wasn't the storyline her parents spent years creating. Once they realized Brooke's big mistake, just before she was supposed to finish high school and begin her summer before college, her parents went into damage control, preserving the pristine family name, and avoiding tarnishing the church-girl reputation they created and had been able to maintain. Nothing, and in her case, no one, was going to interrupt their plan for Brooklynn's success, and that plan did not include walking down the streets of their gated neighborhood behind a stroller, or with a bastard on her hip. They'd been impatient, too. At exactly seven months, just when the fruit of the forbidden started to show, they whisked her to the hospital, induced labor, and gave her baby away to parents-in-waiting. For seven months Brooke and her baby were one, and they didn't even give her a chance to see his beautiful face, because certainly, he couldn't have been anything but.

"They were afraid you were going to change your mind." I reached across the table and massaged her hand with tender strokes.

"I gave him up without a fight," Brooklynn spoke with pain on her face, which I hated to see.

"Sweetheart, you were young. Your parents made the decision they thought was right for you."

"And they ignored what I knew was right for me." Brooklynn sat back and folded her arms. The tears fell as she cried without sound. The patrons turned their attention to the display of emotions at our table, but I did not appreciate the attention. Regardless, I had to be there for my sister. I wanted to help her remove the cinder block from her shoulders.

"Why don't you tell him, assuming he doesn't already know?"

"Of course he doesn't know," Brooklynn assured.

"Then have the conversation with him, Brooke," I proposed in a soft, persuasive tone. "Tell him about DeMarco. Tell him about the contraception…"

"Are you serious?" she interrupted.

"And then tell him exactly why you're reluctant to start the family he so desperately wants," I continued. I ignored her intrusion.

"And risk my marriage?"

"Brooke, you're already risking your marriage with the lie you've told. Everything you've done to cover it up has only added to the pile you'll have to dig yourself out of." I paused. "Unless you don't ever plan on telling him anything."

"You know Stetzen."

If there was one thing on this earth I could bet my life on, it was the depth of Stetzen's love for Brooklynn, and I doubt this one lie—assuming it's only one—would be the straw that breaks their marriage's back.

"I know Stetzen loves you," I assured. I stood, pulled my chair closer to her, and sat. I took her hand in mine and continued. "Of course, he'll be upset when he hears about your deception, and you won't have a choice but to deal with that. But, I know he won't be in that place for too long. Lead the conversation with DeMarco. Maybe hearing about what you've already lost will temper his reaction."

"And if he doesn't?"

"Then we need to plan for me to be there when you confess your sins. If he wants to act like he's lost his damn mind, we can beat that ass together." Finally, a smile came from my best friend. "Seriously, we don't need to think about that, because I'm sure he'll understand."

Brooklynn and I sat back and allowed ourselves time to recover from the emotions that came with our evening together. After dinner, we enjoyed a long embrace before going our separate ways. I had another long day ahead, and Brooklynn had to prepare for an early morning flight back to New York. Our meeting had accomplished one thing: we both rid ourselves of the secrets we kept from each other. What lingered was Brooklynn's decision to actually right the wrong of deceiving her husband, and his impending reaction to her news.

The last thing I wanted was for Brooklynn and Stetzen to become another happily ever after that didn't exactly go according to the script. So far, they'd done everything right, and I hated the thought that her past had precipitated a behavior that could ruin a perfect match.

*T*wenty-five

Michaela...

Life does have a funny way of sneaking up on you, and perception wasn't always reality. Everything I thought about Zachary turned out to be fiction. He mastered the art of deception, frolicking around with the one person who didn't need anyone's permission to stab me in the back. I knew what I did to earn my mother's hate—I finally heard it from the horse's mouth—but, for the life of me, I couldn't think of any reason why Zachary was willing to play Whitney's accomplice, besides the fact that he was an oversexed dog whose dick didn't even pack a punch. Guess we know from whom I got my acting skills. In order to punish me, Whitney had to settle for the same mediocre sex I had to smile through for years. Zachary had gone from being my husband to being the lowest human being on earth.

I came home from dinner with Brooklynn with much on my mind. I wanted to put everything to the side and enjoy a relaxing bath with my hands around a full glass. I set my keys and bag on a chair in the kitchen, then filled the biggest glass I could find. I headed up the stairs with the glass and my phone in hand, removed one shoe at a time and left them on the steps. I was certain to find them in their exact place, unless Alison returned before I woke. I called Brooke to let her know I had made it home safely but was greeted by her voicemail. I placed the phone on the side of the tub and started the water for my bath, added rose-scented bath salt, and then undressed. I stood in the mirror. A depressed feeling came over me. Not since Zachary have I felt a man's hands on my skin, and it wasn't because I still loved him; I didn't. I deprived myself of soft, passionate kisses on my neck. I longed for the feathery touch of his fingertips gliding over my collarbone, between my breasts, and disappearing between my thighs. I desired the shivers as his skin neared mine, and the rise in my chest in anticipation of his pleasure. I wanted his fingerprints all over me. I resisted temptation, and for obvious reasons, but now I needed the arms of temptation to wrap me up all nightlong.

I finally gave up staring at the phone, which wasn't

getting me anywhere close to him. I sat on the side of the tub, sliding one hand up and down the length of my legs.

"You said I should call you if I needed anything," I greeted when I heard his sexiness.

"Is that what you heard?"

"Yes," I answered. I smiled. I scooped the water in the palm of my hand to gauge the temperature, and then allowed the water to cascade through my fingers.

"That's definitely not what I said," he rebutted.

"Then what, Rick?"

"Don't do that," he ordered. I manufactured a naughty smile. He's admitted what it did to him when I called him *Rick.* I guess it didn't take much to turn some people on. "I said," he continued, "you should call me after you've gotten rid of your husband," Kendrick corrected. Damn, I missed him. I missed his voice. After all these years, it still sent my heart racing. "So, did you get rid of him?"

"I'm calling, aren't I?" I stood and stared at my image in the mirror as if he was staring back at me.

"What do you want?" he asked matter-of-factly.

I imagined Kendrick behind me, his hands around my waist, and his breath on my ear.

"I want to wake up next to you?"

"When?"

"Is tonight too soon?" I paused for his response and

hoped what came from his mouth would be music to my ear and my body. He pondered, but the question was simple. "Rick, did you hear me?"

"It's never too soon to see you, baby."

I had Kendrick's heart in the palm of my hands, and soon I would have a firm grip on another important part of him. Oh, the ties that binds.

Kendrick was too close for comfort, but that never stopped his pursuit. He lived in the same community on the far end of the same street until three years ago. Remembering the first time I saw him always made me smile.

That evening, I drove the car slowly so I could gawk at a shirtless Kendrick Prescott as he walked toward his mailbox. He caught me staring, too. Instead of slithering down my seat in embarrassment, I allowed my eyes to continue its shameless travel up and down this man's body. I marveled at what was in plain view, and imagined the unseen. I had no ill intention. I was simply looking at merchandise that was brazenly on display. That day of looking and not touching had been the gateway to our subsequent forbidden encounters. There were two problems: Kendrick wanted more, and I was married. I wasn't upset that my husband cheated on me; he'd only evened the score. I was disappointed that the best he could do was my mother, aged pussy with elastic bands for walls. I was looking for the pleasure that had abandoned my bedroom. What was Zachary's excuse? My secret rendezvous with Kendrick ended because the conscience I set aside and tried to ignore during our moments kept tapping on my shoulder. I could no longer ignore the fact that what I engaged in was immoral. It was good while it lasted. I guess some secrets will always remain just that, secrets.

Kendrick was more than forty-five minutes away, which gave me enough time to prepare for his arrival. The glass of wine was gone before I finished my relaxing bath. I left the bathroom with the scent of caramel between my thighs and on the center of my chest, slipped into a black V-string panty and matching embroidered bra, and not the made-for-granny pajamas I usually wore as I slept next to Zach. While I waited, I thought about the last time Kendrick and I were together. Time did nothing to assuage the memories, and neither did Zachary.

Often, I felt my husband was a stranger in my bed who often fumbled in his attempts at pleasure. Yet, it was the attention I received from a stranger that had my body quivering. All the things my husband did not do, Kendrick Prescott did, and it was his desire to do so. Parts of my body that were too long ignored by Zach were caressed and stroked by unfamiliar hands. He'd licked and nibbled like his very existence depended on it. His fingertips glided over my body with little effort, like a violin's bow over its strings, and together we made music of love. I went crazy for more of his uninhibited love.

I sat on the bed, taming the mane that had finally been uncovered, when the doorbell rang. Although it was expected, it made my heart thump. As I stood, I smiled because my wait was over. The anticipation that had my heart beating like a rapidly played snare drum would soon be tempered by everything this man had to offer. I meandered down the steps as if I were in no hurry to see him, but every part of me craved attention, his attention. I pulled the door open. With one hand extended from the door, I exaggerated the arch in my back, clutched my waist, and smiled wide. His eyes journeyed the length of my body, and I stood there and watched him watch me.

"You know, the closer you are, the better the view." I offered him my hand.

"The view from here is perfect." Finally, the mischievous smile that was a fiber of his beautiful being appeared. His eyes met mine. He grabbed my hand, stepped inside, and then pulled me in close as the door closed behind him. The frantic rhythm of his heart matched mine. "I've waited too long to be this close to you again."

"You're talking too much. Shut up and kiss me," I commanded.

The moment his lips covered mine, my yearn for him intensified. With Zachary, I was never satisfied, and it wasn't because I was hard to please sexually. I was too busy directing him to places that would have me in heaven to actually enjoy the little he was able to deliver.

Kendrick and I had only made it to the stairs before he had my legs over his shoulders and his head between them. He'd unhooked my bra and tossed them to the side the moment his lips met mine. I didn't plan on having them on too long. My panties were left at the bottom of the stairs where I'd stepped out of them. I tilted my head back and grabbed my breasts in both hands the instant his long tongue was inside me. The pleasure made it hard to keep my eyes open. I was going crazy, and that was only a small part of his love.

I was furious when he paused in the midst of his intense assault, interrupted my pleasure, and suggested we moved to the bedroom. My mind was quickly put at ease. Once there, the passion continued. There had never been another man in the bed I once shared with Zach, but it was time to end that curse. Kendrick stood before me with his long, ginger-colored torso. I lay on the bed, propped on my elbows, with my legs spread. I admired every inch of him. His chest bulged like pillows, and his manhood pointed directly at me. I swear this man could make you squirt just

235

looking at him. He crawled onto the bed like a lion ready to devour its prey, and I was ready for him. I was already wet for him, and I needed to feel him, all of him, inside me. I needed to feel his love all over me.

Although he roared like a lion, he was gentle in his assail. His strokes were long and even, and he stared into me with every lunge, as if he were evaluating my satisfaction. He had nothing to worry about. I marveled at the attention my breasts received. He licked and bit, which sent my silent moans up a few octaves. He held my legs back with my knees to my chest. I was wide open, and he hit the very spot he knew would make me climax. His pelvis vacillated like a dancer on rhythm. I wrapped my arms as far as I could around his wide back, inhaled, and then released a long breath. I tossed my head back and became lost in the emotions of the moment. After a few more of his calculated thrusts, I finally allowed my juices to erupt, and so did he.

His sweaty body collapsed next to me. What he served needed to be bottled and sold to Zachary. We took heavy breaths as if we were finally allowed to breathe. He kissed my forehead and lips, and then pulled me on top him. With Zachary, I would've been making my way to the bathroom, ready to wash his lousy performance from me, but I wanted to revel in the moment Kendrick and I experienced, even with his now cold liquid all over me.

"Why aren't you married?" I asked. Not exactly the words I expected to come out of my mouth after great sex.

Kendrick exhaled.

"I guess that means I was good." He smiled, brushed my hair from my face, and then kissed me.

"Was there ever any doubt? Now, answer the question."

"Been waiting on you." He rested his hands behind his head.

"I'm serious." I blushed, and then slapped him lightly on his chest, where my head rested in comfort.

"Ok. No need to get violent." He laughed, and then placed a soft kiss on the top of my head. "I haven't met anyone who appears they would as good at it as I know I will be."

"And I haven't helped."

I stared at him. His mustache mimicked the curve of his soft, pink lips. Thick eyebrows sat above lively brown eyes. His smooth, brown skin felt like silk. Nothing about him had changed.

"I'm sorry," he offered. "I didn't mean…"
"No, it's ok," I interjected.

"See, I tend to stay away from trouble. That's what my mother did after her divorce from my father. I don't think she's been more happy or more free."

"Which is why you had to stay away from me."

"Yes, not because you were trouble, but because I was trouble for you. It was obvious you wanted something else, but you had gotten so used to the dance with the devil."

"Well, the devil cheated on me, with my mother." I was almost ashamed to admit this to him, because I had just confirmed he was right.

"I told you the guy was stepping out on you."

"Yes, but you had no proof."

"Michaela, when a man tells you another man is cheating, that's all the proof you need." He rolled his body on top on mine, kissed my neck, and then stood. "Can I see you tomorrow?" he asked, adhering to rules we established when our relationship first started.

"Yes."

I lay in the bed and watched Kendrick dress. He came just for sex, and I wasn't mad at him. Tonight, that was all I wanted. Still, there was a certain thrill that came with his ride. He pulled on his jeans, secured his man-piece to the side, and then he carefully zipped it closed. His vintage t-shirt clung to him and displayed the hills and valleys he showcased years ago. Still in the nude, I followed him down the steps with my hand in his. At the bottom of the stairs, I slipped into my panties. As we approached the door, he grabbed his light black jacket from the floor in the foyer—he'd removed it just before our session on the stairs—and then slipped into his black loafers.

"You know, I'm really glad you called." He held my face in his hands and then kissed only my bottom lip. "Can't wait to see you tomorrow."

"Neither can I."

I closed the door behind him and was ready to go to bed satisfied. Although I loved the smell of Kendrick on me, I needed to shower. I grabbed my bra from the floor and then began my walk toward the stairs when the doorbell rang. I paused, and then smiled as I turned toward the door. I was ready for a second round with him, and I hoped he returned for just that.

"Is it tomorrow already?" I asked as I swung the door open.

Who stood in front of me wasn't the person who had just left me in a bubble of satisfaction. My smile disappeared. He was good at making that happen.

"Oh, you thought I was him, coming back for more?" he asked. He pointed in the direction Kendrick's car headed. "Sorry to disappoint, but he did actually leave."

"At least you've been consistent at being just that, a disappointment." *Gosh, I wish I controlled lightning*, I thought. "What the hell do you want, Zach? You are not welcomed here."

"I can't stop thinking about you."

"Stop, because I am definitely not thinking about you," I advised. "I wasn't on your mind when you were screwing my mother. You see what I spend my time doing."

"I see. I guess he was everyone's best-kept secret. Well, everyone except your mother."

"What are you talking about?" I asked with little interest in his response.

"Remember when I told you your mother manipulated me into sleeping with her the day I went to break things off?"

"How can I forget your story?" I turned away from him and left him standing at the door. "I'm still disgusted."

"Right, my story." He stepped inside and closed the door behind him. "Well, that time it wasn't exactly manipulation. It was revenge. That time, I had permission to screw whomever the hell I wanted. You gave me permission. Whomever just so happened to be your mother, but all that did was sweetened the pot. It made sense. She already despised you. I just imagined how pissed off you'd be when you finally found out.

"See, Kendrick wasn't just your secret, he was mine, too. Yes, I did hate myself for having an affair. What I hated even more was that the other woman was your mother. I didn't think you deserved either. I'd convinced myself you were a damn good wife and an even better mother. I thought you were the most loyal person I knew. Thanks to your mother, I quickly came to my senses."

"My mother?"

"Yes. She told me all about your extracurricular activities with Kendrick Prescott, and I no longer gave a fuck. I deserved everything you were doing, but so did you. So many nights you lay next to me after being with him. You kept secrets from us, Michaela, so I decided to keep that little gem a secret of my own. Every time we made love …"

"Oh, is that what you call it?" I interrupted. "Surprise, Zachary! Your abysmal performance wasn't love. It was a waste of my damn time, and I got tired of satisfying myself afterward. There were nights Kendrick finished what your lame-ass started."

"Well, dear, I got my nut, and that was all that mattered." He started toward the kitchen. "You didn't care about me satisfying you," he continued. "You knew you had Kendrick in the wings, waiting to pick up where I left off. Your dissatisfaction lasted only as long as it took you to make your way to his bed."

What Zachary said was what men say to jump-offs, and his statement cast a doubt on whether this man ever cared about anyone other than himself.

"Where do you think you're going?" I put on my bra

before turning to follow him. I wished my body was not on display for him. I wanted to run upstairs and cover up. More than anything, I wanted him out.

"To get a drink," he answered, "since you've forgotten your manners."

"My manners are for invited guests, not for unwelcomed dogs like you. Now get out of my house."

"Go to hell!"

"I'm calling the police," I threatened.

"Good. I'll leave when they get here." He pulled a bottle of Makers from under the counter, reached for a glass from the shelf, and filled it with ice. He poured a small portion in the glass and took it to his head, and then he filled it halfway a second time. He turned to face me before he took his second sip. "You should dress like that more often."

"And you should stop wasting your time going places you're not wanted. That was the point of me asking your no-sex-game-having ass to leave, not for you to show up at my house, sniffing the air, trying to smell what good sex smells like."

He brought the glass to his lips and took a final gulp. He set the glass on the counter and exhaled. He smiled.

"At least you waited until I was out of the house before you brought him here."

"Did I?" I turned from the kitchen and headed

toward the foyer to show his ass out.

"Don't play with me, Michaela."

He came running up behind me. I guess what I said had finally hit a nerve. Funny, men have a problem with women bringing another man in their home or in their bed, but they see nothing wrong when they do the same with some nasty-ass bitch who can't hold a candle to your wind.

"Play with you? I stopped playing with you the moment I walked into you playing with my mother. You think I care now if what I say pisses you off or tickle your fancy?

"I don't owe you an explanation, but I stopped seeing Kendrick when I thought about you and my daughter. I started because I was being selfish. You, on other hand, continued screwing my mother because you were finally given a reason to set any guilt you had to the side. You thought only about yourself. You thought about the fact that another man was going to bed with your woman, and rage built inside. You thought about the props you got, from whomever, that you were able to drive my mother and me wild, and I didn't even know about it. I guess, once again, you were the big man on campus."

"Are you done?" he asked.

"With you, yes. Now, I'm going upstairs to get dressed, and when I come back down, I better be the only bitch in my house."

After I said my last piece, I turned toward the stairs. I could feel him staring at me. I hated to treat Zachary this way, but I remember how broken I was over him and the scene of him and my mother that often left me paralyzed. I had no right feeling sorry for him when he never took a moment to feel sorry for me. As I reached the top of the stairs, the door slammed.

Good riddance, asshole. I thought.

Twenty-six

Kennedie...

Sit and wait. This wait had turned into torture. Sitting still wasn't in my DNA, and neither was waiting, not even on a normal day. Nothing about this day was normal, not since I came home and then watched Windsor drive off with my son, after his hurtful accusation, his lies. In front of a muted television, I started on my second bottle of wine. I'd emptied the first bottle as if I were drinking water. The minutes seemed to tick by at a slower-than-molasses pace. It was as if time had stood still. I was more than minutes into my restless wait and still no word from Trent. In fact, the phone had sat undisturbed since Trent and I ended our conversation.

I paced the same path in the living room, from one wall to the next, and when that didn't make the phone ring, I sat on the couch with hands that failed to steady trembling knees. I anticipated a knock on the door, but there was nothing outside but the calm wind that whispered as it passed. I stared at the cell phone in my hand as I contemplated calling Windsor, but Trent's directives were on repeat in my head. *Don't do anything. Don't even call Windsor.* I grabbed the wine glass from the table and began to squat on the couch when the doorbell rang. In a hurry, I placed the glass on the table and spilled the tasty liquid. Shattered clear glass decorated the coffee table, but I ignored the accident I created.

"My baby is here," I shouted as I sprinted through the foyer to open the door.

When I pulled it opened, my nosy neighbor from across the street, Alaine Glassin, stood with a worrisome expression stamped on her face. Alaine wasn't a friend, but she wasn't foe. She wasn't the type of person you let in your house, and she definitely wasn't the person you let in your business, unless your wanted to see your secrets roll down the street like tumble weed in the dry Texas wind.

"Alaine," I whispered. I did nothing to hide my disappointment in her appearance. *Why wasn't it Windsor or Trent? Why wasn't it my son?* I thought just before I questioned

246

her unwelcomed visit to my house. "What can I do for you?"

I hadn't changed clothes since I came home, and it's usually the first thing I did before starting on my evening. The fitted blazer was flung over the couch, and the blossom print pumps were still where I stepped out of them, at the bottom of the stairs just as I started to follow Windsor upstairs. I stood face to face with Alaine in my pencil skirt and blue tank, with a look of doubt in my eyes.

"I don't mean to be nosy..."

Yes, you do, I thought, *which is why you are ringing my damn bell at this hour.* I loved calling bullshit when I heard it, and what she said definitely sounded like it came from a bull's butt. I stared at her.

"Is everything all right?" Alaine asked. She tilted her head to look inside the house. I obstructed her attempt to confirm what had been said about the house Windsor and I once occupied together. I dared to be different, so the structure was a design unlike any within the division. With vaulted ceilings, A-framed roofs, and more windows than walls, it had its reasons to be admired on the outside, but Alaine would never know what's on the inside.

"Everything is fine, Alaine," I assured as I began to slowly close the door. "I appreciate your concern."

What I didn't appreciate was her making what would be a failed attempt to stick her manufactured nose in my damn business. That's right, her business was being talked about, too. If she weren't in my business, she would've been in someone else's. Guess we could say it was my turn. I'm sure she had been waiting on pins and needles for this moment.

She stuck her foot in the door, which got my immediate attention. I looked up at her, struggling to comprehend her persistence.

"You've been pacing in front of your window for the last hour. Are you sure everything is fine?"

I never liked the fact that the window had no draping. It was Windsor's dumb-ass bright idea I apprehensively went along with.

"As far as you are concerned, yes. Everything is better than fine." This woman had mastered the art of imposition. "Have a good night, Alaine."

"He was here earlier. Sat inside his car and stared into your house for a good while before he sped off."

Her revelation peaked my interest.

"Who are you talking about?" As much as I hated to indulge her in her reporting, I gave her permission to continue.

"Mr. Oliver!" She looked at me with inquisitive eyes, as if I should've known.

"Oh, of course."

For once I appreciated her spy practices. How else would I have known my husband was now my stalker? He'd sat outside my house plotting and scheming. I guess this is what men do when they realize what they've lost because of the few moments of pleasure they sought.

"And your son, he'll be back. He's so handsome and free-spirited. I wouldn't worry about losing him. I see you with him every day, and you're a perfect mother."

While I appreciated her confidence in T.J.'s return and my parenting skills, I wasn't going to confirm or deny what she thought was going on in my house. My grandmother had always taught me to keep my front door shut to nosy people. She forgot to warn me about the windows.

"I have to go now. I have something in the oven I must tend to." I lied.

"I have noticed that your husband's sister hasn't been back since that little spat you had with her," she continued, ignoring another attempt to dismiss her.

"His sister!"

"Yes! At least, that's what he said when we were introduced. Of course, I had put myself in a position where he had no choice. See, I've never seen another woman enter your house when you're not there, so when they came out, I strolled on over and struck up a conversation about nothing.

Now, they weren't in there long."

Alaine answered the question that was swirling in my head. I wasn't going to come out and ask. It was one thing that Windsor had this woman in my house, but if I found out he had her in my bed, there would be hell to pay. Windsor may be stupid, but he damn sure wasn't crazy. And why would he bring another woman to the house knowing that Nosy Norma had nothing better to do all day but perch up at her window and fulfill her purpose for waking up that day.

She continued, "I think her name was Alecia."

"Selecia," I corrected. "Her name is Selecia."

"That's it. Nasty heifer."

Immediately I thought, *this woman knows more than she's telling*. Her intent on getting a reaction with her name-calling failed, since I stood in a blank stare. Why did Alaine have such a harsh response to someone she didn't even know?

"Oh, I'm sorry," Alaine added. She put one hand on her chest as if her apology was sincere. "I shouldn't be talking about your family with you standing right here."

"Right, just do it behind my back like you do everyone else." I looked at her sharply. "You and I both know she wasn't family, so cut the crap, Alaine. You gather and report news from your window and front door, and you use the demise of others as entertainment for you and your followers, those that find no shame in laughing at the downfall of the very people you all call friends." I cleared my throat.

Alaine stood with her eyes wide and her mouth open, as if she were hearing my charges for the first time. What I said was nothing but the truth, and as long as she has been in this little community, I was certain her ears had encountered similar words. She had an obsession with other people's business, which she used to hide the pain and loneliness that held her hostage inside her own home. Now, I could've told her that her husband was busy handing out his own share of indecent proposals and was jet setting with those who had willingly accepted, but she probably already knew that. I also could've told her that one of his suitors was the same person with whom she delightedly swapped hearsay, but since she was too busy tending to matters of other people, I'll just sit back and watch her handle stink when the shit hits the fan.

"But…"

"No, Alaine." I dismissed her interjection. "We are done here." Her only response was the same look of astonishment.

With Alaine, I played nice from afar. I waved and smiled during my comings and goings like a good neighbor. But when my business became her target, the niceness went out the window. I stood behind the closed door and processed Alaine's impudence. A few moments later, I posed in front of my living room window and watched her parade back across the street with slump shoulders, and her head toward the ground. I don't know if that was the same demeanor she held when she believed she would accomplish her mission. She'd learned her lesson, for now, but soon she would be back on her porch or perched at her window, searching for someone else's business to meddle in. One thing for certain, two things for sure, she'll never make the mistake of attempting to stick her nose in my affairs.

Twenty-seven

Kennedie...

Waiting patiently was never one of my best attributes, but somehow I managed to keep myself together. I hadn't heard from Windsor. What he'd done was crazy, unbelievable—and he knew that the moment he conceived the idea—but he hadn't completely lost his mind. The last thing on his mind should've been any inclination to dial my number, especially after the stunt he'd pull. Trent hadn't called either, and I had no idea what trick he had up his sleeves. I was on one knee, praying for the Lord to help, and for T.J.'s safe return.

"Lord," I began, "grant me the serenity to accept the things I cannot change, and wisdom to not lose my damn mind and keep myself from snatching Windsor by the throat whenever I see him. Amen."

I ended my prayer and made it back to the couch to continue my wait in a bubble of anxiety. As I sat, I heard a ring. I leaped from the couch, grabbed the phone from the coffee table, and had started a conversation when I realized the ringing sound came from the front door. I raced to the door, this time confident my son would be standing on the other side. It was late, but I wasn't going to close my eyes until I was assured T.J. was safe, and safe meant him and I were both under the same roof, my roof. I had a few hostile words for Windsor that I had been reluctantly swallowing. This time, not even the blood of Jesus could save him. When I pulled the door opened, T.J. alone stood looking up at me, with his overnight bag on the ground next to him. I dropped to my knees and pulled him into me. Finally, I felt like I was breathing. After our embrace, I held him at a distant to examine him.

"Mommy." He stared at me with perplexed eyes. "I'm tired."

He sounded just as he looked. His eyes were droopy, and he bowed his head into my shoulder as I drew him closer. I had so many questions: Where had Windsor been with my son since they left? Did T.J. eat? But T.J. had spoken, and my questions would have to wait. I lifted him in my arms, grabbed his bag, and then looked across the street at the male figure that stood outside the car as I turned back inside. Although he stood in the dark—he purposely avoided the light—I knew his stature was unlike Windsor's. I guess Windsor was too much of a coward to face me without protection from the guys in blue. I closed the door without acknowledging the watchman. From the living room window, I watched this figure as he got in the car and drove away. Any guilt or shame that had come over Alaine after I denied her attempt to meddle in matters that should have been no concern of hers was short-lived. In this late of night, she'd also sat front and center and had unobstructed view to what transpired outside my door.

That my son was safe in my arms—and that's exactly where he was as I sat on the couch thinking about the day we've had—only meant this was just the start of the craziness. My eyes watered as I watched him drift off to sleep. I could not imagine life without my son, and it made me wonder how my own mother could've continued life as usual, not knowing or caring about what was happening to me, her own child. Threatening my relationship with my son was Windsor's version of playing with fire, and he had unknowingly planned his own burn.

I didn't know the tactics Trent used to get Windsor to comply, and so fast, and a part of me didn't care to know. It was unlike Windsor to acquiesce without a fight. My guess, it was made clear to him that reuniting T.J. with his mother was in his best interest.

I grabbed the phone from the table with the intention of sending a quick text message to say *Thank you* to Trent, since it was already late. I made my way upstairs with T.J. still in my arms and eventually laid him on his bed and removed his shoes. After I tucked him in, I sat in the chair next to his bed and stared at him in tranquil sleep. Since I was now sure T.J. was safe, I dialed Windsor's number. I was ready to give him a nasty piece of my mind, but I was greeted by his voicemail.

"You warned me not to involve our son, but that's exactly what you did. You have no idea what you've started with this little game you played. Remember, I can be a bitch. I lived with one for many years, and I learned more than you will ever know," I said in a whisper to avoid disturbing T.J. "And of all the bitches you could've fucked with, you definitely picked the wrong one."

After I hung up the phone, I sat in the dark and pondered precisely how I was going to handle Windsor. I wanted this to be quick and easy, which is why I was grateful Trent was able to help the way he had, but Windsor's performance had added another layer. The white gloves were definitely off. Moments after I hung up, the phone rang and interrupted my thoughts.

"You wanted to get shit started?" I answered, presumably. "Well, I'm ready for you, you sick-ass bastard," I yelled. I walked out of the room to avoid waking T.J.

"Kennedie, it's me," Trent broke in. My assumption that Windsor had received my message and was calling with his retort was incorrect. "I didn't know you had this level of feisty in you."

"Oh my God," I said, and covered my mouth in shame. Yes, I was mad at Windsor, and rightfully so, but I wanted to maintain decorum around Trent. Instead, I confirmed that Windsor had struck a nerve. "I'm sorry. I thought you were..."

"Windsor?" He giggled. "No." His amusement was a relief. "I'm definitely not him." He paused. "Listen, I know it's late..."

"Don't worry about that. I was going to text you." I closed the door to T.J.'s bedroom behind me, and then walked down the hall to my room. "Thank you," I said. I sat on the bed and then exhaled.

"You're welcome. I just wanted to make sure you and T.J. were okay."

"I don't know what you did," I began.

"I told you," Trent interjected, disturbing my speech, "all you had to do was trust me."

"Trust you?" I stood from the bed and walked over

to the window. "That's not easily earned these days. And the fact that I don't even know you makes it even more complicated." I stared up at the calming yellow moon. Its bright shine dominated the otherwise dark sky. "There's something I need to ask you."

"I'm listening."

The silence that followed was deafening. I had been curious since the day I met Trent at the courthouse. I had been waiting for the right moment to satisfy my curiosity.

"Why me?" I asked.

I hoped Trent would take a moment to ponder the simple question, which would've allowed me to prepare for his response. What he said was not what I expected, and it came the instant the last word fell from my lips.

"Why not you?"

"You involving yourself like this, why? I'm going through a divorce, and my husband is obviously trying to make my life hell. I can't offer you anything, and it's way too soon to entertain anyone."

"Wait a minute. You think I..." He laughed, but became serious shortly after. "I want to get to know you."

"Trent."

"Not in that way, Kennedie," he corrected. "Listen." As if he were about to say something for which he could be persecuted, he hesitated. "I'll admit now that my reason for helping you was selfish. Running into you at the courthouse wasn't planned, but I was glad I did, especially after you told me who you were. After you told me what was happening, I knew I had to help you."

"I hear you, but none of what you said answered my question." My breath became heavy. Trying to figure out this man's motives shouldn't be a burden, but his response was nothing, if not evasive.

"I know your husband."

"Huh!" I said with raised eyebrows. "What do you mean, 'you know my husband'? Whatever kind of games you are playing, I never liked games, and I don't have time for it."

"I should've said, I know men who are just like your husband. They use that one thing they perceived to be your weakness, in this case your son, to try and back you into a corner. They force you to fight, hoping you'd be too exhausted and give up."

"And you thought I needed you to help me fight my way out? You think I can't handle the man I've slept with for years? I guess this means I'm indebted to you."

"Handle him?" he questioned. "Seems to me you didn't even know the man you were sleeping next to." He paused. "Look, Ken."

"Please don't call me that," I requested. "He gave me

that name, and I've made the same demand of him."

"Sorry." Trent's voice was cloaked in guilt.

"You don't have to apologize. You didn't know."

"Kennedie," he revised, "you don't owe me anything. My reasons are a little more complicated."

"Complicated! That's the story of my life. I've been dealing with complications since my eyes were at my knees. What's one more? Nothing or no one surprises me anymore."

Trent was quiet, waiting an explanation for what I'd just stated. As far as I was concerned, no explanation was needed. I joined him in his still. I could hear his every breath, as if our heads shared the same pillow.

"Did your mother ever talk to you about what happened?"

"Natalie and I haven't talked about many things. In fact, we don't talk at all. We haven't had a relationship since I was about ten years old. A well-known hate lived between our very infrequent 'Hellos' and 'goodbyes'. See, we have a love-hate relationship." I sat up in the bed with my back against the upholstered headboard.

"What do you mean?" Trent inquired.

"She loves to hate me, and I hate her even more. " I paused.

"Sounds to me like a whole lot of hate and no love at

all," Trent added.

"That's putting it lightly. The woman tried to kill me. Only a hateful heart could drive a person to kill."

And with that, Trent became the third person to hear those words from my mouth; words I'd hurled a few times at the woman who perpetrated the crime. My grandmother had grimaced at the sound of that charge as well. There was nothing untruth about it.

Trent hesitated.

"I was there, Kennedie," he finally spoke.

"Wait. What?" I asked as if his admission was unclear. "What do you mean? Where?"

"At your house, looking into your window. I'd watched your mother from my bedroom window as she casually walk back to your house as if she had just delivered homemade pie to welcome new neighbors when, in fact, she had just done something even worse. Rather than drive myself crazy wondering if you were okay, I made it my business to find out."

"And?" I asked.

Trent had my attention.

"I knew she was lying when she said you weren't there. I walked around to the side of the house to see into your room. I could hear faint moans. From the look on your face, I knew you were in pain."

"She was killing me," I declared aloud.

The memories of that day crept in at a sluggish pace. I had buried them in a space in my mind I thought not even God Himself could unearth. It wasn't God, but man, Trent Ashby, who was about to make me relive the worst day of my life.

"She wasn't trying to kill you, Kennedie," he corrected. To him, my claim was absurd.

"What the hell do you know?" I was bemused. Who was he? What did Trent know that I didn't? "She was the worst kind of evil, and that bitch hated me so much that she tried to kill me."

"I was in the house, sitting at the top of the stairs, when she came over the first time and asked my mother for help. Days later, she returned to ask my mother if she had it. It wasn't until later that I found out what 'it' was."

"You don't know what you're talking about," I asserted.

"But I do," Trent declared, "and so do you." To echo my claim, I remained silent. "Your mother had no interest in trying to kill you. She wanted to get rid of what was growing inside you, and my mother was complicit."

If this was what it felt like to be punched in the gut with words, I had just experienced it. For a moment, I was breathless. The thought that Trent's face had a familiarity about it, the one I had dismissed during our initial encounter, came rushing back, a flash from the past that now made perfect sense.

Easton Trent Ashby lived a few doors down from my mother, on the other side of the street. Although he was a few years older, for some odd reason, we attracted each other. He was a handsome, goofy boy, but he was every girl's crush. He still had those piercing eyes that let you into his soul. The little boy, seemingly too tall for his age, who once navigated life with a recognized inelegance, had morphed into a man who boast confidence that, alone, could be blamed for your wild thoughts about him.

"There's more, but maybe it's not my place to even…" Trent continued.

"Like hell it's not." I exhaled, and then allowed a short passage of time. "You've already crossed the Rubicon. Now is not the time to concern yourself about staying in your place. Tell me what you know. You can't dig up my past like this and then leave business unfinished."

"We should continue this conversation at some other time, in person. I don't think…" He dismissed my request.

"Trent, don't think." I scooted from the bed and stood with my hand on my hip. "And don't you dare hang up. You're not getting off this phone until you tell me exactly what you need to tell me."

I tried to stay calm, but Trent's hesitation had gotten under my skin. He's had plenty of time to think about how he was going to break his news. He should've accounted for my reaction.

"I don't want to hurt you." His concern sounded genuine.

"If what you have to tell me will hurt me, I would prefer my hurt now, rather than later." I exited my bedroom and started toward the stairs.

Whatever Trent had to tell me would probably go down easier with a drink. In the kitchen, I selected a bottle from the stack of reds on the counter, took a glass from the cabinet, and then poured it full. I took a sip and waited for Trent to divulge.

"Do you remember Victor Stephens?" Trent began.

I tilted my head and eyes to the ceiling.

"Yes, I definitely remember him. He was my mother's boyfriend. He was in and out of the house, and was out the day she escorted me to the bus stop. I never said much to him. I avoided being in the same room with him, because I hated the way his eyes violated me. I always felt naked, and I didn't like that he watched me wherever I walked."

"Well, on one of those nights when your mother left him in the house to run a quick errand, he watched. When just watching you wasn't satisfying, he followed you into your room. When your mother returned, she caught Victor closing the door to your room. He turned to face her as he pulled his zipper closed."

"What are you saying, Trent?" I stood at the counter with my hand still clinging to the wine glass.

"He drugged and raped you."

His declaration had me staring at the phone as if it had poison spewing from it.

"But…" I broke in.

"While you slept," Trent added.

Everything went silent, except for my heart, which pounded in my ear. I wanted to run away from a past I barely remembered, but my feet felt stuck in cement. The glass crashed to the floor and unfroze time.

"That can't be true," I asserted. "My mother would've told me if something like that happened."

"Are we talking about the same mother?" He lingered. "There are many things she hasn't told you."

"But that's not something you sweep under the rug."

"Kennedie, that's exactly what she did, right after she shipped you off."

As much as I wanted to respond, I disregarded his statement. I don't remember much, but the disappointment on his face as I trailed behind my mother with hunched shoulders, wondering why I was being sent away swirled about my mind.

"What happened to him?" I asked as I wiped the tears I tried to fight back.

"I don't know," Trent answered without pause. "After you left, I never saw him visit again."

"How did you find out about that night?"

A feeling of shame came over me, and I didn't quite know if I should accept or dismiss it. Why me? What Trent revealed was what he overheard as our mothers sat in his house at the dining room table. His mother had questions, and Natalie was shameless in her answers.

"I know you have questions," Trent spoke. "I'll admit that I don't know everything, but if you're going to ask your mother anything, there's one more thing."

"Of course there is." I'd had enough surprises for one evening, but Trent was positioning himself to deliver one more. I held my breath and braced myself.

"Ask about your father."

"My father?" I asked. My head had just entered a cloud of confusion. I was told about my father before I ever thought to ask. I had no reason to believe my mother withheld any truths. "My father, Leonard Vincent, died in a car accident when I was two years old. Unfortunately, I didn't get the chance to know him, but I'm sure my mother told me all I needed to know."

"Is that the story she told you?"

"That's no fucking story; that is the truth."

Twenty-eight

Michaela...

Val sauntered into my office with his hands behind his back. He held his thoughts until I ended the phone call that began fifteen minutes earlier.

"What are you going to do when you can no longer walk around the corner to bother me?" I asked as I placed my cell phone on my desk.

"Is that what I am now, a bother?"

"What do you mean, now?" I laughed. "You've been a bother since the day I met you. Stop acting like this is news."

He placed his right hand over the left side of his chest in an unhurried gesture. "Oh, I'm hurt," he said. "Anyway," he continued after his action was met with an eye roll, "I have another ten, maybe twenty, years before I have to worry about that." He surveyed the room although it was obvious he and I were the only occupants. He sat at the edge of the desk, and then he leaned in my direction. "So." He stalled. I stared at him as I waited for his inquest to begin. In the past week, it was obvious Val had something on his mind, and I already knew it had nothing to do with Kennedie's case. "What's his name?" he finally spoke.

"I don't know what you're talking about," I answered. I stifled the smile that boiled inside me.

"Come on. You can tell me." He smiled. "Who am I going to tell?"

"Absolutely no one, because I'm not telling you anything." I stood and headed to the door.

"Why not?"

"Because, Val, there's nothing to tell. Listen, you've already wasted fifteen minutes of your day." I brought my lips close to his ear. "Those are minutes you can't get back."

I continued to approach the door. As if I were his escort, Val followed behind. He stepped into the hall and then turned. He flaunted a confident smile.

"What?" I asked. I turned from him and, as expected, he followed.

"Michaela, for the last week, you've walked around here on cloud nine, and I want to know who is responsible for it."

"I can't be the cause of my own happiness?"

"Of course you can, but this has man written all over it. You're going to tell me later," he said. He walked past me and then turned to block my progress. "So, why don't you just tell me now and save yourself from the agony of keeping it all in?" He clasped his hands as if he were about to say the Lord's Prayer. "Please!"

I hated to see a man beg. I was just glad he did not drop to his knees. Val was absolutely right. I was going to tell him later. There wasn't much I kept from him, except the intimate details; those I only shared with Brooklynn.

Brooklynn could hardly contain her excitement when she learned I'd rekindled the old flame that is Kendrick Prescott. She was more enthused about our encounter, as if she had experienced his unbridled pleasure. When I shared our initial meeting, she condemned it, and warned that he was trouble that I didn't need to get into. She was right about only one thing, he was trouble. But he was exactly the trouble I needed to get into. Tired of my complaints about my disappointments in Zach's performance in the bedroom, Brooklynn eventually accepted the errors of my ways.

"All right," I conceded. I turned from him and began to walk leisurely toward my desk. "It's Kendrick."

"The same Kendrick that you...?"

"Yes, that same one," I interrupted.

Clearly, I tell this man way too much, and here I was in my office having more taxicab confessions. Obviously, I haven't learned my lesson. Truth is, I trusted my relationship with Val just as much as I trusted my friendship with Brooke. None of what I disclosed to Val had ever been the topic of water cooler conversations, so I was confident that what I shared was going nowhere.

"So you finally got rid of the cobwebs." He turned and then laughed, which prompted a shy shrug and a smile.

"I am not going to stand here and engage in a conversation with you about my V-spot," I warned, but the smile I displayed softened my seriousness. He stood in silence. I sat behind my desk and waited for his next words, because I knew there were more. I could tell his mind spun in a tangled web of endless possibilities, but that was how Val's mind worked when it came to him, any conversation about sex and me, including innuendos.

With one hand in his pocket, he massaged the well-groomed hair on his face with the other as he meandered toward the desk. The eyes of this imposing figure stared down at me. *Damn, this man is beautiful,* I thought. As much as I hated to admit it, I sometimes found myself getting lost in him.

"Are you ready to take his last name?" he asked. He

interrupted my daydream, but it was a welcomed disruption. I'd almost forgotten he was even there.

"Geesh." I excused his flippant remark, and I answered with the sarcasm his question deserved. "You're already marrying me off?"

"Well." His retort was immediate.

What the hell just happened, I thought. I wanted to believe he was joking. He couldn't be serious. Our usual comical, flirtatious discourse had just taken a turn.

"Val, we both know that's not what I want. It was only one night, a night I seriously needed. I am not ready to crown this finger with anything that indicates I belong to anyone. Plus, I'm waiting for you men to get in formation."

"One night?" he asked.

He dismissed any of the words that followed, as if he knew something else. Whatever he knew didn't come from me. His question was based on supposition.

"Okay, two." I paused, lounged back in the chair, and then smiled as my mind shifted to thoughts of my recent involvements with Kendrick. My skin tingled as I imagined the feel of his fingertips down the length of my spine, his warm breath on the nape of my neck, just before I felt the softness of his lips, and my breasts cupped in his hands as his tongue danced around my nipples.

"Why don't you give me the same chance you gave

him?"

I stood from the chair and walked to the door. It had been left opened since Val wandered in. I processed his question as I tried to arrange the best reply. I closed the door and stood just on the inside; my hand still held the knob.

"Not where I thought this conversation was going," I said. I released the doorknob and started toward him. "Seriously! You are a flirt, and I fall easily. The way I see it, you'll hurt me, and I'll kill you. Let's just say we're saving me from heartache and life behind bars."

"Is that how you feel?"

"That's how I've always felt. That hasn't changed, and it's not going to," I said. I walked back to the other side of the desk. "Now, I don't suppose you want to discuss the Spencer case?" I pulled a notebook from the left corner of the desk and reached for the pen that sat in the center of the keyboard.

"No," he answered and immediately added a smile. "I had my guy do some research on those names she provided. He came back clean, and so did many of the others, but…"

"I like buts." I abandoned the notebook and sat back in the chair.

"Landen Oliver, his brother, has an offshore account in Panama."

———

"There's only one problem, Val."

"What's that?"

"She isn't married to Landen Oliver. How does that help us?" I asked. I tossed the pen back onto the desk and sat erect.

"You're right. But, she is married to the man whose money is in that account." Val sat for the first time since he entered my office. He was elated to share the information.

"I'm listening."

"There's money being deposited in this account on a biweekly basis. Those deposits match exactly the monies that are being deducted from Windsor Oliver's account exactly one week before. Now, we may not be able to get access to that money during settlement, but if we can prove it does in fact belong to Mr. W. Oliver, and he used his brother's name as a way of hiding the money from his spouse…"

"Then we have more to play with at the table," I interrupted. Val nodded in agreement. I never asked Val to reveal his source—because I never cared to know—but many times over, he, she, or they have made liars out of greedy husbands who have cried about shallow pockets.

"This will be music to Kennedie's ear," Val teased.

"That's another problem." I stood from behind my desk and walked to meet Val on the other side. He was still seated, with his legs crossed at the knee. He displayed his yellow and gray pattern socks and brown oxfords. I swore he stepped directly from the cover of GQ every morning and headed into work. "Ms. Spencer is not interested in that kind of musical arrangement."

"Pardon my language, but..." He glanced around the room to observe our surroundings. We were still the only ones in the room. "What the fuck is this woman smoking?"

"Hey." I shrugged my shoulders. "Sometimes women just want to get out. They want to leave with nothing but the dignity they came in with. Their freedom from these men and what they have done to them is all they want. Maybe I'll be able to convince her, but when I asked what she wanted from this divorce, she was clear that she only wanted out, and she's satisfied with getting out with her child and only what she went in with."

Val stood from the chair and walked to the door. "Well, I certainly hope you can convince her. This man has been lying to her since the day they met."

I followed behind him with my arms folded across my chest.

"I guess there's only one honest man left on this earth." I stopped as he opened the door.

"And that would be me." He laughed as he turned. "I do have a question."

"If you're going to ask me about..."

275

"No." He dropped his head and then raised only his eyes to give a taunting glare. He flashed a devilish smile. "How did you manage to get such a quick response to your file? You weren't out there stroking egos again, were you?"

"I know I'm good, and I make Judge Ashby smile, but I don't exactly have him in the palm of my hand."

"Well, I hope we're ready," he said as he exited.

After I watched Val disappear around the corner, I closed the door and walked back to the desk. I don't always think back to my own separation from Zachary, but I remember the agonizing wait like it was yesterday. I had to see my adversary every day. Who wants to be tied to their philandering husband longer than they have to? Yes, I was surprised to have gotten a court date so soon after filing, but that had nothing to do with the relationship I had with one of the best judges on this side of heaven. But, for Kennedie's sake, the sooner we go to battle, the quicker she could adjust to life without Windsor and his distractions.

Twenty-nine

Michaela...

The old fable goes if your ears are ringing, your name is being spat from the tip of someone's tongue. That was probably what prompted this call from Kennedie. That, or she was just a woman with impeccable timing. The phone rang as soon as I reached the desk. Kennedie had dialed my mobile number she was directed to use in case of emergency only. She saved me the trouble of having to contact her about the information concerning Landen Oliver's account, her soon-to-be ex-brother-in-law, and the possibility that Windsor was using that account to hide his money from her. I needed to convince her to ask for a little more from the divorce than just her child and what she entered the marriage with. Kennedie was so definite in what she wanted from her now failed marriage that I was all but certain I didn't stand a chance in getting her to reconsider. I've rarely seen a fair divorce, mine included, but Kennedie had been more than fair-minded during our discussions. Unless there was an ironclad prenuptial agreement that protected one party from being taken to the cleaners—so to speak—they usually went for the jugular. Most of what Mr. Windsor Oliver had to lose, unbeknownst to Kennedie, had been hidden from her, the woman from whom he vowed to keep no secrets. Whatever the reason for her call, I was glad she had.

"Kennedie," I answered. "I was just…"

"Don't leave that son-of-a-bitch two pennies to rub together," she interrupted. The music Val hoped would play in Kennedie's ears was a beautiful composition in mine. Oh, its sweet, sweet melody. My job was already done, and I didn't even get a chance to showcase my power of persuasion.

I walked to the other side of the desk, pulled the chair, and slowly eased my bottom to the edge. I crossed one leg over the other, and then smiled as I silently welcomed Kennedie to the dark side. I guess all she needed was time to reflect on her husband's deception.

"Last we spoke, you reiterated your wants, and all you wanted was out. In fact, your exact words when we spoke were…"

"No need to remind me of what I said. I remember," she interjected. "I've changed my mind. I can do that, can't I?"

"You most certainly can do that." I reclined in the chair and then spun to face the big window. Soon, the view would not be one to admire, with the construction of yet another multimillion-dollar building. Kennedie's reversal elicited a euphoria I hadn't felt since I left Zachary standing in the courtroom, next to his lawyer, looking just as flabbergasted. "You seemed pretty sure then," I added.

"Yes, I was absolutely one-hundred percent sure."

"You must tell me what he did to cause this change, because I know he did something. I can hear it in your voice."

In silence, I listened to Kennedie recap the events that unfolded as she arrived home after she left my office during our initial meeting. She spoke of the two officers who emerged from their car like jump-outs to confront her about abuse allegations that Windsor brought against her. She remembered the look on her son's face as he was whisked away in the back of Windsor's car, and that it had left her feeling like her soul had been ripped from her. She'd spent the time she waited for her son's return in misery.

What she divulged was no surprise at all. Desperate times called for desperate measures, and a worried Windsor resorted to lies and slander. Those tactics would never work in his favor. He poured venom into a woman who was once a harmless snake. Now she was ready to fight fire with fire. Windsor didn't know it yet, but he was about to suffer a really bad burn.

"And how is Tanner doing?" I spun the chair back toward the desk when my cellphone buzzed. I sat up, removed the phone from my ear, and stared at the notification displayed on the screen. I unlocked the phone to display the text messages, and then pressed the name to read the message from Brooke.

Brooklynn Jones: Tonight's the night. I'll let you know after if I'm in heaven or hell. Love you.

I sat back and smiled after I read her message. In my mind, I hoped everything goes well. Before, I was confident in Stetzen's forgiveness in the name of love, but I feared being betrayed by the woman who he would give his life for would trump love.

"Oh, he's fine," Kennedie answered, bringing me back from my momentary distraction. "Of course, he was scared in the moment, but he bounced back like a trooper. He spent a few nights, after the nightmares, asking if his daddy was going to take him away again. I assured him mommy would always protect him, even from men like his daddy."

I'd met the little fellow when I stopped by the house to have Kennedie sign documents and to complete a financial disclosure. Tanner had been a ball of energy, already a little man with swag. He had a smile that could conquer the world, and it was obvious he had his mother wrapped around his little fingers. Without a doubt, he was the apple of Kennedie's eyes. Windsor couldn't have been thinking straight when he thought a charge of maltreatment would stick on someone like Kennedie. Her display of affection was unbound. A blind person could see just how much she adored her son.

Before I mentioned Tanner's name, I heard nothing but disdain in Kennedie's voice as she talked about the actions of her soon-to-be ex-husband. Her contempt for him was profound, and I held the little nugget about the account that was being maintained with money from Windsor. I listened to her heavy breath return to calm, and it was then I decided to let her in on Windsor's big secret.

"I do have something to tell you." I paused. "But before I do…"

"What's the question?" Kennedie assumed. She was still composed, but I was sure it wouldn't be long before she lost it.

"How close are you to Landen Oliver?"

"Not as close as we used to be. He's been in and out

of rehab, bouncing from one member of the family's pillow to the other's post." Kennedie paused as if she realized she'd just aired this man's dirty laundry to a woman who, until a few weeks ago, was a stranger. "Wait, a minute!" she added. "What does Landen have to do with anything?"

"I'll get to that, if you just indulge me for a moment." I waited for Kennedie to protest, but her hush permitted my investigation. "Is he able to sustain a bank account, say, in Panama?"

"With what?" She laughed. "Landen is, as my grandmother would say, piss poor and dirt cheap. I don't know how he would survive if Windsor and his mother weren't supporting him, and they only do it because he's blood. He lived with us briefly, but after Tanner was born and Landen still couldn't keep a job or kick his habit, he had to go."

I listened to Kennedie paint a dismal picture of the life Landen Oliver lived. I needed nothing else to convince me the money held in that account was fair play. Not only had Windsor hid his affair with Selecia Lassiter, soon Kennedie would learn that wasn't the only thing he had been hiding.

"I have to tell you something."

When it was clear I had Kennedie's attention, I broke the news. Her silence was telling. While she was an open book to the man she married, he spent years in their marriage showing her his left hand while keeping his right hidden behind his back. He's a sad liar, that's how Kennedie described him. Divulging what was discovered from Val's research had fueled a now burning fire. She was officially a woman scorned, and she was ready to go in for the kill. I only needed her to keep quiet about our plan, though she was ready to attack him. She agreed to keep her peace, even after she admitted it would be hard to see him and not go all the way off.

"He's about to learn one hell of a lesson," Kennedie interjected.

It hadn't taken her long to go from ten to zero, and I didn't blame her. The damage had already been done, and she had already decided a divorce was the only fix.

*T*hirty

Kennedie...

That my father was deceased—because that's what I was told and didn't know any different—was a valid justification for his absence from my life. I couldn't argue with that. Now I was faced with the possible truth about his existence. Trent's disclosure made me question everything I was ever told. He provided as much detail as he could, or wanted to. There were two other people who could fill in the gaps; one reveled in her hatred for me, the other, I took her word as gospel.

Three weeks and what Trent revealed was still unsettling. Lies were told to protect the lies told to hide the truth. I heard of my parents' willful abandonment, and it was a hard pill to swallow. My mother lied, and my father made the decision to deny me, but Trent wasn't innocent. He was the very cause of it. In a time of desperation, my mother attempted to sabotage the very thing this man had been trying to protect, his marriage. An expecting Natalie's intention when she appeared at the residence of Donald and Chloe Ashby was to kill two birds with one stone: tell Chloe Ashby that the judge wasn't exactly honorable, and that she was carrying his bastard child. When she rang the doorbell and was greeted by a young child, she was furious. Not only was Donald married, but he also had a family. In that moment, she gave a young Trent a message for his father. All hell breaks loose, when they can't have the relationship they want. Since that day, Trent had his father in his back pocket. Although he'd threatened to use his father's infidelity against him, he never made good on those threats. Like his father, he kept Natalie and her bastard a secret, until now. What I did with the information was my decision. I took everything I was told, and the questions that held me captive in my own head, to my mother's hospital room. Until then, I was determined that my mother, whatever her fate, would meet it without ever seeing my face again.

I stood at the door to Natalie's private room and waited for the nurse to finish her check of the monitors and drips connected to either bring my mother to health or soothe her to death. I wasn't concerned when my grandmother first spoke of my mother being sick, and I cant even pretend to care now. I had no desire to find out why Natalie was lying in a hospital bed with life slowly drifting from her. After the nurse exited, I entered the room, set my bag in the beige sofa under the large window, and then sat and waited for her to open her eyes.

The bed linen was pulled to her neck, and she slept with both hands under her face. The room was clean as if it were vacant. Bouquets of flowers sat on the window. One bouquet had been placed on the bed table that was pulled to the side. As I stared out the window, after I surveyed the room, nothing about my mother's condition concerned me. What swirled in my mind were the conversations I had with Trent, and all that he revealed. I shook my head in disbelief when I returned my focus to Natalie. When she turned her head and opened her eyes, she displayed a pain-filled smile.

"You're here." She spoke in a whisper. For the first time, Natalie's displayed delight at my presence appeared genuine. She looked at the roses on the table as if seeing them for the first time. "They're beautiful."

"Don't worry, they're not from me." I paused. Natalie's attempt to raise herself failed, and I sat and watched her in her struggle. "We already know how we feel about each other, so let's not even pretend either of us gives a shit."

I could've listened to my mind and picked up flowers

as I walked past the gift shop, but my heart told me not to waste my time or money. Guess we know which one I listened to. I got up from the couch and sat in the yellow bucket-seat chair in front of her bed.

"Have you spoken to your grandmother?" she asked.

The dark around her eyes told a story of long sleepless nights. She barely kept them open as she spoke. She resembled nothing like the woman who spent nights dreaming of ways to make my life miserable and days making certain my misery was her success. There wasn't a trace of her long black hair left. Her high cheekbones, which once garnered attention and compliment, sagged in her present condition.

"It's been a couple weeks, but we've talked," I answered. "You've never cared anything about her, why do you ask?"

"Kennedie."

She tilted her head from me.

"Anyway." I looked away from her, shifted in the seat, and then crossed my legs at the ankles. "She's not the reason why I'm here."

She pressed the button on the side of the bed to raise it. Comfort was far from her grasp, but pain found her with ease.

"Why are you here?"

287

"Well, I can assure you, it's not out of any concern for you." I could've been sensitive to her situation and save my inquisition for another time, but she didn't look like I had many opportunities left. Furthermore, when her words and actions left me feeling lower than road-kill, where was her concern for me? "Did you hate me that much?" I continued.

"Oh, so you're here to open old wounds?" She closed her eyes, inhaled, and then released a heavy breath. Her eyes opened slowly.

"Since they're my wounds, I can do whatever the hell I want." I paused. "I'm here because I have questions."

"You have questions? You know what, your timing is shitty." She grimaced. "Look around you," she continued, "This isn't a damn cocktail party. We're not laughing and talking about our last visit to a tropical island. I'm not in a boat sailing the blue seas, or sitting on a beach in Aruba, feeling the ocean breeze." Guess her pain wasn't hitting her hard enough to kill the bitch that lived inside her. "I'm lying in a hospital bed with tubes running from me, so damn you and your question."

"I'm sorry. Next time, remind me to give a damn." I stood from the chair and paced. "You just can't help yourself, can you?" Although she had no idea what I needed to ask, I was certain her sick mind was working overtime, pasting together the lies that would come from her mouth. "Look at you," I continued. "The death angel is smiling at you from the side of your bed, and you can't even bow out with grace."

"Death, yes, but I don't see no damn..." She abandoned her thought.

"Go ahead! Finish!" I waited, but nothing. "You don't have one ounce of decency in you."

"I have decency. I'm just quick to reach my limits when it..." she paused again, and then tilted her eyes to the ceiling. "Anyway, what the hell do you want?" Although she was still dismissive, she didn't sound as evil as she would if she actually had power in her voice. I wasted no more time.

"Before you left me in the house with him, did you know he was a rapist?" I stopped in front of her bed, folded my arms across my chest, and stared at her. "Was I his only victim?"

"What are you talking about? Nobody raped you." Her struggle to look at me as she dismissed my accusation had nothing to do with her illness, whatever it is. She just couldn't face me, which was no surprise. Whenever she was lying, she usually avoided eye contact. I knew this much about her.

"Nobody raped me? What is that, his new name? You're lying again, and we know this is what you do best."

"I don't have time for this," she answered.

"You may not have a lot of it, but you've got time," I said. I tugged at her bed sheets. "You caused it. You were too busy with your hate to care what happened to me. You left me alone with that predator to do what he did, and you didn't do a goddamned thing to stop him. Was that the fuel to your disdain? Just how deep did it cut you to know your man craved someone other than you? How bad did it hurt as you slept at night knowing whatever you did wasn't enough, that he needed me to feel fully satisfied?" I stood there with my eyes locked onto hers.

The silence was awkward. Natalie made this encounter more painful than it needed to be. None of what I spoke was what I believed. I wanted my words to hurt her just as much as I was hurting in that moment. I wanted the truth, which never fell from her mouth. I wanted her to open her mouth and confirm what I already knew. I wanted to hear the words: *He raped you;* her confession that she'd left me in the arms of danger. Although impossible to her, that was a simple task, but she remained silent. Again, she took pride in being evasive.

"What happened to him, huh? Say something!" I demanded.

"What the hell do you want me to say?" she managed to yell back. I watched a tear slowly escape from her eyes.

"For once, the truth. Why do you make it seem as if I'm asking you to save humanity?"

"I don't know who you have feeding you this lie, but you better stop. I'm in here fighting for my life, and this is what you have questions about?" she added. "How about asking how I'm doing? How about asking me what's wrong? How about...?"

"How about the life you took from me, did it have a chance to fight?" I interrupted. "And, as far as my concerns for you, I have none, which is exactly how you treated me." My response lacked emotion. "Fine," I yelled, and then dropped my hands to my sides. "You don't want to give me answers." She shifted her eyes to break my gaze. I turned, grabbed my bag from the couch, and then turned back to her. "I'm not going to ask you to bend over so I can kiss your dying ass. Take what you know to your grave."

"Are you done?" Her question was an impassive dismissal.

"I know what Victor did. I just wanted to see if you cared enough to admit it. You lived your life as if nothing happened. I guess I can't blame you for that, because I did the same. I mean, life goes on, right? It had to. I had to live. You had to live. So I guess we took that little piece of our past and vowed never to visit it again. That night I didn't call out for you, not because he'd gagged me with my underwear after I yelled, and then held his hand over it, but because I knew your deep hate for me would keep you from rescuing me. So, I lay there and accepted my punishment for being your child. I gave myself over to him, but what else was I supposed to do. I knew to struggle would've hurt more. I lay there like I was dead, because, that night, life left my body. Your hatred killed me."

That night not one tear fell from my eyes as Victor assaulted my body, but as I stood there talking, the tears flowed. The one person I never wanted to show my weakness witnessed that vulnerability. I started in a quick dash toward the door. I was foolish to think this confrontation would've gone any other way. From the outside, Natalie resembled someone else, but, on the inside, she was the same spiteful, deceitful, and vile woman whose hatred for me replaced the marrow in her bones.

"I protected you," she spoke as I approached the door.

"You protected me?" I suspended my escape and turned toward her. There was no way in hell that was said with a serious face. "How the hell did you protect me? Did you not hear anything I just said? Your boyfriend raped me, and then you aborted what resulted from it."

"Yes, I know that."

Her admission, finally.

"And then you shipped me away so that I wasn't the constant reminder that the man you loved was a brainless prick who preyed on little girls. So, tell me exactly how the hell did you protect me?"

"I'm sorry."

"For what?" I yelled. "What exactly are you sorry for, mother: your lies, your hate, the many times you disregarded me? What are you sorry for?" I repeated as if I expected a response that hadn't come fast enough.

"I didn't mean to hurt you."

There were two people in the room, but only one of us believed the words Natalie spat. I knew better. I knew better than to confuse her feeble existence for sincerity. I laughed and then shook my head in disbelief.

"You know, that's the shit people say, right after they hurt you. Let's not fool ourselves. You put your whole heart into hurting me. Every time you did, you meant it, and when hurting me was no longer satisfying, your boyfriend helped. So don't apologize for something you meant to do."

"So, I guess now you want to see me hurt like you do?" Her eyes moved from one side to the other, like she wished her body could.

"With a heart like yours, that's an impossible feat. I'm not here for revenge. I've gotten over your rancorous treatment, and maybe not as fast as you did, but I've also gotten over that night, and I've gotten over you."

"You wanted to know what happened to him," she said. Her eyes stared in the direction of the door as if she feared her story, whatever it is, would be interrupted.

I listened to Natalie explain her decisions and the events that drove her to them, but my eyes became fixed on the figure who stood in the threshold of the door. I hadn't spoken with her since the day she chastised me about my refusal to visit my mother in the hospital. My grandmother had a way of speaking with her face and, this time, what she displayed was one of disgust and disappointment. Yes, I was there visiting Natalie but not because I wanted to pray her illness away.

"Clearly, God didn't order your steps." She closed the door behind her as she slowly strolled into the room. "The road you took here was paved by the devil." She looked past me as she approached the bed. She placed the small mixed-flower vase she held on the bed table, adjusted the pillow behind Natalie's head, and then kissed her on the side of her face, on her right cheek.

She treated her daughter as if she had been a blessing in her life all her years, and not like the woman who wasn't ashamed to treat her mother as if she belonged under her feet.

"How long have you been here?" I asked. I stood

with my arms folded across my chest. I guess Geraldine meant what she said. Natalie was her daughter, and here she was affirming she was going to be there for her.

"A week," she answered. She still hadn't looked at me. "But I stood at that door long enough to hear you display your selfishness." My grandmother and I exchanged words from our respective corner of the room.

"You've been here an entire week and you didn't even bother to…"

"Stop right there," she interjected. Finally, we made eye contact. "There are much more important things than your hurt feelings about my visit. This isn't about you. You couldn't set your hatred aside for one second, even after I told you your mother wasn't so well. You know that stubbornness says a lot more about the person you are than anything else."

"You're acting as if I don't have valid reasons."

"I'm not acting." She took a few steps in my direction and then matched my stance, with her arms folded across her chest. "For God's sake, Kennedie, she's your mother. She did what she had to do, and this is the thanks she gets? You have questions about Victor, fine, but you didn't even have the decency to close the door behind you. You have every doctor, nurse, and sick person out there listening to the disrespectful way you talk to your mother."

It didn't matter what anyone thought, especially since they were people I didn't know, and won't ever see again. I was concerned about what my grandmother said.

"Wait, what do you mean? You knew about this?" I stared at my grandmother. My eyes pleaded, and I shook my head from side-to-side, hoping her answer would echo that gesture. Her silent stare said a lot. "Jesus!"

"Call on someone you know." She looked at me as if she dared me to respond. "Yes, I knew, but what difference would it have made? Your mother's decision was her decision."

"You watched me agonize over her mistreatment. You saw me struggle to manage the overwhelming sadness. You could've alleviated everything I experienced just by sitting down and telling me there was a method to her madness.

"You said my stubbornness says a lot about me. Well, what does perpetuating this lie say about you?" I asked, "Is that what your bible told you to do?"

"Do not bring the bible into this," she warned. "It wants nothing to do with your mess."

"Oh, I get it," I said as I turned toward the door. "Only you can quote the bible at your convenience." I didn't think my grandmother was like every other Christian, but now I see she wasn't too far from them. She used the parts of the bible that validated their argument, but shun you for pointing out what contradicts them, because you are of the world. I know she didn't say it, but that's exactly what she was thinking. "I can't begin to tell you how disappointed I am."

"That makes two of us," she said. She sat in the chair in front of the bed and crossed her legs. She stared at me with a victorious smirk on her face, and rightfully so, because I walked out of Natalie's room feeling like I had been defeated.

Thirty-one

Kennedie...

Goodnight sweetheart, well, it's time to go. I hate to leave you, but I really can't stay. That's the song my grandmother used to sing as I drifted off to sleep. To believe I hated falling asleep because I always thought I was going to miss something.

Foolishness.

I missed my grandmother. I hadn't seen or spoken to her since the day I stormed out of my mother's room at the hospital like Lot's wife leaving Sodom, but, unlike Lot's wife, I never looked back. I heeded God's warning and left misery in the company of the woman with whom she had conspired in the keeping of her secret. Questions I had about my father were never asked, and I wondered what my grandmother knew or didn't know about him. Was this another secret my grandmother kept as well?

I sat in the living room, talking to T. J, when the bell sounded. I wasn't expecting anyone, so I was hesitant to move on the first buzz. I thought it might've been Alaine, my nosiest of neighbors, but I knew she hadn't lost her damn mind and waltzed her ass across my lawn. The last time she was served a cold dish of mind-your-own-damn-business, with a side of your-shit-ain't-perfect-either. When I opened the door, my grandmother stood. I was happy to see her again. Why was she here? Without an invite, she entered the house. She sat on the chair with her bag in her lap. She held her handkerchief just below her nose to cover lips that quivered between words. T. J. stood and stared at her.

"Why is Nana crying?" he asked.

He looked at me with confused eyes.

"Grandmother, what's wrong?" I inquired.

"It's your mother, she..."

I gestured, showing her the palm of my hand to interrupt her speech. "If you're here about what happened at the hospital, I'm not..."

"She died, Kennedie. She took an unexpected turn for the worst, and now she can rest in peace."

Geraldine had come to bear bad news. I stood and walked to the living room window. I fought to keep my own tears from escaping. I wiped away a lone drop before I turned to assure T.J. his Nana was fine. My tears were not for the woman whose hate for me sustained her, but for the agony in my grandmother's grief. She held Tanner in a tight embrace. After her release, he retreated to his bedroom.

"You better be glad my God is an all-forgiving God." Her words were muffled. She placed her bag at her side in the blue, high back chair, and then stood.

"And what is that supposed to mean?" I asked. I had not seen my grandmother so wrapped in pain since she laid my grandfather to rest. "I'm curious. What have I done that I need to be thankful *your* God forgives all?"

Oh, the nerve she had. She sat in my living room and acted as if the life her daughter lived was holy. You couldn't stretch anyone's imagination far enough. Natalie was evil's namesake.

"All you had to do was forgive her. It wouldn't have been the hardest thing you've done in your life."

"Right, 'cause we both know what that was."

"What's wrong with you?"

"You know what? I'm just about sick and damn near tired of you asking that question. Nothing is wrong with me. You wanted everything to happen in one fell swoop, but it doesn't work that way. And what the hell was my forgiveness supposed to do, save her? Well, I guess you put fate in the wrong hands."

"You know, she did love you, Kennedie," she

claimed as her tears dried.

"Grandmother!" I wanted to hold her hand. I could only imagine what she felt, cause I couldn't even pretend to know. "I'm old enough to know what a mother's love feels like, and to say what your daughter had in her heart for me fell short would be the understatement of my life. It definitely was not love. But, if it makes you feel good, have a field day in creating the woman you want to remember as your child. Whatever you create will not erase what I know to be true about her, or what I experienced because of her."

She was silent. She stared at me as her sadness deepened. I knew my grandmother, and there was something very off about her. She sat in the chair, and then she exhaled.

I stepped closer to her.

"What are you not telling me?"

"Please sit down."

"Thanks, but whatever you have to say, I think I'd rather hear it standing up." I declined her invitation. I folded my arms and waited for her to begin.

"I need you to forgive her, and then I need you to forgive me." She lowered her head.

"Forgive you?" I was perplexed. "All you did was treat me as one of your own when my own mother decided I was the very burden she'd been avoiding. If anything, I should be thanking you, and be glad I wasn't left in a basket at some stranger's front door, with a blanket, a bottle, and a sad *'I'm sorry'* note."

Then, almost in a whisper, she announced, "She's not your mother."

"I mean," I continued, "I despised her for it, but it could've been…" I paused after my grandmother's words became clear. "What did you say?"

She hesitated. She gazed from one side to the other as if she searched for the words she just spoke.

She stood and turned toward me.

"Natalie is not your mother."

This time, she spoke with more confidence, as if she was relieved the burden of holding such a secret had finally been lifted.

I know she saw my heart break. I stood with my mouth opened, and stared into her with wide eyes. In the quiet that gripped us, I shook my head in disbelief. What exactly did this mean? So many questions stormed my mind. I was unable to separate lies from truths because both now came from the same mouth.

"I can't handle this shit sober," I declared. I raised my right index finger in the air and walked out of the living room toward the kitchen as if I were excusing myself in the middle of a sermon. Geraldine's words stabbed at my brain. Just before I entered the kitchen, I stopped, turned, and headed back toward her. "When the hell is someone going to tell me the truth so I can know who the fuck I am, or has everyone forgotten what the truth feels like? My life has been one game with interchangeable players, hasn't it?"

"Kennedie!"

"No. Now is not the time." I thought I had no tears left to waste over this situation, but another layer of confusion had just been added to the mix of dishonesties and secrets. I looked at her from the corners of my eyes. "You are in no position to be bothered by anything that comes out of my mouth. What you need to do is start telling me the truth, or is that overrated these days?"

Geraldine's chest rose as she began a deep inhale. Her shoulders relaxed as she let out an extended breath.

"While I…" Geraldine began.

I was quick to interrupt.

"And please, I've had enough of the symphony accompanied, long-winded explanations. Just get to the point. Whatever the story is, I need the shortest version."

I sat on the couch and gave Geraldine the floor. What she was about to say had to be good. It had to be for her to have lived this lie for so long.

"While I touted my husband as an honorable and faithful man, I can't say the same for the position I held in his life, in our marriage. Though he was faithful, I made one mistake, but I wasn't going to let my marriage end because of it.

"When I realized the consequence of my infidelity was more than I ever bargained for, I became desperate. I needed to hide the fact that adultery existed in my marriage, and I had been the culprit. I was pregnant, and since abortion was not an option, I had to put my Plan B into action. Just before I started to show, I told your grand…" She paused. "I told Russell that Natalie needed me, because she was having a rough time with her pregnancy." She corrected herself because the obvious was now known.

"And I bet that was a lie."

"I moved in with her until you were born," she continued. She ignored my accusation. "And then I left you to be raised by her."

"Don't you mean abuse me? Let's call it exactly what it was. She treated me like I was her mistake when, all along, I was yours." I got up from the couch and stood next to her, on her right. Geraldine's revelation should have devastated me, but my legs hadn't gone weak under the weight of her confession. "Why would anyone believe you? Did you go into hiding?"

"Until you were born, yes. I did. And as far as anyone believing me, that wasn't hard to do. Natalie was expecting around the same time, but she miscarried." She looked at me. "So, that she was having a rough time wasn't a lie, as you suggested."

"And that just worked out perfectly for you, didn't it? I guess your good luck struck again. Isn't that some shit! Her pain and loss was your opportunity to save your own ass and your marriage. Talk about turning someone's misfortune into your personal gain. No wonder she treated me as she did and why it was easy for you to accept the many times she disrespected you. You knew she held your marriage and your image in her hands.

"She had no time to mourn the loss of her own child because, there you were, soliciting her help to hide that you were far from the paragon of perfection and morality you flaunted. You pulled a fast one."

"I know you're upset."

I chuckled. It didn't take a scientist to figure that out. I found out the woman I knew as my mother was my sister, and my grandmother hid that she was my mother because she didn't want her days as a whore to ruin her picture-perfect marriage. What the hell should I be, if not upset? Maybe I should be doing cartwheels, because finding out some shit like this was the reason why I lived and breathed.

"So your husband died believing God and a few bible verses kept your legs closed to everyone but him."

"He died knowing the truth. He died knowing that I

love him, and nothing ever changed that."

"You and your daughter aren't that much different. When death comes knocking, whether it's at your door or someone else's, you want to purge. You go on this quest for forgiveness so that you can feel better about yourselves."

"I didn't have a choice," she said, turning away from me.

"Oh, you had a choice." I followed behind her. "You were a grown ass woman who knew her actions had consequences. No need to feel shame, just accept what you are. You're a fraud who spread her legs from twelve to six, and then you ran to the church to get covered by the blood."

"Now, you wait a goddamn minute," she roared.

"Mommy." T.J's call diverted her attention from the cantankerous verbiage that was about to follow what she already said. "I'm hungry."

His appearance was a reminder that I had not fulfilled any of my mommy duties since Geraldine showed up to cleanse her soul and darken my night.

"That is my cue to leave."

She grabbed her bag from the chair and started toward the door.

"That's the best thing you've said since you sauntered in here," I said as I started toward T.J. He stood at the bottom of the stairs. His eyes looked rested. He was rather quiet since he retired to his room.

"I am sorry," she asserted, but I was done listening.

"I have one last question before you leave."

"Yes."

She beamed as if forgiveness stood just behind those words.

"Is Donald Ashby my father?"

"I know Trent was trying to help you when he told you the Judge was your father, but he got that part all wrong. Your father is Leonard Vincent; that we were never going to lie to you about. He died in an accident shortly after you were born. I didn't have an affair with Judge Ashby, Natalie did."

She sounded sincere, but since lying came with little effort, I no longer knew what to believe. I grabbed T.J.'s hand and began the short journey to the kitchen.

"You can see yourself out," I ordered with not even a glance in her direction.

I busied myself in the kitchen, doing what I'd neglected since Geraldine's intrusion. With everything else that happened, she'd brought more than I wanted to deal with.

I pulled leftovers from the refrigerator, prepared a small plate for my son, and placed it in the microwave. He climbed on the stool and sat. Though he was warned before about this, for fear he might fall, I withheld my admonition because he was safe. When I heard the slam, I paused. My breath became heavy, and my heart beat faster every second. I shook my head, afraid to acknowledge the tear slithering down my face. I removed the dish from the microwave and placed it before him, but his attention was directed at me.

"Mommy," he called, "Are you ok?"

"Yes, baby, Mommy is just fine." I pressed my lips gently on his forehead as an added assurance.

"Where is Nana going?" His questions continued.

"Hopefully, as far away from me as possible." I realized she left without saying goodbye to him, but even that had no effect on my response.

My mouth spoke words my heart did not feel. I loved Geraldine for all she had been, but that evening in Natalie's room at the hospital did cast a dark cloud of doubt over anything she said. Content with my response, if he even thought about it, T.J. returned to innocence. He held his fork in an awkward grip and began to quench his hunger. I was hurt, and that kept me from chasing behind her. What Geraldine saw as her simple mistake caused me unforgettable pain. I felt discarded and unloved by Natalie. Eventually, I accepted her lack of involvement in my life, because Geraldine's love and presence filled the emptiness that once existed. Now that Geraldine decided to speak her truth, all those feelings came rushing back. Until then, I never questioned Geraldine's love.

Thirty-two

Michaela...

There comes a time when you have to stop being stubborn and start listening to the voice of reason. Work could only take your mind away from reality for so long. But at night, when you've closed the portfolios and have finished those boring business calls, there's reality, tapping on your shoulder, reminding you they've been waiting with the patience of God.

Brooklynn had done as I suggested. She'd led the conversation with her experience as a pregnant teen and the void she felt after DeMarco was pulled from her and given away to strangers. Stetzen was compassionate, which was exactly what Brooklynn expected, because that's the kind of man he is. His kisses consoled her. She finally shared that painful moment with him, and it made her feel good. She felt safe in his arms, as she always felt with him. Then came the moment of truth.

As Brooklynn's betrayal fell from her lips, Stetzen's demeanor changed. Better yet, he went into a rage. She heard the heartbreak in his voice. I sat on the phone with Brooke that night. She'd called because she couldn't get Stetzen to say three words to her. That was the worst part. She could deal with him being angry with her; however, his silent treatment drove her crazy.

Brooke had already spent two nights in her self-inflicted misery, lying in a hotel bed she'd gotten used to, thanks to her weekly business trips. Being away from Stetzen and not being able to hear his voice was worst than being in the same state with him and being treated like she didn't exist. I wasn't taking no for an answer when I invited her to spend her last night with Nyla and me, since we had the entire house to ourselves.

Brooke showed up after her late meeting ended. Her suitcase and garment bag were in the master bedroom that had been vacant since I started sleeping in one of the guest bedrooms after Zachary finally moved out. The bed and the room both held memories I tried to forget. After her shower, Brooke and I sat in the living room. She paid more attention to Nyla before fatigue set it. Nyla was tucked in under her princess covers in the empty room down a hall from the living room.

It was obvious Stetzen was on Brooke's mind. He would've called by now to check on her. Under normal circumstances, Brooke definitely would not have gone a full day without hearing her phone ring and seeing 'My Husband' displayed on her screen across his handsome picture. But what Brooke and Stetzen were experiencing was definitely not normal for them. Relationships last because every day you wake you fall in love all over again.

"Michaela, it's been two weeks." She paced the length of the sofa. If I had a stiff neck, watching her pace would've loosened it. Finally she stopped. "He's been avoiding me like a leper. If he comes to the house and I'm there, he doesn't speak. No 'Hi', no 'Goodbye', no 'Dog, here's a bone,' nothing. He comes in, picks up whatever he needs until the next time he decides to stop by, and then he's gone. I feel like I've gone to court and won visitation rights for my husband."

She sat hard as if her pacing had exhausted her.

"He'll be back."

That was the same assurance I gave her when she'd call to tell me she'd had the conversation. That wasn't Hope talking. I knew Stetzen loved Brooke, and love had definitely kept them together. I refused to believe she was equally unlucky, although any end to her marriage would have been her fault.

"Am I supposed to just wait?"

"Honey, what else are you going to do?" I stood from the chair and sat beside her on the couch. "He said he needed a break, some time to cool off. Give him that. Honestly, Brooke, after what you did, you need to be glad he didn't ask your ass for a divorce."

"How long is this damn break supposed to last?"

"As long as he needs to come to terms with the fact that his wife lied to him."

"I'm sure I'm not the first wife to lie to her husband." She pursed her lips, tilted her head toward me, and looked at me with suspecting eyes. She stood. She walked to the window and then looked to the sky. "It was a little white lie," she confessed.

"You are absolutely right. You're not the first woman to lie to her husband, but nothing about your lie was little. A little white lie would've been telling your husband you were on your monthly because you weren't in the mood for sex. No, your lie was a…"

"Whose side are you on?" Brooklynn interjected. She folded her arms like a spoiled child.

"Of course, I'm on your side," I assured her. I stood and headed in the direction of the kitchen. "But you know I don't glaze shit with sugar and call it candy. When you're wrong, you're going to hear it," I affirmed as I disappeared into the kitchen. "And make no mistake, what you did was dead wrong," I continued.

In the kitchen, I grabbed two large glasses from the cabinet, and a bottle from the counter, placed them on a serving tray, and headed back into the living room. Brooklynn sat on the sofa and stared at her phone. She shook her head in displeasure and then tossed the phone on the chair across from her. I looked at the phone and then looked at her. She'd checked for a reply to the message she sent to Stetzen when she first arrived. She was either disappointed in his failure to respond or at the response she'd received. I was convinced the former was true.

"I thought you were immune to acts such as this." I set the tray on the ottoman, opened the bottle, and began to pour into the glasses.

"Yeah, well, me too. I was tired of being pressured. He wouldn't let up. Every time I thought the issue had been put to rest, he'd come baring his soul about wanting a family."

I handed Brooke one of the glasses and then sat next to her.

"I can't drink this," she said. She placed the flute on the tray. I've never known her to turn her nose from a drink.

I didn't have a problem drinking for the two of us. I pulled Brooklynn's glass closer to me. "I haven't even been able to tell him the good news."

"Good news?" I echoed. "Wait a minute. You're pregnant?"

"Pregnant? Of course not, but I am ready for that to happen. No more birth control for me." Brooklynn stood from the couch and started toward the kitchen. "Now, I know your habit, which means you have something stronger in here!" she yelled. "I can't believe you went back here for drinks and came back with some damn wine." She returned with a bottle and two full short glasses and placed them on the tray.

"You poured as if we don't have work in the morning," I warned as I accepted the glass I was handed.

"We'll just do what they've always asked, drink responsibly." She did the familiar gesture, tapped the small glass on the tray, and then emptied the brown liquid in her mouth. I mimicked her actions.

Brooklynn and I sat in the quiet that came over us. She peered over at her phone, but it had been silent all night. She exhaled. No doubt she had a hard time lying in the bed she made. She hoped the strong, brown concoction was the blanket she needed to sleep in comfort, but only the sound of Stetzen's voice could soothe her. She refilled the glasses.

"How do you do it?" Brooklynn asked. She gripped the glass at the rim and then sat back. "I mean, I know you have Kendrick, but…"

"I don't *have* Kendrick," I corrected.

"You know what I mean. How do you begin to live your life without the one person you thought only death could part you?"

"Death did part us." Brooklynn looked on in bewilderment. "Zachary's faithfulness died, my trust died, and so did our marriage. One day he's the man who, even when he's on top of you, is still too far away, and the next you're wishing he would just disappear without a trace. Believe me, you learn to get on with your life, and they have a way of making it easy for you to go on without them." Brooklynn released a long sigh. "But that's not something you have to worry about."

"I do love him."

"He knows you do, and he loves you, too. He also knows hurting him was never your intention."

"It was not my intention."

I stood, and then kissed her on her forehead.

"I know, honey."

I left Brooklynn downstairs in the misery she created. Misery loved company, but my time with her ended as she swallowed her second shot. I stood at the bottom of the steps and watched her. She sat on the couch with legs folded against her chest. Her arms wrapped tightly around them as if she wished they were her husband. She rested her chin on her knees and stared at the still silent phone.

Rather than interrupting her, I allowed Nyla to continue her sleep in the downstairs guestroom. In my bedroom, I sat on the bed and spat a few words in God's ears. I hoped he heard my plea. Brooklynn and I had a lot in common and about as much that set us apart. For her sake, I didn't want to add divorce to the long list of our commonalities. Brooklynn was built to be married and live happily ever after. Divorce wasn't a cardinal sin, but it still wasn't what I wanted for my best friend and her husband. I lay back in the bed and closed my eyes. I needed sleep, since I had another long day ahead, but everything that Brooklynn was experiencing, I now carried on both shoulders, right next to the Kennedie Spencer case.

Thirty-three

Michaela...

Even after sleep, which would've been better if my mind wasn't so occupied, I still had Brooklynn, Stetzen, and what hung in the balance on my mind. Thoughts swirled a mile a minute, picking up exactly where I left off the night before. She checked her phone and had tossed it in her bag before she closed the door behind her as she left for work. She still hadn't heard from Stetzen. Her face was beautifully made up, and her hair was in a neat coil in the back of her head, but she left the house with eyes filled with doubt. Brooklynn never embraced the feeling of not being in control, but that was exactly where she found herself.

I stood in my office behind my desk and stared out the window. As much as I knew not to interfere in

Booklynn's affairs—a rule often broken—I wanted to reach out to Stetzen and plead her case for her. But, I knew I had to leave well enough alone, even if well enough might not be in my best friend's favor. Instead of inserting myself into her marriage, I decided to send a text message.

I love you, girl. Can't wait to see you next week.

I set the phone on my desk and then looked up toward the office door as it swung open. If I thought my morning wasn't going well, her presence had just made it ten times worse. Whitney's brash, nasty attitude was off-putting—and that's putting it lightly—and it walked five steps ahead of her. You haven't changed one bit wasn't always a compliment, and this was the case for Whitney Delgado.

"You're not welcomed here." I walked in haste in her direction. Val stood behind her. "It was made clear the last time you came here and showed your ass. You need to leave."

"Who's going to stop me, him?" She looked at Val and then giggled. "Right, 'cause he's so far up your ass, he'll do anything for you. Anything, except stop me."

Val was an imposing figure. Still, nothing about him made her tremble in her brown open-toe pumps. Val parted his lips to respond. He glanced at me and changed his mind. Whitney wasn't worth it.

319

"Why are you here?" I asked. I had no interest in her purpose.

"Unfinished business," she said as she attempted to step around me. I shifted to block her move.

"You slept with my husband and ended my marriage." I was face to face with my enemy. I stared into eyes where darkness resided. "We don't have unfinished business. We don't have any business."

Whitney stepped back.

"I know I'm good at what I do but, seriously, you've got to stop giving me all the credit." She turned to look at Val again. She examined him from head to toe. "Why are you still here?" Val remained hushed. He stayed because he knew this bitch was crazy, and not because of anything I told him. He's seen her crazy up close and personal. "You don't have to answer that," she continued. "I know you're still waiting on that chance you're never going to get." She refocused her attention to me. "Does he know about Kendrick, that he's back in the picture?"

"What I share about my personal life and who I share it with is none of your damn business," I admonished. I stepped around her and headed to the door. She did not budge. I held onto the door. It was an invitation for an exit that she ignored. Whitney had either been using spy tactics or she had been in contact with Zachary. How else would she have known about Kendrick and I reconnecting?

"Zachary certainly knows about him." I couldn't see her face, but the pride in her speech was loud. "You should've seen the look in his eyes when I told him. She laughed. "Oh, you just had to be there. You know what I would've paid money to see?" she asked as she finally turned.

"Please, enlighten me."

"The look on your face when Zachary told you he knew about your man-toy. You must've thought you had gotten one over on him. Imagine, condemning the man to hell knowing damn well you were out there opening your legs to a man who wasn't your husband. Dirt is dirt, but you thought yours was cleaner than his because his dirt involved me. You thought he didn't know. Played you well, didn't he?"

There was wickedness in her eyes, but it wasn't anything I hadn't seen before in the eyes of Whitney Delgado. Her face was perfectly made, but nothing covered the evil in her stone-cold heart. Whitney was a woman of beauty, and I used to blush at the idea that I resembled her, now it's a strong resentment. We stood like two fighters in our respective corners in the same ring. Val looked on like a bewildered spectator. He's been silent since he walked in behind Whitney. The left side of his mouth wrinkled in disgust, and I could only imagine the thoughts in his mind.

"You continue to take pleasure in my pain." Finally, I closed the door and turned to face her. I paused in my speech and my approach toward her. "Painful as it was, I've accepted your hatred. I've acknowledged that long after you're gone, and I pray it's soon, your evilness will still walk this earth."

"I think I need to leave," Val interrupted, but he looked at me for his cue.

"Yes, please leave," Whitney permitted. "This is a family affair, and you are not family." She placed her bag in the chair and then sat on the edge of the desk. She folded her arms in wait for Val's exit.

"Val, you don't have to go anywhere. Blood don't make you family, and you're living proof of that."

"And you care so much about family," Whitney harassed. "You laid up in that bed wanting people to feel sorry for you, because poor Michaela McKnight had just lost her baby. You acted as if you had lost your soul, knowing damn well you were glad the bastard you carried didn't see the light of day."

"How dare you?" I shouted. For a moment, I forgot where I was.

"How dare I?" she repeated.

"Do you know how crazy you sound? Why the hell would I be glad? A part of me died that day."

"Bullshit. A part of you rejoiced that day. Why? Because then you didn't have to tell your husband you were carrying your lover's child."

I looked from Whitney and caught Val's questioning eyes, but I had questions as well. How could she have known? No one else was privy to this catastrophe, not my doctor, and definitely not Brooke. It was a complicated pregnancy from the beginning. The doctor had already warned me of the possibility that eventually became my reality. My intent was to come clean with both Kendrick and Val, but after my miscarriage, I decided some things were best left unsaid. I enjoyed the feel of my child growing inside me, for as long as I could, and not rob myself of that feeling with unnecessary drama. God had his plans, and I had mine. No harm done, if neither Kendrick nor Zachary knew what happened. I hoped for the best, but I was more than prepared for the worst. I had made a mistake, and that was one I was going to take to my grave. So what if Zachary had mourned the loss of a child that wasn't his? So what if Kendrick didn't know he was almost a father to my child? I lost a part of me that I was never getting back.

"I bet you think now is a good time for that one to leave," Whitney continued. She nodded her head in Val's direction.

"Why? Isn't this your intention, another stop on your

smear campaign?" I said as I began a slow, but deliberate, approach. "Why don't I give him a summary? Well," I said. I turned to Val. "What my mother wants you to know is that I have blood on my hands, my brother's blood. Why? Because he raped me, and when my cries for help were ignored, I stabbed him, and I didn't stop until I was sure he couldn't hurt me anymore. I watched my brother take his last breath." I refocused my attention to my mother. "On top of me," I added.

My eyes fogged with moisture. My heart raced. My body shivered as I disclosed the story that accompanied images I've tried to let die.

"You killed my baby!" Whitney screamed. She wiped tears from her eyes.

What do you know, the devil cries, I thought.

"Your baby was almost a grown-ass man. He knew exactly what he was doing and, just like you, my pain satisfied him. He was a heartless, narcissistic bastard with a momma's boy complex." I looked at Whitney as I walked past her. I stood behind my desk and watched as the words I spoke sink in. "Now you can cross my husband and Val off your list. You've gotten them to hear the vile rhetoric that flows from your mouth with ease. I guess now you'll try to get Kendrick and Brooke to hear the poison in your heart and get them to see me through your hate-filled eyes. Well, good luck!"

"I don't need luck." For a moment, she stood quiet with an inward gaze, as if she realized the daunting task of attempting to convince Brooklynn I wasn't the woman I claimed to be. "Brooke is just like you. Birds of a fucking feather."

I ignored her low jab at Brooklynn. Whitney already knew she couldn't hold a candle to my best friend. She checked her watch, looked up, and flashed a smile a mile wide.

"As for Mr. Kendrick Prescott, he's probably mad as hell, sitting at his kitchen table, reading the letter I gave him. I have a copy, if you want it. On second thought, you probably should wait until he mentions it.

"My God, when will this end?"

"You know, it wouldn't hurt to say 'thank you.'" I gazed at her. She'd lost the last remaining piece of her mind. "I did that for you. The hard part's already done. Now you just have to get ready for the many questions I'm sure he has," her voice resonated in delight.

"You know, you really are sick."

"Please, stick to what you know, or barely know." She surveyed the room. "You're nobody's psychologist, so stop trying to diagnose me."

From the other side of my desk, I stared at this

woman. Over time, she had become a stranger to me, but she was familiar with the alter ego she kept hidden for so long. She had beauty on the outside, but the scorn that lived inside her was indescribable. What she harbored for me should have eaten away at her over time, but she lived for the purpose of retaliation. Whitney Delgado was what happens when hate grabs a hold of your soul and refuses to let go.

"You've won," I declared. I sat in the chair and pulled closer to the desk.

She laughed.

"This isn't about winning. That implies a contest between you and me, and although you're a regrettable part of me, you are no competition." She stepped closer to the desk and then positioned her face just inches from mine. "My plan is to destroy you, just like you destroyed my life. That will be my retribution. Isaiah was my everything. He was everything I went through, the relationships I lost from the day he was conceived. He was a result of all that I sacrificed. You took away my everything."

"And what the hell was I, Mother?" I asked. I jumped to my feet. "Was I anything to you?"

"Let me impart this little bit of knowledge to you." She grabbed her bag from the chair and paced toward the door. "You may have forgiven yourself. Your confession might have finally earned you a few nights of good rest. Your bosom-buddies may have given you a pass because they love you. But as long as I have breath and my eyes can see, I will always see you as exactly what you are, a murderer." She held her head high as if her visit ended in victory. She paused in her exit. She surveyed the entire height of Percy Valentine. She smiled when her eyes met his. She shook her head. "Don't get yourself entangled in her mess. Guilt by association won't work in your favor, and I don't fight fair. You better watch yourself," she warned.

"Why?" I intruded. "Aren't you doing enough watching for everyone?"

Whitney opened the door and then slammed it behind her. Val and I stood in silence. His eyes wandered from the closed door to me. I lowered my head in shame. I knew the airs my mother put on around others, and I wished the world knew the lunacy I was exposed to. How could a woman call herself a mother and then, in the same breath, vow to spend the rest her remaining days on this earth destroying her own child? Unfortunately, that was the sick reality of Whitney Delgado.

Finally, Val abandoned the space he held since he unwillingly accompanied evil into my office. His mouth widened into a bright smile as he approached. He stood behind the desk next to me. He reached around my back, cradled my shoulder, and pulled me into him.

"Don't even ask," I cautioned as I rested my head on him.

"I wasn't," he said. He kissed the top of my head and then squeezed my shoulder.

Time was supposed to heal all wounds, but the only thing time had done was transform Whitney into a pillar of hate. Her soul was owned by the devil. She sold it and began her quest for revenge. My supposed demise was the one thing that sustained her. I wasn't going to win this fight sitting down. I didn't have the kind of time to sit and worry about Whitney's next move. What could she do? I no longer had a husband for her to sleep with. By her own admission, what happened to the child I carried for Kendrick was no longer a secret. Whitney had done to Kendrick exactly what I had avoided, and that was hurt him.

Thirty-four

Michaela...

Ever find yourself in a moment where you wished you could fold your arms across your chest, blink your eyes, nod your head, and just disappear? That's where I found myself the very instant Whitney, her hate, and her anger walked into my office and interrupted the harmony I was in after I sent my message to Brooke.

One part of me hoped—actually, prayed—Kendrick was far away from home so I wouldn't have to dig myself from under the mountain of questions I knew he had. The other part of me just wanted to face the music Whitney composed. They said every cheater was a liar, and now, with my mother's unsought help, both were now my claim to fame. The latter I avoided, though omitting the truth still qualified.

On previous occasions, my entrance into his driveway was in haste and, as my heart raced, I would ring his doorbell, anticipating the two of us becoming one once the door closed behind us to seal our secret tryst from the rest of the world. This time was different. With reluctance, I turned into his driveway, and, after I parked, I walked in a foot-dragging pace toward his front door. I wished I had some whiskey to numb me to what lay ahead. After I rang the bell, I stood with my back toward the door. *Please don't be home,* I thought. As soon as the thought ended, the door opened. When I turned, he leaned against the door, and crossed his legs at the ankles. He folded his long arms and stared at me. His face was devoid of emotions. His jaws were tight, his nose was wide, and his forehead wrinkled in that space between his eyebrows. He remained non-responsive, even after my smile, which usually garnered a compliment from him.

"Hey," I greeted. I stepped closer to him.

"Hey?" Kendrick questioned. "Is that really how you're going to start this?" I shivered from the cold he emitted. "Why are you here, Michaela?

"You know why I'm here."

"I do? Just so we're clear, or at least on the same page, why don't you tell me."

He parted his lips to do everything but smile. What should I have expected? By now, he must've read my mother's painful words in her letter, and they didn't give him any reasons to.

"Can I come in? It's getting dark, and it's a little chilly."

"I think we're fine here." Why should he be concerned about me, after what I did to him? The goose bumps on my arms were either a reaction to the chill in the air or the effects of his dispassionate welcome. He tilted his head and looked at me from the corners of his eyes. "I don't have anything to hide. Do you?" he added.

I didn't expect this to be easy, but I didn't think it would be this hard. Kendrick and I stood in a moment of weird silence. His hush was his patience as he waited for an explanation. My silence was my search through my own confusion. I turned away from him, from his heartless gaze.

"I wanted to tell you," I began. "I wanted you to know, even though I was with my husband, I was carrying your child, our child. I didn't know or care if you wanted it, or if I was going to be taking care of it all by myself because Zachary was definitely on his way out, once he found out it wasn't his. I was happy, and I wanted you to be, too. But then I was heartbroken.

"I stood in my doctor's office and wept, and then

spent the rest of my days counting down to when I no longer felt my child. My world, Zachary's world, was turned upside down. I knew what my pain felt like, and I saw his ache for a child who wasn't even his. I didn't want to see you go through what we were going through." I turned to face him with wet eyes. My heart raced. My palms sweat. "I grieved for both of us."

I wanted him to say something, but he just stood there and held his tongue. His breath was heavy.

"You…" he paused.

"Please," I said. I grabbed his arm. "Say something."

"You grieved for us?" He stood in the middle of the doorway. He wiped his eyes and exhaled. "What makes you think I didn't want to grieve for myself? It was my baby, Michaela. He got to celebrate with you, and then he got to grieve with you. What did I get? I got robbed. I should've been there telling you everything was going to be okay. I should've been the one lying next to you, kissing your ear, caressing your face, telling you we'll try again."

"I'm here hurting you, which is exactly what I was trying not to do. I made the decision to keep this loss from you."

I turned away from him and headed to the car. My pace was slow. I wanted him to stop me. I wanted him to tell me he understood, but I heard nothing.

"I know." He finally spoke.

I exhaled as I made an about-face and quick-paced back to the door. I looked at him with wide eyes. He reached into the back pocket of his pants, and then he extended an envelope.

"Your mother certainly thought I needed to know. She hand-delivered this. After I wouldn't listen to anything she had to say or take it from her, she left it in my mailbox. The damn woman blocked me from entering the door. Since I didn't want to put my hands on her, I threatened to call the police. Look, I don't care what you do with it, but I definitely don't have any use for it."

I observed both sides of the envelope. "It's not open," I said. "You didn't read it?"

"I didn't need to." He stepped inside and gestured his hand to invite me in.

"Why not?" I asked. I looked up at him. "Why didn't you read it?" I repeated as I stepped inside.

"I wanted to hear it from you, not from someone who would've kept it a secret, if not for her quest for revenge."

"How do you know she wanted revenge?"

"She wasn't doing it because of any love for you, that was for certain. I'm not sure what you did to her, but the woman hates you."

I laughed. "Hate is an understatement. I can tell you just how much she hates me. Maybe over coffee?"

"You mean no alcohol tonight?" he asked as we headed toward the kitchen.

Kendrick was the kind of man you dreamt about coming home to. Though he was also the kind of man who slept with a married woman—me—that didn't cause him to lose any earned stripes. I was unhappy, and he more than made up for all that was missing in the bedroom I once shared with Zachary. Hell, he was single, and he definitely wasn't going to let a ring that meant nothing to the woman who wore it stop him from finding out if she was what dreams were made of.

Kendrick and I sat in two of the white high-back chairs that lined one side of the white countertop kitchen island. Our hands wrapped around large coffee mugs he placed on the counter a few moments after we sat. Although I loved the feeling I got from just the smell of coffee, the taste of alcohol always brought special warmth to my heart.

"Gosh, I could use a drink," I said out loud.

"That took longer than I thought." He sprung from the chair.

When Kendrick returned, two glasses replaced the coffee mugs. His drink of choice—and mine whenever I'm with him—Scotch whiskey on the rocks, filled each glass.

After my first taste, the edge the day created was lifted. Thanks to Whitney, I was forced again to let someone into a part of my life I wished I could hide from myself; a part I wished never existed. But, also thanks to her, these conversations became easier to have. I now believed the only reason Whitney hasn't killed me was because it wouldn't equate to the satisfaction she got from her taunts. The thought that she made my life a living hell made her heart sing.

Thirty-five

Kennedie...

With a family like mine, I definitely did not need any enemies. The list of people who meant anything to me, those I knew and loved, and those I thought loved me, now had one less name. So much for keeping family close. The feeling that no one was on my side was one of the worst things to feel. I could always hang my hat on Geraldine being there for me, so imagine the disappointment when it was finally revealed that, not only had she masterminded this cover-up, but also what I experienced in life as a young child was all her doing. I always found comfort in Geraldine's arms. It hurts to know I rested my head on a cheating heart and listened to a lying tongue. The solution to one problem had created another.

My son was the one constant that brought continued peace to my life. I stood at his door and watched him sleep. My pride and joy was all wrapped up into this amazing little person. It was hard to believe the man I now despised— Windsor—contributed to the creation of this beautiful human being. I loved T.J.'s innocence. I hated that being a part of this world came with inevitable encounters with men like his father, or women like Natalie and Geraldine. I vowed to protect him the way Natalie never protected me, and the way Geraldine did, before I knew the truth. Of all I had accomplished, being this little boy's mother had been my greatest success.

"My sweet baby," I whispered as he began to awaken from his slumber.

I could stand and admire him all day, but I looked forward to the imminent war of words at the days proceeding. I get to sit and entertain myself with unflattering thoughts about Windsor. I hadn't seen Windsor since he attempted his chumped-up charge of child abuse and left my house with my son. His behavior gave me all the rights to act like the bitch he accused me to be. Still, I planned on playing fair in anything that involved our child. Both attorneys, Michaela McKnight and Delaire James, negotiated Windsor's visits. Despite Windsor's attempt to turn the court against me, I wasn't going to keep his son away from him. Windsor had been picking up and dropping T.J. off at school. I didn't want him close to my home or me, and he needed to be counting his blessings that I didn't want him to be close to my son. The stunt he pulled earlier had led to a few precautions, including a restraining order that kept him one thousand feet away from me. Somehow, Michaela was able to prove Windsor's unsubstantiated accusation meant he was willing to do just about anything to hurt me, and that was just a first step. His attempt to punish me had been a miserable failure.

There's never enough time in the morning to get both T.J. and myself ready, even when I'm up earlier than normal. This was the only time I ever wished his independence was right around the corner. I planned to drop him off at school and then meet Michaela for breakfast before heading to court. After I'd dressed T.J. and prepared his breakfast, I took my sweet time pulling myself together. I wanted to make sure Windsor couldn't take his damned eyes off me when I walk into the courtroom. He probably wouldn't admit it to himself now—and definitely not aloud—but he lost a damn good woman. Listen to Windsor's story and he would try to convince you I'd lost a good man. Nothing makes a man feel better than to see you crumble under the weight of him leaving you. They want to hear you scream, "I can't live without you!" without you even opening your mouth. There will never come a day when Windsor would have that satisfaction. Regardless what he thinks, Windsor was not the best thing to ever happen to me.

I entered the kitchen, set my red shoulder bag on the stool next to T.J., and finished fastening the second pearl earring in my right ear. It matched the double-strand pearl necklace that rested against my coffee skin, my something borrowed that I was ordered never to return. I held T.J.'s face and kissed his cheek before I pressed toward the Keurig in the corner of the counter and removed the cup of coffee I brewed earlier. He sat watching cartoons while he ate breakfast. After my first sip, the recognizable tone on the cellphone sounded. I stared at the number before grabbing the phone from the counter. I knew the number that displayed and who it belonged to, though I hadn't saved it to his name.

"Hey! Sorry I haven't called you," I answered after his greeting. I sat on the stool next to T.J.

"Listen, if I said anything that has caused you hurt in any way, let me know so I can fix it," Trent pleaded. "It was not my intention."

"I know your intentions." I removed the phone from my ear to read the text message that came in, and then continued. "Please, no feeling like you caused me any pain. I've had to deal with my world being turned upside down

339

before, and it didn't kill me. I've just been busy."

"Busy?" Trent repeated with a chuckle, "Or were you avoiding me?"

"I needed to take a step back. There's so much to tell you."

"You've spoken to your mother?"

"Can't exactly call her that now, can I?" I glanced at T.J., smiled, and then peeked at my wristwatch. I still had some time before I had to get T.J. to school and meet Michaela. I lounged back on the stool, and then took a sip of the lukewarm coffee. I returned the cup to the counter and continued. "I got some answers though. Look, I know you're not supposed to speak ill of the dead, but Natalie was no good to me alive anyway."

"She's dead?"

"Yes, she's very dead. Not a breath left." There wasn't even a hint of grief in my response, and rightfully so.

"Are you okay?"

"Of course, I'm okay. She died, I didn't." I didn't care if punishment awaited me for the glee I displayed as I spoke of Natalie's demise.

"Kennedie!"

"Before you go feeling sorry for me or anyone else, she wasn't my mother. My mother is alive and well."

"I'm confused."

"Now, just imagine how I felt when I found out the woman I've known as my grandmother my entire existence is actually my mother."

"I know I was young, but I distinctly remember the woman who showed up at my parents' house."

"The woman you remember seeing wasn't the woman who raised me. They look a lot alike, which was a part of the reason they were constantly at each other's throat." I paused. "So, you should know, Judge Ashby is not my father."

Trent absorbed every word I spoke without further interruption. As the story unfolded, I began to accept the dysfunction of the people who were, unfortunately, family. The truth is a hard thing to swallow, and I had a tough time accepting the reality that was unveiled. This was definitely stranger than fiction. Yes, I could've blamed Trent for opening the gates of hell, but he wasn't the one who pushed me in the fire. What I did with the information he presented was my choice. I wanted to know more, even though the more I got wasn't what I bargained for. You won't get answers to questions kept to yourself, thinking people can read minds. The answers I received had fractured a bond I thought could never be broken and a trust I never doubted. What Geraldine had done in the dark had finally been brought to light, but the light cast a long shadow over the relationship that meant so much to me.

Until now, I was silent about the reveals after my visit with Natalie. She was truthful about two things: I was raped, and Donald Ashby was not my father. But, the secret she took to her afterworld was the one that cut the deepest.

Geraldine's impromptu visit that ensued had done nothing but dirtied muddied water. She'd unloaded her burden at a most convenient time—for her. Now, she had nothing to lose. She withheld her revelations at times when my happiness, sanity, and wellbeing depended on it. She held her tongue, protected her image and her marriage, and caused the pains that Natalie inflicted. All I had to say to Natalie was said as she lay in the bed in her hospital room. I didn't have to go to her funeral to say any last words. I didn't need a moment to say things I wanted to say because I didn't have the opportunity to do so while her miserable self walked this earth. She's fine. She died with a clear conscience, which is all she ever wanted.

"And now you have to face Windsor in your divorce."

"Wait a minute," I said, I hopped from the stool and placed the coffee mug in the dishwasher. "How did you know that was happening today?"

"How soon you forget who my father is," Trent teased. "And I'm also a clerk," he whispered. I could imagine that wide smile on his face, his smooth, pink lips parting to display the top row of beautifully maintained teeth. "Are you ready?"

"Is Windsor ready is a much better question."

"I can be there with you, if you want. If your grandmother isn't able to make it, I don't want you to be there alone."

"Geraldine isn't going to be there," I corrected. "But, I won't be alone. I have an attorney, remember?"

Geraldine and Natalie robbed me of so much. You can't choose your family, but how you treat them is your decision. I would've been better off taking my chances with strangers, if family was going to treat me the way Natalie did. Natalie had abetted her mother, hiding her illegitimate child from the husband who, by her own admission, had been the epitome of loyalty. And, as if she couldn't have said no, Natalie spent years hating and hurting me. I was punished for everyone's mistake.

Thirty-six

Kennedie...

I learned many things in the years I spent with Natalie Lamar. I learned to not speak unless spoken to, not to cry, even when I'm given something to cry about, and I became a pro at hiding my feelings because "no one gives a damn about you or your damn feelings." Of course, I did all these at Natalie's request. Although I knew better, my survival as Natalie's daughter depended on it. Years after I was shipped off to live with Geraldine, I took advantage of the newly-found freedom to speak my damn mind—as long as I was respectful—whenever I felt I needed to, and know my feelings and I mattered to those who love me.

I shook my head after I read Windsor's text message. *I hate you! This is what you wanted. Don't be sorry when things don't turn out the way you think they will.*

What I also learned from Natalie was that a person usually hates you long before they make you aware of it. The day I learned of Natalie's hatred, I also learned she's hated me since the day I was born. Windsor's words reminded me that I didn't give a damn about what he thought. He was just like a man: always making beds they don't want to lie in. Windsor's feelings about me didn't keep me from sleeping at night. Yes, someone was going to be sorry when it's all over, but it damn sure wasn't going to be me. He should have been worrying about violating his restraining order, because that's what he had just done by his contact.

Michaela and I stood in a corner in Café Bliss on Massachusetts Avenue, a few blocks from the courthouse, where we decided to meet after leaving T.J.'s school. I stared into my latte after my first sip. We had some time to kill before making our way to the courthouse. We laughed and talked as if we had nothing to worry about, because, honestly, we had nothing to worry about. Michaela had just asked about T.J. when Windsor walked into the café with his attorney in tow. I guess he, too, had not lost any sleep. The bastard actually looked good. His dark-green jacket fit snugged at his waist. His bowed legs in his slim fit pants would've made him irresistible to a woman who didn't know better. I'm a sucker for a tall man in a suit, but no matter how you dressed up Windsor, he was still just a dog in a nicely tailored suit. He spoke in his attorney's ear before he strode to where Michaela and I stood.

"So, here we are." He had his back toward Michaela, and didn't even acknowledge her. "Did you get my text this morning?"

"Yes, Windsor, I did," I answered without giving him my attention.

"And?"

"And, what?" I asked, looking him squarely in his eyes. "I ignored it, which is what I should be doing right now."

"Oh, is that how it is now?"

I know he saw the depth of my detestation for him in my eyes, but that still wasn't enough to repel him.

"It's been like that since…"

"Do not say another word to him," Michaela counseled. This wasn't their first face-to-face meeting. By association, Windsor's dislike for her was instant. He turned to look at Michaela after she spoke. "You do know you're violating the restraining order my client had you served, and, to my understanding, this isn't the first time," Michaela added. She hinted at our conversation about the text message Windsor sent earlier.

"You're talking to me as if what you say matters. I'm

talking to my wife." He barked at Michaela. "Just stand behind me and mind your business, like you've been doing." He stared at Michaela and waited for a response. She allowed his blatant disrespect to disappear. "You're not even going to look at me?" he asked as he refocused to me.

"Mr. James," Michaela called out. Windsor's attorney stood a few feet from Windsor where they stopped after they walked in and our eyes met. "Can you please advise your client of his violation?"

Of course, Michaela didn't need Windsor's attorney in order to stand up to him. Windsor was just another bully who liked to roar like a lion, even when he's best known to purr like a cat.

"Mr. Oliver," Attorney James began as he approached, "We don't need this right now, man. This is not what we came in here for. Come on, Windsor. Let's go!"

"You go!" Windsor shouted. "I'm still talking to my wife."

"I'm not your damn wife," I corrected.

"On paper, you are still Mrs. Oliver," he said as he reached for my hand.

"Isn't that funny. Did that paper matter to you when you were screwing Selecia?"

"Mr. Oliver," Michaela interfered. She stepped closer and placed her palm in the middle of my back. She turned to

347

face Windsor.

"Why are you still here?" Resentment echoed in his voice. They stared into each other's eyes since she matched him in height. "And why do you insist on speaking to me?"

"Mr. Oliver," Michaela repeated with a sterner voice, "we are here to make sure that, as far as my client is concerned, you can never use those two words again. I understand that may not be what you want, but right now, what you want doesn't matter. Now, you keep piling up on these violations and you won't be available to defend yourself."

"To hell with you. Neither you nor some worthless piece of paper is going to tell me when I can or cannot talk to my wife, or how close I can be to her."

I stared at Windsor as if he lost his goddamn mind, because, clearly, he was behaving like he had.

Michaela sipped her coffee and then spoke, "It ain't the coffee that's bitter." She smiled and then took another sip. She stepped close to Windsor. Yes, she never backs down. "Since you won't allow your attorney to advise you, let me say this, not as Ms. Spencer's attorney, but as a woman who knows all too well about men who walk in your shoes. You keep chasing rainbows, even though you already have your pot of gold. You cheat even when you don't have enough dick to satisfy the woman you have at home, so now two women can claim your mediocre sex game.

"You want us to take a backseat to your midlife crises and pretend to be satisfied with memories of an unfilled past. You want forgiveness. You want us to forget because, to you, your infidelity only bent us, though we've screamed how broken we feel. And then, you want the heart you've broken to stay faithful."

"You don't know a damn thing about me," Windsor interrupted Michaela's one-woman performance. She was already ripping him to pieces and we weren't even on her turf, the courtroom, yet.

"Oh, but I do." Michaela smiled. She enjoyed their colloquy. She made him sweat, though he tried to appear unbothered. "Like I said, I know your kind. You beg for the second chance you don't deserve, and you're confident you'll get it because you know her heart. Guess what? Her heart knows you. You'll get your second chance, prove ain't shit about you changed, and then we get to live a word of I-should-have-known and how-could-you-be-so-stupid. So, here we are. Your good thing is gone, and, just to be clear, I'm speaking about my client." She paused. Windsor stared at her. "Your wife."

Windsor stood. The words he searched for to respond to Michaela eluded him.

"Let's go, Mr. Oliver," his attorney commanded.

"Yes, Mr. Oliver. Go!" Michaela cosigned. In that instant, hate resonated in Windsor's eyes. As Windsor turned and mirrored Mr. James in his departure, Michaela took another sip from her cup. "Yes, it's definitely not the coffee."

I looked at Michaela and smiled. She returned the expression, and then winked.

"Are you ready?" I asked. The question was rhetorical. If Michaela was anything, she was ready.

Thirty-seven

Kennedie...

Michaela and I sat on the pew-like bench in the long second-floor hallway. Our attempt to pass time, drinking coffee at the café a few blocks from the courthouse, was interrupted by Windsor, his rudeness, and his blatant disregard for the order I had in place. I witnessed Michaela berate Windsor and all men like him, and it made my heart smile.

As time ticked slowly, we watched lawyers walk by with their rolling bag in one hand, and their box of artillery in the other. Some traveled the known path unaccompanied, others walked in unison with their equivalents. Missing was the enthusiastic grin, even as they bid good morning to those passing by, some of the very same persons they prepared to oppose. They appeared as if they wished they could be anywhere but here, if wishes were actually granted. The clients they met, after they strolled pass, seem to share the same sentiment. Their dark suits—the consensus uniform of choice—were starched crisp and looked fresh out of yesterday's dry cleaning pick up. We hadn't seen Windsor or Mr. James, although they departed the café before Michaela and me.

When the courtroom opened, we stood to enter. I exhaled. The day was finally here. Michaela folded her white jacket over her arm, secured her bag over her shoulder, and then grabbed her case. She smiled. She was either a woman scorned or a woman impassioned by her love for her profession. Regardless, I benefitted from her two faces. After we sat at the plaintiff table, I kept my focus forward, even as the judge entered the room and ascended the stairs to her imposing bench. She looked as if where she stood was exactly where she belonged. Her striking pose as she demanded your attention said it all. Her short crop framed her oval-shaped face. The collar of her crisp, white shirt hung over her long robe. Her soft pink lips parted into a wide radiant smile that exposed near-perfect teeth. She appeared to have aged gracefully.

I knew at least one of the men who occupied the two chairs behind the desk to our right. Windsor Oliver was a man-whore who had been caught with his pants at his ankles, after his sidepiece all but told it on the mountain. The other, Delaire James, I knew by name only, until earlier at Café Bliss when Michaela addressed him. He stood and approached the bench, walking in stride with Michaela when they were summoned by Judge Sarai Williams-Bell, as the nameplate on the front of the bench confirmed.

"Ms. McKnight," Judge Sarai Williams-Bell began a few moments after the two attorneys returned to their respective desks. "The floor is yours."

Michaela uncrossed her legs and rose from her seat. She adjusted the slim-fitting blush-colored skirt that was pulled up just above her knees. She swayed in her pink floral pump to the other side of the desk.

"Thank you, Your Honor." Michaela turned toward me. She smiled. "You're on."

I emphasized the sway in my hips as I strutted to the witness box, navigating the short trip like I was finally given a long-awaited moment as a Victoria's Secret model. I knew Windsor watched. Although I was tempted, I didn't have to turn around to prove I was right. Windsor Sebastian Oliver couldn't help himself. As much as he hated me now, he still loved me just as much. Gosh, I loved the tug-of-war his heart was in, even now as I raised my right hand.

"Do you swear to tell the truth, the whole truth, and…" the bailiff began.

"Nothing but the truth," I added, finishing the oath, an accidental interruption, which was a no-no, even for the most obtuse. My interference was admonished the instant I spoke.

Judge Sarai Williams-Bell lowered her glasses and peered at me from above the rim. "Please allow the bailiff to finish before giving your response," she recommended.

I widened my eyes and refocused on the handsome bailiff. His smooth baldhead glistened under the fluorescents, and his undecorated ring finger led me to conclude he was very available.

He repeated the oath without my disruption.

"Yes, I do." I smiled. "I have nothing to hide," I added as I sat. This time I received a warning side-eye from the judge.

"Please state your name," Michaela began. She sat against the desk with a notepad and a pen in one hand.

I leaned nearer to the small microphone that sprouted from the corner of the witness stand. "Kennedie Leanna Spencer-Oliver."

"Is it okay if I call you Ms. Oliver?" She winked.

In that I was comforted. She knew how much that name brought unwelcome knots to the pit of my stomach.

"Sure."

"Thank you, Ms. Oliver."

Michaela eased from the desk, walked back to her chair, and sat. She placed the pad and pen on the desk and then sat back.

"I have no further questions for Ms. Oliver, Your Honor."

What the hell! I thought. I looked at Michaela, and then at the judge. If she could read my eyes, they had questions.

"Ms. McKnight." The judge tilted her head. "Are you sure?" She asked exactly what I thought. Michaela and I had not discussed her tactic.

"I have no questions for Mrs. Oliver, Your Honor," Michaela restated her position. Her reassertion was assuring, and I took comfort in knowing there must be a method to her calculated madness, even if I had no damn idea what it was.

"Okay then." Judge Williams-Bell slowly turned her head to the other side of the room. My gaze followed. I witnessed the baffled expression on the faces of both Windsor and his attorney. "Mr. James, you have the floor. I'm sure you have some questions for Mrs. Oliver?"

Attorney James tossed the pen he held onto the desk. He glanced at his client, and then he stood. He buttoned his jacket as he walked toward the center of the courtroom. He stared at Michaela who returned a smile, which only made him more unsettled.

Mr. Delaire James had a Napoleon complex; actually, he was just short. He wore a blue suit, a yellow tie, and I'm going to assume, from the brown ring around the collar he thought no one could see with a naked eye, the same white shirt he wore in the very near past, like yesterday past. His brown shoes looked thrift-store worn. Still, he swaggered like he was Gentleman's Quarterly ready.

"Mrs. Oliver," he began. I sat back in the chair and waited for his question. Mr. James's voice trembled. Everyone in the room could claim calm and collected, except for him. "Do you love Mr. Oliver?"

I leaned closer to the mic. "As what, a human being?" I asked. "Yes. A wise woman taught me to love everyone, including my enemies."

"Thank God for wise women," he whispered with his head hung to the floor. He paused before he looked up. "And your feelings toward him now, Ms. Oliver?"

"What do you mean?" I asked, not soliciting an explanation from Mr. James. "We're not here to renew vows, sir. We're getting a divorce. He's the father of my son, that's about all the feelings I have for Mr. Oliver. I always appreciate the truth even if it was forced out of the mouth of the serpent I called my husband."

"So you're saying..."

Jesus, this man is as dull as a butter knife, I thought. I wasn't asking him to read between the lines. Still, he acted as if dust clouds surrounded my response.

"I'm saying Windsor is a vile, self-absorbed dunce who never had respect for our love or our vows. He tries on his lies and then presents you with the one that fits him best, hoping you're gullible enough to believe him."

"Mrs. Oliver." The judge called out.

"Well, you're only as good as the man you marry," Mr. James murmured.

"Mr. James," Judge Williams-Bell called out. She removed her glasses in preparation for a speech that never came.

Mr. Delaire James raised his hand to acknowledge the judge's cautioning.

"Maybe you should've done a better job vetting Mr. Oliver before you went skipping down the aisle to holy matrimony." He ignored the judge and continued his muffled, asinine remarks. He walked to his desk and flipped the pages of his notebook. During his pause, I executed my own blow.

"And I'll surmise you didn't afford Mr. Oliver that same advice, seeing he ended up with you." I lounged back in the chair and folded my arms. Mr. James raised his eyes from his notebook, glanced at me, and then looked at the judge.

"Mr. James," the judge began, "no one is here for your personal opinions. If you have no relevant questions for Mrs. Spencer-Oliver, now is a good time to…" She paused. "Stop."

I anxiously waited my turn, but the judge didn't even look at me. She folded her arms and reclined in her chair. Whatever Mr. James hoped for was not received. He tapped on the desk. Disappointed, he hung his head.

"What about your son, Tanner?" he asked. He raised his head and smiled, as if the question brought him satisfaction.

"What about T.J.?" I sat up and scowled at Windsor.

"Do you love your son, Mrs. Oliver?"

"Is that a serious question, Mr. James?" I shot another menacing glance at Windsor, but his eyes were fixed on his attorney.

An angry Windsor stated that our son was not a part of our disagreement, and although the scheme he pulled was unforgivable, I agreed. He shrugged his shoulder as if his attorney had ventured into shark-infested water despite his warning.

"Just answer the question, Mrs. Oliver." Mr. James redirected my attention to him.

"My son and my love for him are not up for debate;

not now, not ever. Of course, I love my son. I gave birth to him, and my heart beats because of him."

"Mrs. Oliver, there are a lot of women who give birth to children they hate."

"Well, I'm not..."

"You love him, yet you abused him. Is it not true T.J. was removed from your home because of abuse?"

Only the good Lord kept me from standing up and telling this little bit of a man which part of hell he should go. Mr. James had wandered into uncharted territory, and that should have been the first warning Windsor gave him.

"Yes. That was the invented charge levied by your client's desperate attempt to get me to change my mind about the divorce. But did he tell you my son was back in my house that night? Guess he got in a little over his head."

I continued to field questions posed by Windsor's quasi-witted attorney. If the best he had was a botched plot by his client to get custody of my son, then this argument was dead on arrival. I experienced every emotion possible talking about our storied past. I gave my heart to a chameleon. Windsor wooed his way into my life with his bass-laden admission of love. He proposed, and, believing he was someone who held the sanctity of marriage in high regards, I accepted. I daydreamed through sex he thought took me to heaven, and relied on fantasies and Kendrick to supplement the underperformance I'd come to expect. Until Selecia's decision to expose his secret, Windsor had convincingly lived our years together as a devout husband and father. At least I can applaud him for the latter.

Thirty-eight

Michaela...

I sat at the desk next to Kennedie in the small courtroom. Thoughts about my last night with Kendrick kept my mind busy, and if I wasn't in court, next to him is where I wanted to be. It had been a few days since our last encounter, but I was still feeling fulfilled. You know a man is a keeper when you still have a smile on your face days after the sex has faded. That day did not go as planned, but that was not always a bad thing. At the end of the night, Kendrick provided what I needed. Only to laugh in Whitney's face at her failed attempt to derail another relationship would have brought me more pleasure.

Reminiscing on days not too old provided a temporary reprieve from my fiery discussion with Mr. Oliver at Café Bliss. He was as stubborn as he was dishonest, but he'd found his match. He couldn't manhandle me as he had his attorney, Delaire James. Mr. James worked for him, so he had no choice but to tolerate him. I didn't like him, and although I could be a great pretender, I was going to save what would have been my best act for a more worthwhile cause.

I looked at Kennedie, who sat next to me in the ash color wingback chair, and then took a quick glance over at Windsor. That he was still fuming from our earlier argument was evident as he sat tight-faced next to his attorney at the desk a few feet from where Kennedie and I were. Until his extramarital affair was brutally brought to her attention, Kennedie took pride in calling him her husband. Sometimes we don't know we could do so much better until we are put in the position to know we could. Once again, that moment stared at her. She dazzled. Her button front black and white shirt and black ankle length pants helped her flaunt her eye-catching figure, and it was done on purpose. Her double strand pearls sat on her skin. She added a pop of color with her red velvet pump. She had a sway in her hips that could hypnotize snakes, and she had caught one in Windsor Oliver.

Windsor must've been her lapse in judgment. I wondered what the hell she saw in him. Yes, he was handsome, even sexy—I'll give him that—but that was the depth of him. His first impression had left me wanting a lot more, but I presumed he had no more to give. That he was a man hadn't predisposed him to the hate I harbored. That he was a man like Zachary McKnight did.

We stood as Judge Sarai Williams-Bell entered the courtroom and mounted the three steps to the platform. She stood behind the bench in front of the oversized black leather chair. She surveyed one side of the small room to the other, eyeing yet another couple that something other than death did them part. She was older, very respectful, and a divorcé as well. After her own public divorce, Williams-Bell traded in the long mane that once grazed her shoulder for a short crop with auburn highlights where gray used to be. I was as surprised to see her as she was to see me sitting in front of her. Judge Williams-Bell respected my dogged determination to unmask the men that sat across from me.

"Attorneys, approach the bench, please," she summoned as she sat. Attorney James stood from his chair. He looked in my direction and then shrugged his shoulder as if he'd read my mind. Judge Williams-Bell covered the microphone as we neared. "Now, I know I don't have to remind either of you about courtroom decorum. Some things I will not tolerate. The grandstanding, keep it for your guest appearance on *Law and Order*. I don't want it in my courtroom. We're clear."

"Yes, Your Honor." Our response was in unison.

"That was a statement, not a question," she explained.

Judge Williams-Bell's warning must've been for Attorney James because I've always behaved my best, at least until an attorney decides their sex made them superior, or that my client was beneath them. At that point, I eighty-sixed the politesse and apologized for my disrespect later, not to them, but to the court. As we marched back to our respective desks, Attorney James looked like a schoolboy who had been scolded by a schoolyard bully. I let her warning roll from my back. I knew that was a part of her courtroom procedure. I was surprised he stood erect. He didn't even have a spine.

When directed, I called Kennedie to take her place on the stand. She wore her confidence well as she took the stroll at my request. It was show time. Her sexiness was undeniable, and Windsor's stare was a testament to that. He couldn't help himself, even if he wanted to. His willpower was no match to the hypnotic moves of her hips. Yes, maybe he did love her; however, his love and honor had been put to the test, and he failed.

Kennedie swore to tell the truth, but not without comedy that earned her a warning from the judge. Of course, she had nothing to hide, as she'd broadcast. She had been forthcoming since the day we met.

"Kennedie Leanna Spencer-Oliver," she announced. Then, with my asking, she gave me permission to call her the one name she hated even more than being called a bitch. In my own way, I assured her this was the worst the day would get. Otherwise, I had no other questions. I wanted to waste no time getting to Windsor. So, I handed my client over to Attorney James, and although my decision received questioning stares from the judge, Kennedie, Windsor, and Attorney James, I knew Mr. James, when given the opportunity, would play right into my hand. That's just how Delaire Lawrence James operated. He'll dig the very hole in which his client would be buried.

Attorney James never disappoints, and I sat back and watched him steer this train to a wreck. He clearly had no plan, and when he stood before the court, the shenanigans began. His client could have made this process much easier, but his stubbornness wouldn't allow him to agree to anything proposed. Windsor declined the use of a mediator to divide their acquisitions. He said no to a proposed collaborative divorce. He wanted to make this hard for Kennedie simply because she originated the idea of a divorce. Though his attempt was futile at best, he concocted a claim of abuse in hopes Kennedie would recant her request for a divorce. In being vindictive, he set himself up to lose more. When Kennedie wanted to leave with only what she brought into the marriage, his misguided scheme infuriated her. She had a change of heart, and didn't even want to leave him with a window to throw his piss out of.

*T*hirty-nine

Michaela...

Kennedie held her head high and smiled as she descended from the witness stand. Windsor wouldn't see her do otherwise, because his infidelity and false claim had not caused her to lose her way. Windsor avoided eye contact with Kennedie as she strolled past him. After she sat, she crossed her legs. Her smiled hadn't left her face. Mr. James sat next to his client. He glanced over at Kennedie, whose mind now seemed to be everywhere but in the moment, and then shook his head. I wish I knew his thoughts.

At his attorney's invitation, Windsor stood from his seat. He removed his suit jacket from the back of the chair and dressed. He adjusted his tie as he walked to take his seat in the box next to the judge. When he was instructed, he had his hand on the bible, and with his right hand to God, he swore to tell the truth. I didn't know Windsor well, but I knew enough to know in that gesture, his lies began.

"Windsor Sebastian Oliver," he spoke in a hushed tone into the microphone, following his attorney's request to state his name.

"Thank you, Mr. Oliver." Mr. James remained seated at the desk. He appeared uneasy. He tapped the point of his pen against the writing pad. "Do you love your wife?" he asked. He allowed the pen to fall.

Hush followed Mr. James's inquiry. Windsor lowered his head, but his eyes traveled to Kennedie. He kept them fixed on her as the moments passed, and then he returned his focus to the microphone.

"Of course, I love Kennedie," he began. If he expected his stoic delivery to convince anyone, he had failed miserably. "It was the only reason I married her. Love was the only reason I would marry anyone. I'd avoided the conversation of marriage, because I wasn't certain I could be a faithful husband. Then I met Kennedie. I listened to her talk fantastically about love, like it was something that could never happen to her. I wanted to change that. The first few times I looked into her eyes, I saw into the soul of a woman who deserved to be loved. She deserved the happiness that had eluded her.

"She was a beautiful mystery." He laughed. "Yes, she told me no more times than I had ever heard from anyone in my life, but they only made me more determined. My persistence was never so we would end up here." Windsor sat back in his chair. He exhaled as if his short travel into yester-years had exhausted him.

Mr. James finally vacated his seat. With his hands in his pockets, he walked, and then he posed in front of Windsor. He smiled as if he had just stepped into his own ray of sunshine.

"You had your son removed from the house you once shared with Ms. Oliver?"

Windsor hesitated. His eyes danced from side to side.

"Yes," he answered.

"Why?"

Windsor paused, and then he leaned closer to the microphone. "Because I was concerned about his safety. But he was returned later that night."

"So...?" Mr. James's question lingered.

"So, what? Kennedie loves our son. She does an amazing job. She makes being his mother look easy. She would never harm him or allow harm to come close to him. I was angry, and that anger made me entertain this crazy idea. Kennedie, I'm sorry."

Windsor's remorse earned Kennedie's attention. He

held a crestfallen demeanor, contrasting the brazen, condescending persona he presented earlier. He returned his gaze toward the floor as he lounged back into the chair. When he looked up, his eyes brightened. He smiled. I followed his stare and wondered what instigated his reaction.

"What do you want, Mr. Oliver?" Mr. James asked.

She stood at the back of the courtroom in front of the doors that had closed behind her, as if she'd just made a grand entrance into a President's Inauguration Ball. Kennedie must've noticed the change in Windsor's demeanor as she, too, followed his focus to the back of the room. I had an idea who she was, until it was confirmed. Selecia Lassiter had once again put her boldness on display by showing her face and giving support to her man. Her presence was unexpected, and it twisted the knife Windsor had lodged in Kennedie's back. That her husband had accompanied her had tripled the shock value.

Garen Lassiter, partner at Lassiter, Larson, and Beale, stood behind his wife. He looked more like her escort and a lot unlike the man who had her heart. Although they walked with her hand in his, her eyes were locked on Windsor's. It was obvious Garen was in love with Selecia, but the man who had her heart sat in the testimony box answering questions in his divorce. Their presence caused a shift in the atmosphere.

"Mr. Oliver," Mr. James called out. The couple assumed their seat on one of the benches behind the desk occupied by Windsor and Attorney James.

"What do I want?" Windsor repeated the question asked before his distraction walked in. "Initially, my wife back, but we're here. Clearly, that possibility is dead," he answered. He glanced up and over at Kennedie. "What I want is to be a part of my son's life, and I know Kennedie wouldn't have it any other way. Give her whatever she asks for. I just want to put this behind me and move on with my life."

"Are you sure?" Mr. James asked in a whisper.

"Of course, I'm sure."

Mr. James tapped his hand on the witness box before he began his promenade toward his desk. He paused in a moment of contemplation before he sat. I wondered what he pondered.

"Mr. James." Judge Williams-Bell sat with her hands clasped atop her bench. "Do you have anything else you need to discuss with Mr. Oliver?"

The Judge was right. This was nothing but a discussion, and we could have done this over facetime or conference call. In fact, we would not have gone down this road had Windsor agreed to what was offered.

"No, Your Honor," he said. He sounded as if

Windsor had just helped him lose a fight.

"Attorney McKnight, Mr. Windsor is all yours," she instructed.

"Thank you." I stood from the chair and, in an unhurried pace, approached Windsor. "Mr. Oliver, I'm sure my client appreciates your generosity. But, I want to be clear we have the same understanding."

"Yes." A nod of his head in the affirmative complemented his response.

"What my client requested, and what you have now graciously agreed to, is half of what you have amassed since the marriage, after all debt that the two of you incurred have been paid off. Of course, that includes all you revealed on your financial statement, and this." I retrieved the document from the desk and handed it to Windsor.

"What is this?"

"It's a statement from an account we have unearthed." Windsor surveyed the document, but confusion was the only expression on his face. "Let me save you some trouble, Mr. Oliver. It's your account statement from Banco National de Panama."

"What are you talking about?" He looked over at his attorney, who could offer no help. The shrug of his shoulders indicated that truth.

"See, my firm did some digging and discovered an

account that belongs to Landen Oliver. I'll spare us the back and forth. Obviously, you are not Landen Oliver, the name on the account. We also know Landen, your brother, does not have the means, and hasn't had the means in quite some time, to contribute the kind of money we see flowing into this account."

"Are you asking if I have any knowledge of this account, or…"

"No, I'm definitely not asking about your knowledge. We know the money in the account belongs to you. We have been able to cross-check the monies being deposited in that offshore account and it consistently matches the amounts you withdraw from your own."

"You greedy, selfish bitch," he admonished. Just like that, his composure became undone. Oh, how the tides change. The same woman he had just sung praises was now the target of his derogatory-filled rant. "Don't think you're going to sit there looking pristine, as if you didn't whore your way through our marriage."

"Mr. Oliver!" Judge Williams-Bell screamed.

"Yes, I disrespected our union with my affair," Windsor continued. He ignored the judge's attempt to silent him. "But you had your share of fuck-friends, too. So, you can perform for these attorneys who only know you from what you've told them, but I know the real you."

"Mr. Oliver," the judge yelled again. "You will respect my courtroom, and all women within."

Unfazed by his accusation, Kennedie stared at him with unblinking eyes. She shook her head in embarrassment for the father of her child. Windsor had done what most do when they can't defend the truth. They turn to ersatz and pernicious slurs they hope anyone would believe. Unfortunately for Windsor, his indictments had fallen on the ears of those who saw through his desperate outburst.

Forty

Michaela...

All's well that ends well are words I don't think losers ever get to say, and those were words you will never hear come from the mouth of Windsor Sebastian Oliver, Adulterer. It's definitely cheaper to keep her. Zachary McKnight learned that lesson. Although his money was never needed, he had to learn there was a price to pay for pissing on women like me. I was his spine when he needed one. I was his rock when he found himself in a hard place. Windsor learned that lesson, too. Sure, we could've stayed with our husbands, sweep their transgressions under the rug, stifle the reminders that came in dreams and nightmares, and hoped to never become the other woman in our own marriage. Truth is, we can't let men determine our worth. When you let them get away with lying and cheating, or think we were what drove them to these deceptions, that is exactly what you do.

It felt good to get back to what I did best. It hadn't taken Judge Williams-Bell long to decide how to divide Windsor and Kennedie's assess. Half of what was divulged on the disclosure form was given to Kennedie, and seventy-five percent of the monies he had in his offshore account was now hers, too. She was given sole custody of Tanner, but her heart wouldn't allow that. Regardless of what came from Windsor's mouth about her in court, she wanted Tanner's father in his life. She'd shared all with the judge in her plea on Windsor's behalf.

I came home to the delight of Alison and Nyla sitting in the living room. Usually Nyla was awake for her morning kisses, but when I left for court, she was still in dreamland. She'd spent the previous day with her father, and whatever they did, left her too tired to even ask me to read her to sleep.

"I haven't seen that smile in years," Alison greeted. "Yes, I know I'm exaggerating, but it has been a while." She stared in Nyla's face; her hand smoothed the hair on her head. She looked up. "It's good to see."

"Today was a good day." I stood behind the large couch with my jacket in one hand and my bag in the other. I stared down at my beautiful daughter. Nyla looked up and smiled. Her eyes held the love and innocence I hoped would never disappear, but I know the state of this world. In spite of this, I keep praying for a change, for Nyla's sake. "I feel like we haven't talked in weeks," I said. I held Nyla's face in my hands and kissed her forehead.

"Well, if it makes you feel better, it's only been a few days. I know you're handling business, and I like that. I won't hold it against you." Alison smiled and then turned her attention to the television. "You know what else I like?" she asked as I started toward the kitchen.

"Flatter me please," I encouraged.

"You are wearing that dress."

As if I'd come to the end of the runway in a fashion show, I stopped, gave my best Ajak Deng pose, and then smiled. I appreciated Alison's compliment.

In the kitchen, I rested my bag in one of the bar chairs, tossed my jacket over the back of the chair, and set the cellphone on the counter. I stood lopsided on one heel when the phone vibrated. I picked up and stared at the name and picture on the screen. It made me smile again. I had implored my best friend, Brooklynn Jones, to confess her deceit to her husband, give him her backstory, and then work on building her family. She'd been apprehensive, and before our last conversation, she'd been closed-mouth.

"Just when I thought my day couldn't get any better," I answered. I finally removed the second heel. "Hey Love!"

"Hey sis!" she greeted. "I guess I don't need to ask how you are." There was something different in her tone. "I'm glad I could add to the already phenomenal day."

"You better be a bearer of good news." I blindly pulled a bottle of wine from the rack, grabbed a long stem glass, and poured it half full.

"I love this feeling," she began.

"Which feeling is that?"

"The feeling that I'm going to be a mother again."

I wanted to scream into the phone, but I didn't want my outburst to startle Alison and Nyla, who were zoned in on the T.V. "Get out of here. You're pregnant?"

"Yes, and I'm feeling so good."

"I'm happy for you." I paused and took a sip. "So that means you told Stetzen everything." I assumed. She was silent. I placed the glass on the counter. When Brooklynn goes silent, it only meant something was afoot. "Brooklynn," I called. "You said you told him everything."

"Everything he needed to know. He knows about my son and what my parents did. We finally talked about the family he wanted, the only difference is that I now wanted that family, too."

"But you were supposed to tell him everything, about replacing the pills with the injection, and about having difficulty conceiving. I'm glad he knows part of the story, and that you weren't being entirely selfish, but…" I paused. "You lied about something that many couples struggle with."

"And I do feel horrible."

"Then tell him, Brooke."

"Trust me, I wanted to. I saw how he reacted to the little I did tell him, and I got scared," she explained. "I'm not losing my husband."

What if he finds out later?"

"Find out how, Michaela? You're the only other person who knows. Are you going to tell?"

Her question couldn't have been anything but rhetorical. Still, I decided to entertain her with a response.

"Of course not." Regardless of what I thought, it was not for me to tell. My loyalty was to her, not to Stetzen. Yes, he was a great person, but my love only extended to him because of her.

"There was no harm done," she continued. "In the end, Stetz still gets what he wanted."

"After years of unsuccessful attempts, all of a sudden the stars align, the kinks worked itself out, and now you're expecting. And he just…" I paused. "He just believed you?"

"You said it, the stars align. Michaela, miracles

happen. Stetzen has been praying for this baby, and I've been praying for His guidance to do the right thing."

"I'm sure God didn't talk you out of telling Stetzen the whole truth."

"Tell him the whole truth, and then what? When he gets mad as hell and asks for a divorce, do I come to you to make sure I get half of everything?" I stayed hush with my wine in my hand as she continued. "Honey, I've loved Stetzen for so long, I wouldn't know how to love anyone else. I wouldn't want to love anyone else."

"You're being presumptive. You don't know how he's going to react. I just don't want this on your conscience."

"Thank you for your concern, Michaela, but can you let me and God worry about my conscience?"

"Fine! I'll leave it alone. I still think you should have told him. You can't risk giving other people the opportunity to tell your truth. You have a better chance of forgiveness if…"

"You're not leaving it alone, Michaela," she interrupted.

A big part of my heart was happy for Brooklynn. I knew she would be a great mother today, just as she would have been a great mother to the son her mother forced her to give up during her teenage years. Stetzen vowed to help her find him. The other part of my heart still worried about her misleading deeds. My happiness for Brooklynn wasn't void of caution. I just couldn't shake the feeling this wasn't going to end well.

Before she hung up, Brooklynn assured me my worrying was in vain. Her confidence should've been enough to defeat any trepidation I had. Still, I was unsettled. It brought no ease to my mind that Brooklynn professed to know the man she slept next to each night, because I knew so many who, unbeknownst to them, slept with strangers and enemies.

"Sorry. I didn't want to interrupt," Alison announced. She stood against the entrance to the kitchen. "Nyla fell asleep." She walked closer to where I sat. "Do you want some company?"

"Of course, although you know I have no problem finishing this bottle all by myself."

She laughed.

"That I know," she agreed. She pulled a bottle from the rack, and set it on the island. "We could make it a competition." She winked.

Alison uncorked the bottle and began to pour. I smiled after the red liquid passed the halfway mark. I guess she needed to catch up. We held our glass high for a toast.

"To love, friendship, and life," Alison began.

"And to getting rid of people whose only intent is to bring you a portion of their misery."

"Amen," Alison replied. She smiled.

When our glasses dinged, my phone vibrated. An unknown number appeared on the screen. I teetered between ignoring or answering, but my curiosity made the decision.

"Can I help you?" I answered.

"Oh, it's going to be a sad day in hell, and by hell, I mean Brooklynn's marriage, when he finds out." Whitney's voice was filled with malice. She was one form of the devil none of my prayers had been able to defeat. "Seems Brooklynn is a pretty little liar."

How could it be that a few minutes after getting off the phone with Brooklynn, I would get a call from Whitney? What did she know, or was she just casting a line to see what she can hook?

"What do you know?"

"About as much as you, but a lot more than Stetzen. All that will change. One way or another, everyone will be in the know." Whitney released a heavy breath.

"You never give up, do you?" I didn't expect anything from her mouth to address what I asked. Alison held the glass between her lips. She didn't have to ask who had interrupted. My demeanor had turned to gloom, and there were only two people who could have caused this change.

"Give up? But I have so much of you left to destroy. Remember, Dear, what's done in the dark."

"Brooklynn and her marriage are stronger than anything you think will destroy her."

"Girl, please. Stop telling yourself something Brooke doesn't even believe. I have some news for you. If she thought her marriage could survive this little white lie, don't you think she would've told Stetzen?"

"You won't succeed."

"O ye of little faith. Just in case you're not keeping score, I already have two wins under my belt."

"What the hell are you talking about?" Finally, I set my glass on the table, stood from the chair, and began to pace the kitchen floor. Alison's eyes followed.

"I've succeeded in ending your marriage to Zachary. Remember you thought that was solid as a rock, too. And I killed two birds with one stone in ending your friendship with Patience and your relationship with Drew."

"That had nothing to do with you." I paused.

"Baby Girl, it had everything to do with me. I know it seemed like Patience went from being your best friend to being your worst enemy overnight. But nothing happens overnight. She took time to cultivate. Jesus! It wouldn't have been so exhausting if she didn't worship the ground you walked on. All you had, she wanted for herself. I just had to make sure she wanted your man, too. It didn't hurt that she had the reputation she did.

"So I planted these little seeds in her head. You know, how you were tired of coming to her rescue, you didn't trust her around Drew, and that you needed to distant yourself from her before she tries to sink her claws into him. She wanted to confront you, because you knew she wouldn't do what you were accusing her of to her best friend. But I told her you would only deny everything."

"You're right. I would've denied it, because none of it was true."

"Of course not, but Michaela, Patience didn't know that. So, she did what she did best, she went in for the kill. She got into Drew and the rest, as they say, is an amusing history." She laughed. "Tell your sweet, conniving Brooklynn Jones to tell her husband about her deception. She could risk losing him now, or she can wait and risk losing him later. Remember, until I have no breath left in me, you and everyone connected to you won't live a day in peace."

I slowly removed the phone from my ear and stood in disbelief. Once again, my mother had raised her ugly head. She was busy keeping her promise to make sure everyone I loved and I experienced a semblance of the misery she has lived in since I killed my brother.

Forty-one

Kennedie...

You're damn right I hollered inside my head, but I sat back folded my arms, and smiled as Windsor's walls came tumbling down. Michaela had pulled the pin and, like a bomb, Windsor exploded. I was honored to wear the badge I was given. I'd been selfless, but where exactly has that gotten me. Everyone I'd put before me betrayed me. My entire existence had been a lie. Everyone did what they needed to cover up their mistakes. I couldn't care any less about their internal struggles. As far as I was concerned, I was the only one who suffered, because I was born into a situation created by those who were supposed to love and protect me.

Nothing was exactly what it was. Geraldine was a slutty Christian who thought she was saved by the King

James Version of the Bible; Natalie hated me, though she had willingly agreed to ease her own mother's burden; I cried at the tomb of the unknown, and purged my heart because I was told the man whose bones were within was my father— the one truth in a bed of lies; and if that wasn't enough, the man I vowed to spend the rest of my life with had betrayed my trust in him and shared what I thought only belonged to me with another woman. I gave him everything he wanted. I knew getting pregnant wasn't the best way to keep a man. Geraldine always said all dogs stray. Well, Windsor can't call her a liar, because he was one dog who proved her right.

Windsor's spectacle was amusing at best, an embarrassment for him at worse. He paved the roads that led us to here. Greed caused him to risk losing his wife, his family, and it was funny to see him act as if Selecia was not worth it. She witnessed his explosion, too. She'd walked into the courtroom with her husband next to her, and stood at the back as if she were waiting for her round of applause. She alluded to her husband not caring what was happening between her and Windsor, but watching them for the few moments I did as they walked to their seat, he was clueless to his wife's transgression.

Selecia brought with her my realization that I was going through this alone. Natalie had succumbed to her illness, but it's not like she would've been front and center cheering me on anyway. Geraldine was in Georgia minding her own business. Yes, I was stubborn. I ignored urges to call her. So, the woman I thought was flawless had her imperfections. That she wasn't a saint hadn't stopped her from loving me, and there was no denying that she did.

At the end of Windsor's tirade, both attorneys were summoned to the judge's chamber. I gathered my bag and started my exit from the courtroom. Selecia and her husband kept their eyes on me as I waltzed out. When I pushed the door open, my eyes widened at the figure that stood with her back toward me.

"You're here."

When Geraldine turned, I wanted to fall to my knees. Her eyes held a sadness that rarely visited.

"As long as I am alive, you will never go through anything alone." She stepped closer and reached for my hand. I obliged. "I'm sorry."

With my eyes fogged by tears, I lowered my head into her chest. When I felt her arm around me, I exhaled.

"How did you know?" I asked. I raised my head and stepped back from her.

"I called her," Trent answered. He stood from the bench along the wall. "She said she hadn't heard from you, and was already planning on coming out here. When I told her about the hearing, she changed her ticket, and, well, here she is." He paused. "My dad is here, too." Trent held my other hand, and then kissed Geraldine on her forehead.

I stood in my own silence. My heart raced, but I knew exactly what I wanted. I'd lived my life never having anyone to call my daddy. I believed lies told to cover lies and protect those who perpetrated them. I had nothing left to lose.

"Where is he?"

"I'm right here." He turned. He hadn't moved when Geraldine turned to greet me, so I didn't pay any attention to the figure. He stood unbothered by anything that occurred behind him, until I responded in the affirmative to Trent. I released Trent and Geraldine's hand. I strode slowly toward him.

"Hi!" I said. I smiled nervously through tears. "I'm Kennedie Spencer." I extended my arm and expected him to do the same. He grabbed the sides of my face in both arms and stared into my eyes. He smiled as he lowered my forehead toward his lips. I closed my eyes to the touch of Trent's father's lips, and then he pulled me into him. With his arms around me, I exhaled, and then sunk into him. He wasn't my daddy, but I finally felt secured in the arms of another man.

National Sexual Assault Hotline

Call 1-800-656-4673